Bile rose in Kate's throat. Her eyelids became as heavy as velvet curtains preparing to drop at the end of a show. Holding the edge of her dresser to steady her balance, she focused on the necklace she'd laid out before showering. She picked up the thin gold chain and clasped the locket in her hand, tighter and tighter, as if meshing the keepsake into her skin could bring her mother back to help her through this.

"Kate?"

She heard Drew calling, his voice distant, searching for her in a deep mineshaft. Her mouth opened to answer, but no sound followed. Perhaps she didn't want to be found.

She tried again to speak, but the sensation of hot tears streaking her face intruded on her effort. The protective wall surrounding her soul had split in two. A lifetime of denied emotion had broken through the dam, and there was no holding back the flood.

"Daddy, please, not yet," she whispered, then crumpled to the floor, wilting like a rose in her mother's forsaken garden.

"Be warned: do not start this novel if you anticipate any pressing obligations - a need to sleep, say - or without a handful of tissues within arms reach. Flaherty's Crossing is a compelling and imaginative story, not just about death but about life and emotional growth, a broken woman's journey towards learning to trust again. Beautifully written, heart wrenching yet inspirational, this is a 'must read' for anyone who has loved and lost."—ELIZABETH JOY ARNOLD, *USA Today* bestselling author of *Pieses of My Sister's Life*

"Before you start reading Flaherty's Crossing, clear your schedule. You will not want to look up until the last page is turned. Suspenseful, poignant and ultimately soul-satisfying, this life-affirming tale of shattering secrets will keep you on the edge of your seat. Don't miss it!" - JOY NASH, *USA Today* bestselling author of *Deep Magic*

"FLAHERTY'S CROSSING immediately engages the reader with lyrical prose, a plot equally moving and suspenseful, and real, compelling characters. The writing is as fresh as it is evocative. From heart wrenching to heartwarming, inducing laughter and tears, this virtual roller coaster of a tale won't let the reader go until reaching the final turn of the ride. A superb novel bearing a message not easily forgotten." -ANGELA FOX, Publisher of *Oregon City News/Clackamas Review*

"FLAHERTY"S CROSSING is a beautiful story. It made me reflect on my own life, and how I shouldn't wait until it's too late to let people that I love know how I feel, or to apologize if I need to. Readers will truly enjoy this story."-PAIGE LOVITT for *Reader Views (www.readerviews.com)*

Flaherty's Crossing

Champagne Books Presents

Flaherty's Crossing

By

Kaylin McFarren

This is a work of fiction. The characters, incidents and dialogues in this book are of the author's imagination and are not to be construed as real. Any resemblance to actual events or persons, living or dead, is completely coincidental.

No part of this book may be reproduced or transmitted in any form or by any means, electronic or mechanical, including photocopying, recording, or by any information storage and retrieval system, without permission in writing from the publisher.

Champagne Books
www.champagnebooks.com
Copyright © 2009 by Linda Yoshida
ISBN 978-1-926681-19-1
February 2010
Cover Art © Amanda Kelsey
Produced in Canada

Champagne Books
#35069-4604 37 ST SW
Calgary, AB T3E 7C7
Canada

Dedication

At 2:30 AM in the morning, I completed this story —a story I've contemplated writing for the past sixteen years. I poured myself a generous glass of Merlot. I reveled in the moment, toasting a complex man who wasn't a great communicator, whose intentions were not always understood, but yet, a father whose generosity and compassion never failed to amaze me. I toasted my mother, a tireless soul who opens her heart unconditionally, seeks no regrets in her life, and who dreams of being reunited one day with the love of her life. My third toast was extended to my husband. His enthusiasm, encouragement, adoration, and patience are beyond imagination. He is, indeed, my dearest friend and confidant. My final toast went out to my beautiful daughters: Kristina, who continues to be my greatest fan, my hero, and inspiration, Amanda, whose compassion, sincerity, and God-given talents amaze me to this day, and to Erika, whose acceptance, inner strength, and rebellious nature have spurred me to pursue new experiences and adventures in life I would have never otherwise considered.

When all was said and done, the glass was empty, but due to my incredible friends and family, my life will always be full.

I love you all.

"Faith is being sure of what we hope for and certain of what we do not see." Heb. 11:1

Flaherty's Crossing

One

The journey begins...

    The last grain of sand was about to drop in her father's invisible hourglass and there was nothing Kate Flaherty could do to stop it. The realization launched a shudder up her spine.
    She'd known this day was inevitable. Yet it still came as a shock when she'd learned, only hours ago, that his final days had arrived. She should have come back sooner.
    No—it was his fault, not hers. She'd had every right to stay away after discovering the truth. So why did she feel remorse encroaching on her anger, his gurgling breaths draining strength from her limbs?
    In his curtain-drawn bedroom, she perched on the edge of the mattress, a few inches away from what had become a mere sketch of a man. The lamp's amber glow cast shadows across his features, accentuating how much he'd deteriorated in just under a month.
    Surgery, chemo, radiation therapy. For two years she'd watched his heavyset frame shrink with every trip to the hospital, his sixty-three year old body blast through a time warp. But never ravaged to this extent. She barely recognized the sheeted man beside her. Mussed strands of thin, ghost-white hair, matching jagged mustache, and stubbly chin were all that remained of the father she knew. He was more of a

stranger than ever before.

Slowly, he lifted his eyelids and turned his face. When their gazes met, a spark of recognition flickered. "You're here," he rasped as he reached for her hand.

She accepted, reluctantly. His palm was cold and clammy, his skin sallow and tissue-thin. She swallowed hard, wanting to pull away, but the child in her resisted, the part of her that had never stopped longing for his affection.

"Where've you been?" He inhaled a labored breath. "I was waiting for ya."

"I..." A lump of guilt formed in her throat, blocking any answer.

"Is the baby ready?"

She stared at him, shocked. His words made no sense. "What, Dad?"

"We gotta go. Don't wanna hit traffic, Iris."

Kate's heart plummeted before she could remind herself of what he'd done. She slipped her hand away and clenched her fists, her nails biting into her palms. She tried to reignite the rage she was entitled to, but he appeared so defenseless, she summoned only the foreboding of imminent loss.

She leaned toward him. His gaze fixed on the ceiling. All she had to do was say good-bye, just as she'd done countless times throughout her youth. It would be a relief—for both of them.

"Dad, it's me, Katie."

"Mmm. Smells so good."

She sniffed automatically, half-expecting the aroma of her father's favorite rosemary-garlic potatoes roasting in the kitchen down the hall. Instead, she inhaled only the nauseating odors of disinfectant, bodily fluids and medication. Her stomach reeled.

"Dad, can you hear me?"

"How long till supper, darlin'?"

The question caught her off guard. "Are you...hungry?"

"He can't eat anymore, dear," a woman reported from behind her. Kate turned toward the doorway where Doris Shaffer stood. The portly hospice nurse, her knotted hair as white as her smock, looked on with kind eyes.

When Doris's comment sunk in, a wave of horror rolled over Kate. "What about his protein drinks?"

"He isn't able to keep any food down, I'm afraid."

As though cancer wasn't bad enough. Now he was starving.

"You're welcome to give him some ice chips. I'm sure he'd like that." Doris pointed at the nightstand next to Kate. There, on the corner of the table, his thick-rimmed glasses rested beside the remote control for the small television he'd watched during her last series of visits—visits in which *The Price is Right* appeared more interesting than any conversation she had to offer. But then, after all these years, why had she expected anything different?

In the center of an aged doily sat a metal soup bowl dotted with condensation and filled with a mound of ice slivers. She glanced at the raw corners of her father's mouth. Compassion guided her hand to retrieve the spoon poking out from the bowl.

"Lamb, corn, potatoes..."

As he rambled off the menu, Kate pictured her apron-clad mother peeking into the window of the heated oven. But just as her mom had vanished from their lives, so did the image.

"Think I'll need a bigger belt," he said and chuckled, a sound Kate hadn't heard in years.

She placed a spoonful of melting ice on his tongue, and without taking her gaze off his face, she asked Doris in an even tone, "Isn't there anything else you can do for him?"

"At this stage, we're just trying to keep him comfortable."

At this stage. Such finality in those words. Kate fought the tremble in her hand as she transported a second scoop toward his mouth, but a good portion landed on the crumpled sheet. Immediately, she set down the spoon and brushed the ice off the bed in frantic sweeps.

She had to get this over with. "Dad, can you hear me?"

"The showerhead needs changing." He'd begun to slur.

"Dad?"

"Closet door needs oiling…" He trailed off in a gurgle.

"It's the morphine," Doris explained. "Sends him off on tangents that don't make a whole lot of sense."

Not always the case. Sometimes those tangents made all too much sense.

A cavernous moan caused Kate to jump. It took her a second to realize the sound had actually come from her father. This wasn't fair. How could she maintain resentment for someone enduring such suffering?

Just then, fluctuating numbers on a green screen captured her gaze. Resembling a large calculator, the morphine pump parked between them blinked to attention. A timed dose of truth serum flowed through the tube, disappearing under the white bed sheet.

"He'll sleep for a while now," Doris said. "I've put some tea on. You're more than welcome to join me."

"Thank you." Kate shot to her feet and led the way. She needed to breathe, to escape the stifling weight of the room.

The walls lining the narrow hall spoke through symbols: empty nail holes her father had never filled and rectangles defined by contrasting shades on the faded floral wallpaper. All evidence of where framed photographs had hung when she was a kid. Memories her father had done his best to erase.

Upon reaching the family room, Kate edged around a low coffee table and slid into the cushy sofa chair, her favorite seat in the house. She recalled her mother saying she'd purchased the avocado-green furnishing to match Kate's hazel eyes. Together, they'd spent countless evenings in that very chair until Kate had insisted she was too old to sit on her mom's lap for bedtime stories.

If Kate had known what was to come, she would have cherished those sweetly spoken tales, those moments nestled in the safety of her mother's arms.

"Lemon or milk, dear?" Doris asked.

"Excuse me?"

"For your tea."

A standard question, yet it suddenly held no significance. "Either is fine."

Doris smiled as she strolled into the adjacent kitchen. Kate watched as the woman lifted the whistling kettle from the stove and reached in the cupboard.

Kate cringed at the sight of another female roaming the house with such familiarity. To dilute her discomfort, she focused on her surroundings. Decades-old books, collectable antique glassware, and stacks of magazines littered shelves like a garage sale display after the Friday morning rush. Lint appeared woven into the brown shag carpeting. Alcoves bore patches of spider webs, and pine needles on the skylight strained grey rays from the early evening sky.

Her mother's only sibling, Aunt Sophie, would have had a conniption if she'd seen the house in such a state. Even after Sophie had moved out following Kate's graduation, the place never looked so neglected. Kate had offered to hire a housekeeper months ago, but her father wouldn't have it. He said he didn't need a stranger meddling with his "Lil' Bit O' Heaven," or so the place was called according to the engraved sign above the front door.

She shook her head at the irony. Her father's handmade cabin, hidden in the serene woods of Washington's Olympic peninsula, featured traits no more heavenly than an Antonin Gaudi mosaic—a vision of beauty from afar, but in reality, a composition made of broken pieces that had once been part of something whole. A deceptive masterpiece.

"Mr. Flaherty told me about all the collectors you have," Doris called from the kitchen. "You must be a very successful artist."

Kate glanced down at her tattered jeans and oversized umber sweatshirt, both splattered with an array of paint colors from the new commission she'd been working on when Doris phoned. Not until she had hit Highway 101 did she realize she'd left without scrubbing the acrylic residue from her nails. Certainly not the ideal picture of success. "I'm doing all right, I suppose."

"So what type of art do you do?"

Experience had taught Kate that the average person wasn't genuinely interested in hearing a detailed definition of multimedia abstract naturalist paintings. "Modern."

"How fascinating. You know, I once took a tole painting class at a friend's house, but all my hummingbirds ended up looking like roosters."

Kate's lips flirted with a smile, until a dull moan from the bedroom reminded her of the purpose of her visit. "Is my father ever lucid?"

Doris reentered the room balancing a pair of teacups on saucers, each piece bearing blue and white colonial scenes. "He has his moments, though they've gotten less frequent since we had to increase his dosage." She handed over a teacup set, then sank into the lumpy russet davenport across from Kate. The scent of peppermint sweetened the room's burly smell of pine.

"I hope he hasn't been too much of a challenge for you. Accepting help has never been one of his strong points."

The corners of Doris's mouth curved up. "Well, as they say, 'Pride's been known to bring down empires.'" She winked and sipped her tea that surely contained a spoonful of sugar. All she needed was a twittering bird on her shoulder and she could play Mary Poppins on the forty-year reunion special.

"It's so nice to finally meet you in person," Doris continued. "Mr. Flaherty has raved on and on about you and your husband."

Kate passed over her words, confident the woman was embellishing to be polite. "How often have you been taking care of my father during his…"

"Transition?"

Kate lowered her gaze to the tawny liquid before her.

"I've been relieving Sarah three or four days a week."

Sarah. The Energizer Bunny with the hypnotic unibrow.

"Has anyone come to visit?" Kate asked.

"I don't believe so. Not while I've been here anyway, but I could ask Sarah for you."

"That's all right. It's not necessary."

"On second thought, a nice fellow did drop by last weekend. A tall gentleman. Silver beard. I don't recall his name, but I think your father knew him from years ago."

An old trucker buddy, no doubt. Kate raised her cup to hide her frown and blew on the steaming tea. She tested the temperature with a cautious sip. The balanced flavors of citrus and mint skimmed her tongue and warmed her throat. When she took a second sip, her necklace clinked against the saucer.

"My, that's a lovely locket," Doris remarked.

Kate glanced down at the violet-jeweled keepsake. Inside, cut into a heart shape, was the only photograph of her mother she had managed to salvage. "Thank you. It was my mom's."

"She passed on, I take it?"

Passed on. Kate hated when people used that phrase, as if they were referring to a passenger on a bus who'd decided not to get off at their usual stop.

"She was killed by a drunk driver," Kate said as coolly as the reporter had on the six o'clock news. That was all Doris needed to know.

"I'm sorry."

"It happened a long time ago."

Silence settled densely around them, like fog blanketing a cemetery. Kate snuck a subtle glimpse at her watch, wondering how soon her father would be awake. She drank from her teacup. "I imagine your job is tough, being surrounded by death all the time."

"Well, I must say, it's never easy letting patients go. But I take pride in easing their passage. Often, when I tend to their needs, I end up feeling much like a member of the family."

Kate felt the unspoken accusation hanging in the air. She shifted in her seat.

"I suppose it's always been my calling," Doris continued, "to offer support for souls crossing over. And for the troubled ones left behind. Losing a loved one can be a traumatic and confusing time for even the strongest people. Thankfully, God never gives us more than we can bear."

Her spiel sounded suspiciously like something memorized from a hospice employee manual. The evangelical bonus chapter.

Doris tilted her head, her brow furrowed. "Was it something I said?"

Kate's face must have betrayed her distaste for religious adages. "I think we have very different beliefs, that's all." She hoped that would end the topic.

"You don't believe in God, dear?"

Spectacular. "It's not that I don't believe in Him, I just don't…" Surely, Doris wasn't someone who would agree with the rationale behind agnosticism. "Forget it."

"No, go on." Doris set her cup and saucer on the round oak table beside her. Clasping her hands on her lap, she looked at Kate with interest. "I'd love to hear your thoughts."

Religion and politics. Two subjects destined for disaster.

Kate shrugged. "Let's just say I've never been a big

believer in angels floating around with feathery wings and harps. Or in a guy named Peter who stands at a gate in the clouds, checking off names like a restaurant host. To me, it's all a bit...farfetched."

Surprisingly Doris giggled. "I admit, when you put it that way, it does seem a bit silly. But I suppose that's where faith comes in."

"Yeah, well, faith tends to run in short supply in my family." In fact, with every man in her life.

"I'm sorry to hear that." Doris sighed. "Life can be a challenging journey without faith to guide you. My husband and I would've been two lost souls for certain." She patted the silver cross that hung on a short chain encircling her neck.

Kate rolled a handful of darts around in her head, debating which Judeo-Christian belief she should target next: the claim that Noah was able to not only gather, but squeeze a pair of every animal species on earth into his handmade boat, or the alleged miracle Jesus performed because a wedding couple couldn't afford cases of cabernet at their reception. They all made for great childhood stories—water to wine, staff to a reptile—but so did Santa Claus and the Tooth Fairy. Part of growing up meant separating fact from fiction, no matter how much someone wished for proof to the contrary.

"More tea?" Doris asked with a smile.

"No, thank you." Kate tucked her darts back into her skepticism box. Clearly, Doris's stance wasn't going to change any time soon, and taking potshots at the kind woman's gullibility was hardly necessary.

"How about a snack?" Before Kate could refuse, Doris rose and toddled toward the kitchen.

As Kate waited, she caught sight of a hardcover book next to the caregiver's abandoned teacup: *Heaven's Light*. Had her father sought a soul-redeeming insurance policy by joining Doris's book club? Was he seeking forgiveness for his sins?

Kate quelled the notion as she shoved her fingers

through her hair. The feel of small dried clumps prompted her to pull a lock into view. Snowy streaks of paint had artificially aged her long auburn strands. She was thirty-four, not sixty-four. Unfortunately, it would take more than a good shampooing to remove the fine lines permanently framing her eyes.

"Here we are." Doris sauntered back into the room. She placed a platter of sandwiches and a bowl of green grapes on the marred table dividing them, then resumed her position on the couch.

"Iris," her father's gravelly voice called.

Kate stiffened. It was time to do what she had come for. Whether he recognized her or not.

"Iris!"

"Yes, dear!" Doris replied.

"I love you."

"I know, dear."

Kate stared at the stranger in disbelief.

"It keeps him calm. Usually puts him right back to sleep." Doris gestured to the sandwiches. "You should eat something, honey. It won't do you any good to get sick."

Kate studied the dainty triangles of crustless bread, her stomach too knotted to eat.

"If nothing else, I do have broad shoulders." Doris smoothed her hand over the top of her dove-white hair. "So if there's anything you'd like to discuss, I'm more than willing to listen."

Thanks, but I'm fine. Kate's standard response sat on the edge of her tongue. Brief and versatile, it had proven effective in countless situations with her husband, Drew, when she wanted to be left alone. Instead, she pressed her lips together.

Here was an opportunity to finally receive affirmation that her feelings were justified. That even as Collin Flaherty's death coach neared, his only child's absence was perfectly

understandable.
    She couldn't resist.

Two

Drew Coleman scowled as he pulled his BMW into the spacious garage of his stucco suburban house. He rolled to a stop before his custom-made workbench and glared at the empty neighboring stall.

"Welcome home," he grumbled. He stepped out of the car, grabbed his suitcase from the backseat, and slammed the door. As he tramped through the laundry room, his gaze cut to a plastic bin in the sink where a collection of fanned paintbrushes soaked in murky water.

A thousand TV episodes featuring detectives investigating crime scenes had taught him how to estimate the amount of time that had passed since the suspect had fled the area. He touched a glossy drip of dark red paint with his finger. His thumb circled over the spot on his fingertip, intensifying the artistic fumes. From the tackiness of the liquid, he guessed she had come out of hiding several hours ago. Long enough to have missed his ultimatum.

He strode toward the living room and dropped his bag on the marble floor at the foot of the staircase. He tossed his keys onto the kidney bean-shaped, frosted glass table. The answering machine on it indicated two messages. He hit the playback button.

"Hey, Drew. It's Brian…"

Drew listened as he headed for the kitchen sink to scour

the paint off his hand.

"Just wanted to let you know some of the guys from the department are coming over tomorrow to play cards. Not sure how long you're in Chicago. Give me a call if you're back and want to join. We're starting around seven. See ya."

Great. Another night of surrendering his piggy bank to a group of cops dishing out as many wild cards as annoying lawyer jokes.

Drew turned the faucet on full-bore and immersed his fingers in the stream. A hint of red flowed like blood from his hand and slithered over the stark white sink. He rubbed his fingers together, then pulled them out of the water. A patch of paint was still there. Why wasn't it coming off?

"Kate, it's me."

In an instant, he recognized his own voice. Thankfully, his suspicion had been correct: she'd left the house before hearing his message. No wonder there wasn't a note on the entry table or a return call to his cellular. She didn't even know he'd flown back yet.

"I'm at O'Hare," his recorded voice went on. "I got done early, so I'm catching a flight back in about an hour. When I get home…well…I've been thinking, and…"

Just say it already! When did he become so weak? His chest tightened, the thought like a vise around his lungs.

"Maybe we need to take a break. Look, I'll be there soon, if you want to talk."

Talk? Yeah, right. Hearing the words out loud made the very idea they could have a productive discussion about their relationship seem laughable.

His focus fell back on his fingertips, now dyed pink. He pressed on the built-in soap dispenser. Nothing. He pumped it a few more times. Still nothing.

"Come on already!" He pounded the dispenser, but of course it was empty.

He closed his eyes and exhaled. *Just take a deep*

breath...

The entire flight, his mind had tossed around hopeful images of Kate at home awaiting his arrival. His suggesting a trial separation was precisely the drastic measure needed to get her attention, to recover the woman he missed, to force an overdue dialogue that could finally settle their issues. Now all he had to do was pose his unexpected threat when she returned and hope for the best.

He shut off the water, dried his hands on a kitchen towel, and moved toward the arched staircase. As he climbed the steps, he gazed up at Kate's artwork hanging on the walls. He couldn't recall when he had last looked at the pieces. Really looked at them. Not until now did he notice that the color combinations of splatters and frenetic brushstrokes darkened with each canvas he passed. From vibrant hues, to pastels, then muted shades of grays and black. The fate of their relationship had been laid out in front of him every day, and he hadn't seen it.

In Chicago, he'd spent the majority of the weekend with one of his firm's VIP clients, a man whose waistline was as large as his appetite for extramarital activities. While preparing documents for the guy's fourth divorce, Drew couldn't help but mull over the argument he'd had with Kate the night before he flew out.

"Kate, how many times do I have to explain?" Exasperated, he'd tossed his undershirts into the suitcase on the bed. "I had to pick up the bill. There was no way I could've left the dinner meeting early."

"Naturally," she'd mumbled from the doorway of the walk-in closet, tying her bathrobe belt into a tight knot.

"You think I deliberately missed the opening of your show?"

She turned to him with a steely expression. "As a matter of fact, I do."

He crumpled his brow. "Why would you say that?"

"Because you always come up with some convenient excuse not to be there."

"That's ridiculous."

"Oh, so now I'm being ridiculous?"

"I didn't say that," he grinded out. "I said, *that's* ridiculous."

She laughed humorlessly. "Thanks for the clarification. Be sure to get that one on the record."

"Like I told you, the dinner ran longer than I expected—"

"Until *midnight?*"

"Yes! What, do you think I'm lying?"

"I wouldn't know, Drew," she replied dryly. "*Are* you lying?"

He leaned on the corners of his suitcase, exhaling breaths through his nose like a trapped bull. Nearly six months had come and gone since the incident with Lindsey. Was Kate ever going to let it go?

"Believe me or don't believe me, Kate—it's up to you." His neck muscles tensed more with every shake of his head. "It doesn't always have to be this hard, you know."

Kate's eyes turned to daggers. "Well, if I'm so hard to live with, I don't know why you bother sticking around."

He wanted to object, but no words came to mind.

"Have a good trip," she said under her breath and left their bedroom.

"Kate…" He didn't follow her. He didn't have the strength. Instead, he watched her sequester herself in her studio across the hall, where he presumed she'd remain until he left for the airport and the coast was clear for her to cross enemy lines.

He had to admit, she'd raised a valid question. Why *was* he sticking around? What was he holding on to? The memory of how they used to be? The convenience of the familiar?

He just wished he knew how on earth they'd ended up here.

A hiss drew his attention downward. Kate's Persian cat had joined him on the landing. Glaring at him, she trailed her long tail across his leg. Then she pranced off, bell tinkling and nose high in the air, as if she'd deliberately shed her white hairs on his black Armani pants.

"Thanks a lot, rug rat," he told Sofo, short for some longer name he couldn't pronounce, the namesake of the first female artist of the Renaissance. The finicky cat was also a real work of art. She had a fit whenever Drew put her food in the wrong bowl or tossed her catnip baggie too far out of the foyer. Kate's companion since high school wasn't the type to build a bond with anyone else. Either too much independence or not enough trust. "Must run in the family," he muttered.

He took two steps before tripping over a ratty toy mouse. He grabbed hold of the closest door frame to catch his balance and found himself facing the room he'd made a habit of avoiding. Shipping boxes, bubble wrap, blank canvases, twisted empty frames. The space he'd once believed would hold their future had become a mere storage closet for overflow from Kate's studio down the hall.

He straightened, flicked the toy aside with the tip of his shoe, and proceeded toward their bedroom. At the gaping door, he froze. The bedding was only disturbed on his side, just as he'd left it. He knew exactly where she'd spent the weekend.

Ironic that it was *his* devotion being questioned.

The headache forming behind his eyes swelled, slightly blurring his view of the custom-designed master suite. Silk draperies, art deco furnishings, and eight-hundred thread count sheets. He would have given her the world if she asked, and all he'd ever wanted in return was her love and trust. But one mistake, one lousy mistake, and the cool tract between them had expanded into a frozen wasteland.

He headed toward the closet, tugging his necktie loose.

While passing the bed, he nabbed the cordless phone poking out from the bunched covers and dropped it onto the charger atop his nightstand. As he stepped away a revelation hit him, reaching inside to wrench his gut.

The message numbers on the answering machine hadn't been blinking when he arrived. They'd already been played. She'd heard what he said. She knew he was contemplating a break from their marriage, yet she didn't care enough to show up and give him a solitary reason to stay.

His bruised soul folded at the hands of her indifference. No, not merely indifference—worse. She would know the suitcase he had with him was already packed. Maybe she hoped he'd take a hint.

Was he jumping to conclusions? Shouldn't he wait to find out for certain when she returned from whichever errand she saw as more important?

Would it change anything?

"That's it," he said with conviction. He refused to continue a marriage with the way things were. Strangers sharing quarters. The time had come to act.

He took a deep breath and turned around. *Go. Don't think. Just go.* The command drilled through his mind as he descended the long, cold stairs. Yet when he paused to grab his suitcase and keys, a framed photo on the table gave him pause.

Tahiti. Shell necklaces. Their dream honeymoon six years ago. His shaggy hair bleached blond from the sun, his smile reflecting their newlywed bliss. And Kate, his gorgeous bride, with her salt water-slicked mane and shapely, bikini-adorned figure, as sexy as she was witty, laughing at the quirky man who'd taken five minutes to find the right button on their camera. They were tanned, relaxed, happy. Naive enough to think their future would always be as perfect as that moment.

How very wrong they were.

"Good-bye, Kate," he whispered, blinking back tears. And before he could lose his nerve, he walked out the door.

Three

"How much has my father shared with you about his life?" Kate asked, measuring her words.

Doris reclined further into the davenport. She crossed her legs as if welcoming a lengthy heart-to-heart. "Not very much, I'm afraid. But I would venture to say he's a kind man with a great deal of love to give."

Kate raked a nub on the arm of the chair with her thumbnail, a dull ache building inside her. Obviously, the caregiver hadn't been privy to his loose-lipped confession.

"Truth is, Doris, my father doesn't understand the first thing about love. He…"

What was she doing exposing her heart like this? Really, it didn't make a difference what anyone else thought. But then, wouldn't it be nice to have one other person on this planet who could see through her father's self-sacrificing, widower charade? One other person to reinforce the anger Kate was trying to sustain—needed to sustain—now more than ever.

She continued hastily before her courage waned. "After my mom died, the dad I'd grown up with disappeared too. I'm not just talking about him always being on the road driving a semi, which by the way, made him miss almost every important event in my life. I mean, any warmth he once had was gone. Unless it was a lecture, he had no words left for me."

Doris sat in silence.

The unreadable quiet hindered Kate's momentum. She rose and moved toward the open window, drawn to the sounds of early spring, of a brighter life existing outside her father's dark walnut-paneled walls. She closed her eyes. Meadowlarks chirped at a cawing crow, and the rushing water of a creek struggled to merge with the neighboring lake. Even nature was at constant odds with itself here.

Opening her eyes, she gazed past the rough cedar deck at what was left of her mother's beloved rose garden, recalling the years it had taken to adjust to seeing her aunt pruning her mom's pride and joy. To the side, lining the dirt road only lightly marked with treads, decaying blooms clung to bare stalks and overgrown wisteria branches weighed on a weary ash arbor.

Doris interrupted Kate's thoughts. "If I've learned anything, it's that men have a hard time expressing their feelings. I'm sure he only had the best of intentions."

"Maybe in *his* mind he did," Kate blurted. She perched sideways on the windowsill and allowed a few key memories to seep to the surface. "After all, he did teach me about taking responsibility—by giving my puppy away the second time I forgot to clean up after it. And canceling my birthday party because I'd thrown his truck keys in the lake, when the only reason I did it was so he'd be there to see me open my presents."

Doris's expression remained unfazed, neutral as Switzerland.

Kate would have to delve deeper to sway her opinion. "Of course, he *was* there on my wedding day."

Doris smiled warmly. She smiled because she didn't know what was coming.

"I was in my dressing room, all ready to go. Aunt Sophie had just gone to cue the musicians when in comes my father." The recollection reopened a concealed wound, exposing her soul like a cut that might never heal. Yet she charged on. "Five minutes before he's supposed to walk me down the aisle, he tells me I'm making a huge mistake. That all I had to do was give the word and we'd drive home right then. Just up and leave Drew, the pastor, the guests." Her father's objection was so unexpected she hadn't been able to articulate any heartfelt reasons for her choice. To this day, she regretted not being prepared for that moment.

"Well..." Doris seemed to be hunting for suitable words. "Perhaps he wasn't ready to give you away."

"Yeah, right." Kate's voice faltered. The instinct to leave the pain of her past unshared threatened to bar her words. She turned back to the window—the same one she used to gaze out each time her father drove away—and placed her palm on the cool glass. "For so long, I worried he'd never know who I became, or what I accomplished. I spent all this time craving his approval, and for what?" For a brief moment, Kate forgot she wasn't alone in the room.

She glanced over her shoulder to gauge her progress on Doris's face. Still neutral, completely unfazed. Evidently after raising three girls, Doris had mastered the invaluable skill of listening to each party's arguments while remaining impartial, or at least appearing as such.

There was only one bullet left in Kate's bag of ammunition. More than a bullet—a grenade her father had only recently supplied. Tossing it would surely destroy any possible excuse Doris could conjure up on behalf of her patient; for how could the God-fearing woman defend an act that broke one of the almighty commandments?

Kate was about to reveal her father's secret when fear intervened, fear that she herself might crumble in the explosion. "Look," she said. "I'm sure I've given you more information than you wanted. There's really no point in—"

A moan echoed from her father's room.

"Goodness, what time is it?" Doris's brows pinched. She turned to the grandfather clock in the corner. "I'd better check on your dad. Sounds like he's waking up." She pressed on her thighs to stand. "Would you like to come along?"

The moment had arrived. To say good-bye.

Reluctantly, Kate trod behind, as if following a warden down death row. Upon reaching the bedroom, she spied a lone tear trickling down her father's cheek. Her clenched jaw slackened.

They say hearing was the last to go. Could he have overheard their conversation?

Watching Doris adjusting his pillow, Kate regretted the harsh words she'd uttered. Right or wrong, good or evil, he was still her father.

"Hand me that blanket there, would you, dear?" Doris motioned to the Celtic throw on the hope chest at the foot of the bed.

Kate retrieved the folded fabric. As she handed it over, she asked in a cautious whisper, "How long do you think, before…?" The question caught in her throat.

"You never know for sure," Doris replied, once more sparing Kate from finishing. "But my guess is a day or two until—"

Another moan trumped the nurse's answer. Kate's father's body doubled up from a convulsion that resembled an epileptic attack.

A surge of panic shot through Kate. Blood hammered her temples, a drumbeat of helplessness. "What's happening to him?"

Doris grabbed hold of his flailing arms and pinned them to his sides.

"Doris!"

"He's having a seizure," she answered evenly. "It happens when cancer reaches the brain."

Kate clutched her chest, the sight of his restrained spasms nearly ripping out her heart. "He needs more morphine."

"He can't have any more. He's had all he's allowed." Her impartial tone made Kate's Irish temper flare.

"What difference does it make? Are you afraid it'll put him out of his misery?" Kate snapped her gaze toward the morphine device, mentally willing it to light up with a sequence of numbers that would bring her father's battle to an end. "*Please* give him another dose."

"I can't."

"But he's having a seizure!"

"Morphine won't stop the seizure."

"What will then?"

"He has pills that control them, but we ran out this morning."

"What?" Kate exploded.

"Don't worry, dear." Her voice was infuriatingly calm. "Sarah got held up with another patient, but she'll be bringing more over in a few hours."

As if responding to the nurse's assurance, her father's body suddenly relaxed. But then he let out a hollow moan that cut through Kate like a winter gale.

Doris released his arms and pressed a stethoscope to his chest. She gave a nod confirming he was still imprisoned in his ruinous shell.

Kate gazed into his constricted pupils. His empty eyes offered no answers, no peace.

"Will you be staying overnight?" Doris asked.

"I, um..." Kate had been so stunned by the woman's phone call she'd forgotten to pack a bag. Now she was glad she hadn't. She couldn't say good-bye to him tonight, not until he'd had his anti-seizure pills, not until her emotions were put back in check. "I left without my things. I'll come first thing in the morning."

"That's just fine." Doris patted Kate's hand. "You go on home. I'll let you know if anything changes."

Kate nodded. She rushed out of the room toward the

front door, holding her breath as though her dad's illness were contagious.

Once outside, she climbed into her black 4Runner and started the engine. Gripping the steering wheel as tightly as a safety bar on a roller coaster, she pulled out onto the old mountainside road, fearful of the twists and turns about to unfold—and the steep drop that surely lay ahead.

Four

The tires on her car squealed, their traction briefly slipping around the sharp corner. Kate tapped the brakes. The vanilla-scented pine tree freshener swung like a frantic pendulum from the rearview mirror. She glanced at the speedometer and realized her angst had weighted her foot on the gas pedal. Her heart pounded as her eyes averted from the edge of the winding road where a guardrail was needed but lacking.

On a dark Sunday night, with only an occasional car zooming by in the opposite direction, how long would it take for someone to discover she'd plunged down the side of the mountain? How long before Drew would even notice she was missing?

Drew...*shoot!* She'd meant to leave him a note, but Doris's call had sent her mind whirling. Glimpsing her watch, she realized how late it was.

She fumbled through her purse with her free hand. Her sudden desire to keep her eyes glued to the road hindered her ability to find her cell phone amidst the wadded receipts and other clutter of her life. For a moment, she imagined living without sight, attempting to search for an object using only the sense of touch. The thought was horrendous: an existence without vision? Without art? To never study the beautiful chaos of Jackson Pollock's drip paintings, or the vibrancy of

Rauschenberg's masterpieces? It was unthinkable.

For so many years she'd dreamt of the day she would take Drew to see those ingenious works of art in person. Not in a local museum, but somewhere more magical, like Europe, where art and life were one. Together, she and Drew would nibble on crepes, tour the Parisian halls of the *Musée Picasso*, dance in the Latin Quarter; they'd conquer the spiraling steps of the Duomo, inhaling romance from the Tuscan air like a steaming cappuccino. They'd ride the train to Amsterdam, home of the Van Gogh Museum, and giggle like children at the "colorful" world of the Red Light District.

Now, of course, Kate knew better. It was an imaginary trip she'd grown to accept would never happen. Instead, she'd found a way to live out her dreams on a fresh canvas with its endless possibilities. No words were necessary to express a feeling when a stroke of paint could say it all. And alone in her studio, like the wardrobe entrance to Narnia, she could lose herself in a world where plane tickets weren't needed for passage.

Just as the road straightened, her fingers found the phone at the bottom of her purse. She pulled it out and pressed 2 on the keypad to speed dial the house.

Ringing, ringing. Drew's voice on the answering machine: "Hi, you've reached the home of Drew Coleman and Kate Flaherty."

Kate had appreciated her husband's understanding when she wanted to keep her maiden name due to her blossoming career. Tonight though, something about hearing him state their names separately only underscored the fact they'd become little more than roommates. Her spirit sank a notch.

"Sorry you missed us," he continued. "Please leave a message, or you can connect to our cell phones by pressing one for Drew or two for Kate. Thanks."

A long silence. Then a beep.

"Hi, it's me," she said. "I got a call today about my father. His health...he isn't doing well." How was she going to explain this? She'd never told Drew her father's "cured" status hadn't lasted, hoped somehow she'd never have to. But after the message he'd left, she had no choice. "I thought you'd be home by now. Just...call me when you get this."

Where could he be? His flight should have landed hours ago.

Impatience increased her speed. She drove through the little town of Hoodsport so quickly that if she'd blinked, she would have missed it. For the next few miles, the scattered remains of Fourth of July stands and unkempt yards filled with rusted vehicles speckled both sides of the highway. On her left, the florescent sign of the Lucky Dog Casino promoted huge jackpot winnings, reminding her that for others happiness was a mere pull on a slot machine away.

When she came around the next bend, a bright orange sign jumped in front of her car.

DETOUR.

She stomped on the brakes and veered off the main highway like a criminal in a high-speed police chase, barely missing a lineup of red flares and orange cones from a broken-down semi. Her pulse raced as she straightened the wheel.

Where the heck was this taking her?

A small white highway sign answered in unsympathetic black letters–*106.*

She huffed at the inconvenient route, one she hadn't taken in years. Cracking the window, she took a deep, sobering breath. In came the smell of damp fir from the trees stippling the sides of the remote road.

For twenty minutes, not one vehicle followed her or passed in the oncoming lane. Street lamps became rarer, each yellow light shining dimmer than the last. A drive never felt so long.

As her car jounced over the rough highway lining the

Puget Sound, a layer of fog lifting from the dark waters swallowed the beams of her headlights. The ocean welcomed her back with its hazy abyss. The sounds of undulating static evidenced waves crashing on the shore. A crisp breeze brushed against her face, delivering a trace of salt to her tongue.

She tried to remember how many years it had been since she'd spent time near the sea. Crabbing, fishing, water skiing: all her happiest memories with her dad had taken place by the water. As well as the most terrifying day of her life.

Kate closed the window. She turned on the radio and flipped through the channels, all crackling between towers. A political debate. Advice for the lovelorn. The brain-itching chorus of "Gypsy Soul." She clicked it off.

Her wheels screeched as she flew around another curve and onto the connecting highway. She released her foot from the gas pedal but, resisting the instinct to use the brakes, she shoved her foot back down to accelerate. Perhaps her way of defying death, or a desperate search for control.

She lifted her phone and called home again, only to hear the same message on the machine.

Where was he?

Suddenly, Drew's words came back to her: *"Maybe we need to take a break."*

They'd had plenty of arguments in the past, but never before had he mentioned separating. What if he viewed her unexplained absence tonight as blatant apathy?

Apprehension raised her blood pressure, burned the tips of her ears.

She speed-dialed Drew's lifeline—his cell phone. It went straight to voicemail: "You've reached Drew Coleman with Milton, Sidis, and Stricklen. I'll be out of town until Monday. If this is an urgent matter, you can reach my assistant at…"

As Kate anxiously waited for the beep, she noted darkness in Drew's voice, a seriousness that had replaced the fun-loving spirit she'd fallen in love with.

"Drew, I'm on my way home," she said. "I'm heading back from my father's. I'll explain when I see you. Anyway, there was a detour. I just took highway sixteen off one-o-six, so I shouldn't be more than forty minutes away."

The glow of her headlights bounced off something ahead.

It was an animal. A deer. Standing sideways in her lane.

Kate dropped the phone. "No, no, no!" she yelled, jamming the brake pedal to the floor. She yanked back on the steering wheel as if pulling a B-52 out of a nosedive.

In exaggerated slow motion, the deer turned its head toward her. No fear in its eyes. No attempt to move. Either at peace with its fate or unwavering in its defiance.

The car's beams elongated the creature's shadow across the road, the distance between them vanishing. There wasn't time to stop; they were going to collide.

Kate screamed, swerving into the hole of blackness off the edge of the highway. Every muscle in her body clenched, preparing for impact.

Five

Kate's neck muscles strained as she slowly raised her head from the steering wheel. A sharp pain flared in her forehead. Opening her eyes, she touched the tender spot above her left eyebrow and brought her fingers into view. No blood. She blinked hard to clear her bleary vision.

Her mind replayed the moments just before her car had slammed to a stop. Adrenaline flooded her body, her pulse pounded like the bass beat of a stereo. She drew a long breath to calm the vibration in her hands. Based on the dirt covering her windshield and the angle of her locket dangling in mid-air air from her neck, she had landed hood-first in a ditch.

Her day couldn't possibly get any worse. Oh, what was she thinking? Of course it could.

At least the car hadn't flipped over. But shouldn't it have released the airbag? Apparently, the massive vehicle Drew had insisted she drive for safety's sake had never been tested in a face-off with a Bambi blockade. Another lawsuit to keep her husband busy. Just what he needed—a new case to consume his time.

She raised her hand to find the overhead light. Finally, the switch. She clicked it once, twice. Darkness. Not even a glow or flicker from the dashboard panel.

She hated to call for reinforcements, but she had no choice. She patted the passenger seat, then the floorboards in search of her cell phone. Feeling something beneath her heel, she reached down and her fingers closed around it.

With her free hand, she struggled to push the angled car door open. The second she climbed out of the vehicle, her lungs gobbled up the pine-scented air as though she'd resurfaced from a deep-sea dive with an empty tank.

Surveying the area, she half-expected to find the deer lying in the ditch near her car. But there was no trace of the animal. Kate was alone.

She heaved a breath of relief, and her thoughts returned to her husband. She dialed Drew's number and got the *No Service* indicator on the digital screen. Phone held as high as her stiff body would allow, she zigzagged on the gravel road, like a ghostbuster on a quest for supernatural beings.

Still no service.

"Come on!"

Call forwarding, call waiting, caller ID, deluxe voicemail. A handy gadget if you weren't in the flippin' boonies.

She turned to her vehicle with a damage-assessing gaze. Her auto body knowledge didn't extend past oil changes and flat tires, but that had never stopped her from portraying otherwise at the local repair shop—not when she could see the damsel-in-distress estimate multiplying with every nod from a scruffy mechanic. Of course, with the left rear wheel suspended several inches off the ground, it didn't take a genius to determine the car wouldn't be going anywhere without the aid of heavy-duty equipment.

She looked up and down the moonlit highway. Trees, trees, and more trees. She thought she would recognize the area she'd grown up near, but nothing appeared familiar. Between the drifting fog and her shaken nerves, she might as well have been in the Amazon.

Her eyes flashed back to the phone. No signal. She hit *Send* anyway, just to be sure.

Nothing.

Frustration skyrocketing, she hit the key with her thumb again, harder, harder, beating it into submission. Like punching an elevator call button to demand its instantaneous arrival. Her final strike sent it tumbling to the pavement.

"No, no, no!"

She scooped up her cell only to find a black screen. She depressed the *Power* key repeatedly, trying to resuscitate the device. All she got was an empty square, punishing her for its undeserved abuse.

It was official. She had killed the phone.

The moment called for a bellowing curse that would ricochet off every tree in the vicinity, sending forest creatures scurrying for safety. But what good would that do? It certainly wouldn't change her situation, other than signaling her whereabouts to a pack of hungry wolves or a psychiatric ward escapee with a hook for a hand.

She pitched the cell phone into the car and shut the door, tried to think like a guy. Problem—solution. There had to be a solution.

She remembered passing a lone house sitting back off the road, a light shining inside. But it had to be a mile, if not two, behind her.

Turning the other way, she saw something in the distance. A metal glint, just past the concrete bridge—a railroad track running parallel to the highway. A memory rushed to her aid. Her father used to take her to a diner near those tracks. She recalled the joy that came with the bumping and rattling of her father's pickup truck as they rode over the steel lines, alerting her to the proximity of her favorite sundae. The heavenly creation had such a thick pool of warm butterscotch and chocolate syrup she could barely find the ice cream. Hopefully the old joint was still there.

As she strode across the bridge and toward the rails, the lunar glow above brightened through shifting clouds. She didn't have to raise her eyes to verify it was a full moon. What else could it be on a night like this? A Stephen King fantasy.

Her boots crunched pebbles as she turned left onto the dirt road and stepped over the tracks. A light blinked up on the right. She walked toward the beacon, trying her best to block out notions of what might be skulking in the dense woods around her, ready to lunge at its vulnerable prey.

Why was she allowing such notions into her mind? Too many of her dad's ghost stories by the campfire. And, according to her mother, too many roasted marshmallows on those same nights, priming her mind for sugar-high nightmares.

Kate hurried toward the neon sign. She could finally make out the name— *Gordy's Diner*—minus a few burnt-out letters.

"Please be open."

At last she arrived at the parking lot. The absence of cars worried her until she saw a figure through the lit window of the nostalgic café. By all accounts, it was in such great condition she wouldn't have been surprised if it had been a shooting location for a movie or two. At least that's how it seemed in the dark. A perfect set for a passé film. Or maybe a horror flick.

A twig snapped nearby. Or did it? She halted.

Silence. Eerie silence.

Breath held, she quickened her steps.

Six

"Freeze! Put your hands up!"

The woman's voice from behind, nearly stalled Drew's heart. Spinning around, he fumbled his glass on the metal railing, nearly dropping it off Brian's balcony. "Dang, Lindsey, you scared me."

"Breaking and entering is a felony, you know." Her body, draped in a bathrobe, filled the space between the jamb and open sliding glass door. "Any concealed weapons you want to tell me about, or am I gonna have to frisk you?"

Of all people to see tonight. He'd come here to get away—from Kate, from all of life's troubles—and here was Lindsey, the very person who'd kicked off the downward spiral of his marriage.

"Door was unlocked," he replied coolly.

She angled her towel-turbaned head back over her shoulder as if studying the front door of the condo for proof. "I see." She turned her chestnut brown eyes back to Drew. "Just illegal entering, then."

"Very cute." He leaned his hip against the two-tiered railing and took a drink of his whiskey. The liquor flowed hot down his throat while his eyes graced Lindsey's body. The kitchen lights shining through the window outlined her curves beneath the silky white robe, her runner's figure just as fit as the last time he'd seen it.

He forced his gaze back to his tumbler.

"Prowling around the place?" Her voice was as smoky and smooth as a Cohiba cigar.

"When I got here, I heard the water running. I thought Brian was in the shower."

"Dee, we're in Washington, not the Ozarks. Here, brothers and sisters quit showering together once they're in preschool."

"You should be a comedienne. Really." He offered a weak smile and took another sip. "I assume he's not home, then."

"No, he's at the gym. He...." She covered her nose with her hand as she sneezed.

"There's number one," he muttered.

Right on cue, a second sneeze squeaked out. For some reason, her sneezes always came in pairs. Maybe it was an Italian thing.

"Linds, you'd better close the door before you catch cold." The cool wind whistled as if in agreement.

"You joining me?" The corners of her lips curled up.

"In a bit."

She nodded and slid the pane closed.

A drop touched his hand, then his cheek. The sprinkles multiplied. A Northwest native, he should have been a meteorologist. *Tomorrow's forecast, 100 percent chance of showers followed by a downpour with periodic breaks of drizzle.* Now, there was a stress-free job.

He glanced around once more. The golden lights of the city twinkled in the distance as moonlight dripped a white jagged trail over the black water of the Des Moines marina. Brian's fifth-floor balcony boasted a 180-degree view from Tacoma to Vashon Island. Only a twenty-minute drive from Drew's house, but still worlds away.

Finishing off his whiskey, he noted the faint sputtering of an unseen motorboat interwoven with pop music and giggles, the sounds of carefree youth he and Kate no longer possessed. "Ain't this the life." He issued the sigh of a man twice his age before reentering his best friend's haven.

Lindsey stood behind the small, black Naugahyde bar, pouring herself a glass from the bottle he'd left open. "Jack Daniel's, huh?" she said. "I thought you only drank Wild Turkey."

He shrugged and stepped around a pillar of squashed pizza boxes. "It was the closest thing I could find."

"See? That's why I'm never getting hitched. Men have no loyalty whatsoever."

If it weren't for her playful tone, he would have slung an angry retort. He was tired of standing accused of a crime he hadn't committed. Sure, he wasn't completely innocent. In hindsight, mentioning a spontaneous dinner with his old flame would have been wiser than leaving evidence on his nightstand. Kate had undoubtedly fumed all day after finding the restaurant receipt he had folded around Lindsey's phone number, before finally confronting him.

Regardless, there was a big difference between a misdemeanor and a felony.

Drew moved into the living room and plopped down at the far end of the couch. The rust-colored cushions reeked of stale beer and cigarette smoke. But with the furnishing's ability to accommodate his six-foot-two frame, it would make a decent bed until he figured out what he was going to do with his life.

Soon Lindsey rounded the single rattan chair piled with clothes. She stood before him, gripping the bottle of JD in one hand and a quarter-filled tumbler in the other. "You mind?" She lifted her pointed chin toward the couch, the glint in her eyes implying she was after more than an invitation to sit.

Seven

Kate approached the diner's entrance, trying to ignore the soreness in her left shoulder and hips. Side effects from the seatbelt restraints.

Inside she was sure to find a chatty, gum-popping waitress in a white jumpsuit with a pencil stuck behind her ear and a nametag reading "Madge." On a lonely night like this, the woman would undoubtedly have spent the last two hours of her shift enjoying the free landline and unlimited cups of watered-down coffee. And with a pot-bellied chef engrossed in a comic book in the back, Madge would love fresh company.

Kate groaned, then smoothed her hair and pinned on a smile.

When she reached for the door handle, pain shot through her hand like a surge of electricity. She grabbed her wrist, held it until the burning sensation passed. As she released her grip, she noticed a crack splitting the face of her treasured watch.

Her stomach dropped.

She raised the timepiece to her ear. No ticking. She looked at the hands. Frozen at 6:17. The graduation gift from Aunt Sophie was ruined. Like so many other things in Kate's life.

She carefully stored the watch in her pants pocket and opened the metal door bearing a circular window. Behind the long, white Formica bar stood a tall, lean man who she presumed answered to a name other than Madge. Kate waited in silence as he finished laying out his till; a request for a favor would be better received if she didn't ruin his count.

He raised his head. "Sorry, ma'am, kitchen's closed." In a boyish gesture, he used his hand to comb the bangs off his face. His eyes matched the color of his cinnamon brown hair. He looked roughly Drew's age, thirty-five or thirty-six, but he had the golden complexion of an outdoorsman.

"Actually, I just need to use the phone," Kate said, massaging her wrist. "I ran my car off the road avoiding a deer."

"Good to see you're all right." His concerned tone complemented his demeanor, his faint accent bearing evidence of a Midwest upbringing. "I hate to tell ya, though, the telephone line's about as useful as your car likely is right now. I hear someone hit a pole on the highway earlier and took down some wires. Who knows, maybe they were trying to miss the same ole deer."

"No, that can't be," she said.

"Well… I was kidding about the deer. I doubt it was the same—"

"No, that's not what I meant. I just have to use the phone. Are you sure it's out?"

"Afraid so. Just tried it again a few minutes ago."

Fabulous.

From the side came a familiar melody. She angled her head toward the bubbled Wurlitzer jukebox in the corner. Andy Williams was crooning "Moon River." That cheesy record had been played in the house so many times while she was growing up she could name it after only a few notes. She faced the man behind the counter. "Do you know if there's a tow service close by? Or anyone who'd have a working phone?"

A smile slid across his lips. He scooped up a handful of ice from a bin and laid the cubes in the center of a white bar

45

towel. "There's an auto shop a few miles up the way, though I'm guessing Fred's home with his family at this hour. I'd give him a jingle, but..."

"But the lines are down."

"You got it." He closed the cloth over the icy mound and handed it to her. "Here. Looks like you could use this."

She glanced at her red, swollen wrist. "Oh, right. Thank you."

"I still have a few things to finish up. So you're welcome to stay till my ride shows. I imagine the phone lines should be up and working soon. I'd be happy to keep checkin' if you'd like." He reached into a corner window and flipped over the *OPEN* sign. "Feel free to make yourself at home, ma'am."

Ma'am. She felt too young to warrant the title. Still, she smiled in acknowledgement.

His prediction didn't sound all that promising, but waiting for a prompt repair of the phone lines was better than holding up her thumb on the side of the cold, dark highway.

She headed toward the row of black booths running the length of the windowed wall and chose the one at the end. Sinking into the cushioned vinyl, she scanned the mnemonic café.

At the bar, the guy began to refill saltshakers that were lined up as perfectly as the diner's padded swivel stools. Black and white, Kate's favorite combination, was the dominant theme of the room. The simple tones colored everything from the checkered floor tiles to the photographs hanging on an adjacent wall.

"Your first time in here?" the man asked as he screwed tops on the shakers.

"No. Haven't been back since I was a kid, though."

"Meatloaf surprise scare you away?" He winked.

"Maybe," she replied.

When *had* she been here last? She must have been

only…what, seven years old?

That's right. She and her parents had just come from an antiques auction in Alderbrook. There, a large-nosed man with white ear hair had blown cigar smoke in their direction, causing her father to wave his bidding card to clear the pungent cloud. Her dad ended up accidentally buying an overpriced, cracked chamber pot destined for the Salvation Army, or as her mother had said cajolingly, "the most expensive planter" they ever owned.

Kate caught her lips smiling and drew them in. She was amazed she'd retained any joyful memories from her youth at all, even of times prior to her mother's death, as she'd convinced herself none existed.

"If the phone's still out when my wife gets here," the guy's voice pulled her to attention, "we'd be happy to give you a lift somewhere."

Accepting a ride from a stranger defied one of the most basic common sense rules ingrained in her since kindergarten. But with his wife in the car, the situation made for an exception. Kate only hoped he wouldn't recant his offer once he knew how far away she lived.

Timidly she asked, "Auburn on your way home?"

"Not our usual route, but it shouldn't be a problem."

"I'd appreciate that." Relief spilled over her.

He motioned toward a half-filled coffee pot. "How about a cup of Joe while we're waitin'?"

"Sure." Opposite of Madge's, his brew was likely strong enough to wake the dead. But if all went well, they would be leaving before she had time to drink much of it anyway.

Almost instantly, he arrived at her table with a ceramic mug and a glass pot emitting the scent of fresh roasted coffee beans. As he poured steaming dark liquid into the cup, his sidelong glance implied he was studying her.

"How's that for ya?" he asked.

"Plenty, thanks." She answered without confirming the amount he'd poured.

He returned to the back of the bar where he filled a cup for himself. He took a drink, then grabbed a straw broom propped in a corner and began sweeping the floor.

Kate removed the damp towel resting on her numb wrist. The swelling had already started going down. She sipped from her mug, finding the drink more comforting than she'd expected. At least the detour would give her time to contemplate what waited at home—assuming Drew was even still speaking to her.

"So what brings you out this way?" the man called out.

"Just...heading home," she said, gazing at her mug on the shiny white table.

"Everything there okay?"

She glanced up, taken aback. "What do you mean?"

"You just seem to be in a hurry. I'm hoping it's nothing urgent."

What could she say? That her husband might be clearing out his side of the closet at this very moment, sticking around just long enough to say good riddance?

"My apologies, ma'am. Don't mean to pry. It's simply my nature. Can't mind my own business most days." Sympathy shone in his eyes.

Great. She might as well have hung a sign around her neck to make her turmoil a little more obvious. Time to deflect with some lighthearted sarcasm. "Is it always this crowded on Sunday nights?"

"Not sure. I'm actually the new guy here."

"So you're not Gordy, I take it."

"Me? No, I'm not the head honcho. Just a fella trying to earn an honest living." He returned his broom to the corner and started toward her with his cup in hand. "May I?" He motioned to the seat facing her and sat down before she could reply. "The name's Mick." He extended a large, callused hand across the table.

"Nice to meet you." She reached out for a brief shake, but his other hand closed over hers and held it tightly, a look of satisfaction in his eyes.

A chill trickled down her back. The hair on her neck stirred.

Something wasn't right.

Eight

Lindsey settled herself sideways on the middle cushion of the couch, pressing her knee against Drew's thigh. He subtly shifted a few inches away.

"Refill?" She faced him, raising the bottle.

He held out his tumbler which contained only melting ice cubes. As he watched the whiskey streaming, something just beyond the rim of the glass arrested his gaze. The crisscross of her robe had gapped open enough to verify that her firm breasts were indeed free of a constraining bra. Always a front hook, as he recalled. His hand volunteered the memory of her soft olive skin. His abs tightened with the vision of her hair brushing against his stomach.

"Enough?" she asked.

"What?"

"Whiskey." She smirked, deepening her devilish dimples.

He nodded briskly. "Yeah, thanks."

Maybe it was *his* turn to take a shower. A cold one.

He drowned his primitive instincts in a gulp, then asked, "You forget to pay your water bill?"

"Not quite." She set the bottle on the table and took a generous swig from her tumbler. When she sat back, her garment fell into place, harboring her cleavage and shoving temptation aside. "My bathroom's getting remodeled, so I'm stuck using Brian's for a week."

"Gotcha." Seeking a distraction, Drew scanned the disarrayed magazines on the coffee table: *Sports Illustrated, Maxim, Men's Fitness.* Every cover featured a half-naked woman with silicone enhancements and airbrushed curves. What the heck was a blonde bombshell in a bikini doing on the front of *Men's Fitness*?

"So?" She arched an eyebrow.

"So...what?"

She downed the rest of her booze and set the glass aside. "So what was the fight about?"

"What fight?"

"With the little wife. Must've been some spat to get you to move in with my brother."

Lindsey couldn't possibly know. She had to be joking around.

"What makes you think I'm moving in?"

"Well, let's see...it's black, has two wheels and a handle, and is stuffed full of clothes folded as neatly as a Neiman Marcus display."

He'd forgotten he'd parked his suitcase beneath the armrest beside him. "You should consider becoming a private eye."

She chuckled.

Lindsey was still as feisty as when they'd first met during his freshman year at the University of Washington. Brian, who was then his roommate, had warned him about the rebellious older sister who was coming to visit, and she'd certainly lived up to her reputation. Skydiving, bungee jumping, mountain climbing—the riskier the better. Lindsey would challenge a biker to a game of nine ball, then wink as she tucked the sucker's cash into the back pocket of her low-rise jeans.

"How much do PI's make, anyway?" she asked.

"Varies, I guess."

"Just ballpark."

He shrugged. "I can't imagine it's more than what you already pull in. Stick with bartending. Believe me, it's a cleaner living."

"It can't be any worse than the summer I spent working for a nine-hundred line."

"I don't think I need to hear any more."

"Oh, calm down." She waved her hand dismissively. "It was for a psychic network."

"I didn't know you were psychic."

"Never said I was." She unwound the towel on her head and ran her fingers through short black ringlets. "Of course, if I were, I might know what your little tiff was about. *And* I'd know why you'd pick this place over somewhere like the Four Seasons."

Her example was far from random. They'd been dating a month or two when they'd spent a memorable weekend at the elegant hotel in Manhattan. From a whirlpool tub to a grandiose bed and a mirrored elevator equipped with an emergency stop button, they'd enjoyed every amenity the place had to offer.

Back to a safer subject. "I don't get it. What have you got against your brother's pad?"

"Are you kidding? This dive?"

"*Dive?* It's bachelor heaven. HD TV, surround sound, pool table." He had to admit the flickering neon beer signs over the bar bordered on tacky, but the freedom Brian's condo represented often launched a streak of envy through Drew.

"How does Kate feel about you living like a bachelor?"

He stared at the last sliver of ice floating in his drink, wishing the mere mention of her name didn't darken his already sullen mood. "I don't think she'd care. We're...taking some time."

Silence. As heavy as his head now felt.

"You wanna talk about it?" she asked.

"Not really."

More silence. More whiskey. More emptiness, facing the fact that he knew, deep down, he and Kate wouldn't just be taking a short break. He'd been a divorce lawyer too long not to know that separation was just one step and one brutal court battle away from a final farewell.

Lindsey grabbed her purse from the foot of the couch and retrieved a lighter and a pack of cigarettes.

"I thought you quit smoking," he said.

The corners of her eyes curved up as she smiled. "Some habits are too hard to break." Her sultry tone thickened the air.

She placed a cigarette between her lips and flipped open the top of her lighter. Two rolls of the metal wheel under her thumb produced only small sparks. Drew relieved her of the silver monogrammed device, a lavish gift from a guy no doubt, and in one swift motion presented an orange flame. He felt like James Bond, minus the tux and Walther PPK.

She pursed her lips together and inhaled as he lit the tip. He wasn't a fan of cigarettes, but even during the year they'd dated on and off, he never pushed her to quit. Lindsey always did whatever she wanted anyway, so long as it felt good and didn't require a commitment.

They were perfect for each other back then.

"What about you?" Drew asked, desperate to confirm all was well with her and her nightclub bouncer boyfriend—a guy who, according to Brian, had a roadmap of tattoos on his arms that hinted at prison time served.

She pulled the cigarette from her mouth and blew a stream of smoke to the side. "What about me?"

"How are you and your boyfriend making out?" The second the words came out, he regretted the unintended pun.

"Which boyfriend?"

"The resident of Cell Block Four."

She laughed. "We split up months ago."

"Sorry. I hadn't heard."

"Doesn't matter. Wasn't anything serious." She exhaled another stream that expanded into an enveloping grey cloud.

Drew rubbed his watering eyes and coughed.

She crushed her cigarette in the plastic ashtray on the table as she added, "He ended up moving back east to work with some of his old buddies."

"Laundry duty at McCreary Penn?"

Her jaw dropped. "Holy cannoli! Drew Coleman still has a sense of humor." When she pinched his side, he jumped as though she'd pressed an eject button. "Hell, Dee, are you still that ticklish?"

"Knock it off," he ordered, trying to erase his involuntary grin.

She pinched his side again, causing his whole body to twitch.

"Look at you," she said, "You're like a little girl."

"I mean it, Linds." He set his glass down hard on the table. "I'm not in the mood."

"Oh, please. I hardly touched you. All I did was—"

When she raised her hands, he reflexively grabbed her wrists and pinned them behind her back. "I'm not joking." He was trying for a firm tone, but he failed.

"Okay, okay, I give up," she said, giggling. "It was an accident."

"*Accident?* That wasn't an accident."

"I swear, I didn't know you were ticklish."

He couldn't help but laugh. "Liar!" She had pulled that maneuver on him too often in his dorm room to believe her allegation.

"Fine," she sang out. "But it won't happen again."

"And I should trust you because…?"

"Because I mean it this time."

He laughed harder, and it felt great. In an instant, he had reverted into a flirtatious teenager who prayed he'd at least make it to second base.

"All right," he said, "I'm letting you go. But with a serious warning." As he relinquished his grip, he realized his body was lying on hers. Their fading smiles were only a few inches apart. He tasted her warm breath. Mint, tobacco, whiskey.

The temperature rose.

He had an urge to place his mouth over hers, to disappear into another world, a place where he felt like the man he used to be. A place where he wasn't alone. And why the hell not? Kate never fully believed his explanation. As far as she was concerned, he had already crossed the line. Guilty beyond a reasonable doubt.

Justifications abounding, he peered into Lindsey's eyes. In them, he found acceptance of his unspoken proposal. She lifted her head slightly, enticing him.

Suddenly they were kissing. Her thin lips felt familiar, but still foreign enough to charge him with a thrill of the unknown.

Just then, morality made its plea: *Do you really want to prove Kate's suspicions were right after all?*

Of course not. That wasn't the kind of guy he was. Regardless of what his wife thought.

He pulled back from Lindsey, pausing the same way he had the first time they'd made out, when his conscience had reminded him he was about to feel up his best friend's sister. That night in his car, just like now, Lindsey's boldness sliced through his hesitation. She laced her hands around his neck and kissed him, deeper, more passionately.

Since the day he'd met Kate, he'd never thought he would so much as consider being with another woman. But now, in this moment, with Lindsey's curves pressed against his body, he couldn't deny the euphoria that filled him. The strength. The desire. The forbidden. The unmistakable feeling that she wanted him too.

What are you doing? The whispering voice came from

inside him.

He refused to answer; he was tired of being questioned. He slid his fingers into her hair, squeezed his eyes tight, and surrendered.

Nine

Mick's hand remained clasped on Kate's, and her thoughts swirled as swiftly as her pulse.

Why wasn't he letting go? Was coming here a fatal mistake? Could she outrun him to the diner's front door?

Just then, he released his grasp. He picked up his mug and leaned back in the booth, giving her the space she craved. A safety zone.

"So you're a painter," he said, and took a gulp of coffee.

Her question nervously squeezed out. "How did you know…?"

"I just hope you got more paint on the walls than yourself."

She followed his gaze to the dried splatters on her sweatshirt. The thought of him observing her body prompted her to layer her arms on the table to block his view. "Yeah, right."

"How about a song?"

What, was he going to serenade her?

She gripped her forearms and echoed, "A song?"

"It won't cost you a dime if there's something you'd like to hear." He pointed to the jukebox, a forty-five record inside clicking back into the vertical rack. "It had a habit of eatin' customers' coins, so the owner jury-rigged it. Now all the songs are free."

"That's okay. I'm...not much of a music person."

"You sure? 'Cause if you don't pick 'em, I'll have to."

"It's your show." She commanded her lips to feign pleasantry.

"All right, but you can't say I didn't offer." He smiled while scooting out of the booth and turned toward the glowing machine.

As he strolled away, Kate realized how foolish she was being. After all, she wouldn't be an artist without a wild imagination. "Overactive," her aunt used to call it. Indeed, this man was her rescuer, not her captor.

"Bing?" Mick called over his shoulder.

"Excuse me?"

"Do you like Bing Crosby?"

"Oh. Sure. He's fine." She drew a long sip from her cup, keeping an eye out for headlights. "How soon do you think your wife'll be here?"

"Should be any time now."

She looked around for a wall clock, but there wasn't one in sight. Perhaps it was better that way. Watching the seconds tick by at a sloth's pace would only intensify her anxiety.

As Mick slid back into his seat, the crooner's unmistakable vocals filled the room. "Swinging on a star," he said. "You know this oldie?"

Yeah, she knew it. All too well. It was one of the tunes she and her dad used to dance to, her feet on his as he rocked around the room, stiffening his legs like Frankenstein's. She responded to Mick's question with a mere nod, attempting to keep her memories bound within the cobwebs of her mind.

"My mom loved it to bits," Mick said. "She'd crank it up whenever it came on the radio. Got so I hated it. But then one day, I'm driving the truck on a delivery and found myself hummin' along with it." His lips eased into a smile. "Funny

how things you think you'll never do become second nature."
Leave the topic alone, she told herself.
But she couldn't.
"You drive a semi?" More of a statement than a question.
"Oh, no, just my own pickup." His gentle tone indicated he didn't catch the edge in her remark, or he'd chosen to ignore it. "I've definitely racked up some mileage with all the furniture deliveries I've made this year. But at least it's got me primed for a job at Consolidated. You know, the freight company?"
She shook her head.
"Well, I applied to work for them anyway. I may have to drive across a few states now and then, but the insurance and pay is worth it. Pretty soon I'll have something put away for my little girl."
In Kate's peripheral vision, she saw a flash of light and felt a flicker of hope. Her hand curved into a visor across her forehead as she peered through the dark window. She strained her eyes as heated air from her nose and mouth created foggy spheres on the pane.
Nothingness. A black hole separated by glass. Must have been a reflection.
Shielding her angst, she turned back to Mick. "I'm sorry, you were saying?"
"Just talkin' about my daughter. She's five, goin' on twenty. It's like her wheels never quit turning. But I guess that's a girl for ya, right?" He lowered his eyes and beamed as if he could see the youngster's image in the glossy table.
"She's a funny little thing. Just yesterday, I was tucking her in and started to act like I was gonna gobble up her cheeks." He looked at Kate. "It always made her laugh when she was a baby. But all of a sudden, out of nowhere, she puts up her hand like so—" He held up his palm. "—and says, 'Daddy, please stop. I am *not* a cookie.'"

A giggle snuck out of Kate.

"I tell ya, it all goes by too quick."

Kate dropped her gaze to her mug. She ran her thumb along the rim as she recalled the emotional gap that had widened with each of her father's cross-country lumber deliveries. Knowing his bedding and a bag of clothes were tucked into the back of his cab had left her in perpetual fear that every good-bye might be their last.

"Did I say something I shouldn't have, ma'am?"

"No, it's just..." She hesitated. "Well, my dad drove a rig for about twenty years. He lived on the road, so I grew up not knowing much about him."

"If you don't mind me askin', how'd your mother manage on her own?"

"My *mother*?" Her brow pinched at the intimacy of his question.

"See, the missus assures me they'll do just fine when I'm away. But if I've learned anything, it's that you ladies don't always tell us when something's really bothering ya."

Kate relaxed her features. "She was fine. More than fine actually..." Sensing where her own betraying words were leading, Kate cut to a tidy conclusion. "I don't think I'm a good resource for you, though."

"Oh, and why's that?"

Why wasn't she giving Mick the appeasing reply he was looking for?

"Mick, I'm sure our family was night and day from yours."

"How you figure?"

She rounded her shoulders. "I suppose you could say my parents had a *When Harry Met Sally* kind of relationship."

His blank expression indicated the love-hate reference was lost on him.

"What I mean is, they'd have petty arguments constantly, some of them screaming matches. Then instantly, everything was wonderful again. They'd sit at the dinner table, laughing and teasing each other like nothing ever happened."

Well…until their last fight, of course. The night when all their fighting ended. The night a cloak fell over Kate's world, leaving her in a darkness that refused to lift.

Ten

Drew, what the hell are you doing? The gentle voice in his head turned stern.

He wanted to do more than ignore it—he'd defy it. He pulled Lindsey's robe back over her shoulder and kissed her neck harder. The crisp smell of soap on her skin and lavender from her damp hair threw his senses into a tornado spin.

Stop! Don't do this!

"Shut up," he growled at his grating conscience.

"What?" Lindsey asked in his ear.

Shit. He'd said it out loud.

"Nothing." He smothered her bewilderment by placing his lips on hers, then slipped his hand between her back and the couch, drawing her body closer. When she moaned faintly, his urge to ravage her soared. To proceed with any act with any woman, so long as it trampled thoughts of Kate and forced them from his mind.

Just then, something pressed into his kneecap. He tried to dismiss it, but couldn't. Without looking, he reached down to toss the object aside.

A female voice boomed from every direction. His head snapped up.

"Then Dr. Robbins will share five effective ways to get your life back on track after a traumatic episode." Oprah Winfrey glared at him through the flat screen television mounted on the wall.

He scrambled for the remote control wedged between the cushions. The volume of the speakers was nearly maxed, likely from the last sports game Brian had watched on his new system.

"We'll also meet a woman," the commercial continued, "who claims her husband's affair turned her into a lesbian."

Drew frantically punched buttons on the remote. *Mute*, *Off*, anything to stop the cautionary onslaught.

"Join us tomorrow—" *Click.* The screen blackened.

Drew bristled in his seat at the far end of the couch.

Several moments dragged until he turned to Lindsey, who was gazing at him with interest. With her temple propped up with one elbow and one knee bent, exposing her smooth thigh through the split in her robe, she reminded him of an exotic Playboy model: posed, sexy, confident. Any warm-blooded heterosexual guy would have gone weak in the knees.

"Linds—I..." Suddenly, he was Dustin Hoffman in *The Graduate.*

She arched her Mrs. Robinson eyebrow and smiled.

"I'm sorry," he said. "I shouldn't have—"

"No worries." She gave a light shrug. "Just got a little carried away is all."

He nodded. Then he ran his hand over his hair and gripped the back of his neck.

She interrupted the awkward silence that followed by cinching her robe and standing up, crunching something on the rug beneath her foot. "Relax, Dee, I've gotta get ready for work anyway." She pivoted and left orange particles behind on the rug, undoubtedly a Cheetoh...cheater...cheat. How fitting.

As she disappeared into the bathroom, Drew noticed he was still clutching the remote. *Goddamn thing.* He flung it at Brian's heap of not-quite-dirty-enough-to-wash clothing.

Drew's pulse slowed as he reprimanded himself for his code of propriety. Outside of formalities, wasn't he a free man

63

already? What better way to make a stand and reclaim his identity? After all, Kate had abandoned their marriage long ago.

He snagged his Tennessee buddy, Jack D. and emptied the last of the guilt-reducer into his tumbler. He raised his glass toward a framed photo on the fireplace mantle: he and Brian with a group of their fraternity brothers, beer cans held on their heads, faces slimy from the blueberry Jell-O they'd used for the sorority's wrestling mixer.

"To the good ole days," he said and threw back his drink. Gulping it down, he envied Brian for the open gullet that had made the guy an icon at their frat house. With a tolerance that others always underestimated due to his short stature, Brian was surely just as revered today at the testosterone-brimming sheriff's department.

Suddenly, as if he'd been summoned by Drew's thoughts, Brian stepped through the front door. "Hey, man. What's up?" he asked, as the alcohol ignited in Drew's chest. Unable to reply, Drew tossed up his hand.

"Wait." Brian paused, his face puzzled. "I didn't say we were playing cards *tonight,* did I?"

"No," Drew managed to rasp out.

"Good. You scared me. Thought maybe I'd screwed up on the message I left." Brian shut the door with his foot and lobbed a stack of mail onto the kitchen counter. By the time he swiped a beer from the fridge, a few envelopes had slid off the pile and landed on the floor. "So you just stop by to hang out or what?"

Drew kept one discreet eye on the hallway, his thoughts racing over the question of whether Lindsey would say anything. He cleared his throat. "Actually, I came over to help you practice for tomorrow. Considering the wad you gave up at the last game, I wasn't sure you knew the difference between an ace and a deuce."

Brian grinned. "Asshole." He twisted off the cap, flung

it into the sink, and tipped the bottle to his lips in one honed motion.

Drew busied himself by snagging a handful of peanuts out of a bowl on the coffee table. He popped several into his mouth as his friend made his way over.

"You and Lindsey do some catching up?"

Drew choked on the stale nuts before forcing them down. Silently, he gave thanks that his buddy hadn't arrived five minutes earlier. He gestured to the half-filled bowl. "These aren't from the last time we played cards, are they?"

"Hard to say. Might be." With one shove, Brian relocated his clothing pile to the floor and reclined in the rattan chair. He wiped the sweat from his black brush-cut hair with the kitchen towel he'd slung over his shoulder. "How's life treating you, counselor?"

Before Drew could answer, high heels began clacking on the hardwood floor in the hallway.

"Hey, Linds," Brian called.

"Just in time," she said. "I was afraid I was gonna have to leave your little friend here all alone."

Without looking up, Drew felt as sure as the starch in his white Oxford shirt that she was smirking. He ran two fingers along the inside edge of his collar and wondered if the condo had air conditioning.

"Thanks for letting me borrow your shower," she said to her brother.

"No problem. I'll add it to your tab."

"Cheap ass."

"Yeah, and who's here for the free hot water?"

"Whatever."

Drew flicked a glance in her direction. He was relieved to see that a black cleavage-boasting shirt and curve-hugging slacks had replaced her silky robe.

"Bye, Dee. Good seeing you," she said.

"You too." The words sprinted out as he returned his

face forward, eyes on a small crack in the wall.

"Oh, and Brian," she added, "take a shower, would ya? I can smell you from here."

Brian raised his elbow and gave his armpit a quick sniff. He shrugged and took another swig of MacTarnahan's Ale.

The instant the door clicked shut, Drew lifted the empty liquor bottle from the table and upended it over his tumbler. Barely buzzed, he hoped a reserve compartment would miraculously deliver a final glassful. Thankfully, a few drops appeared. He hinged the glass on his lips and waited with the desperation of a man in the Mojave who had discovered an empty water canteen.

"Hard day?" Amusement filtered through Brian's voice.

No, Drew told himself, *just a long time coming.*

Eleven

Mick pursed his lips. "So, you're one of those folks who see life as a romance flick, where everything ends happily ever after."

"Yes," Kate replied before thinking. "I mean, no—of course not." Frustration ground at her like the heel of a shoe. "I just think people who truly love each other should find a better way to work things out." Or at least remain faithful when the going gets tough.

As he nodded, she realized how worked up she'd gotten. She had no business unloading on a stranger.

"I imagine you're right," he said. "Goodness knows I don't always say or do what I should. And I admit I can be stubborn as an ox. My wife can attest to that." His eyes sparkled. "But when it comes down to it, I'd say people grow more from venting than keepin' their traps shut. Probably why we're inseparable."

Kate slouched in the booth, unable to challenge his reasoning. Clearly her habit of not voicing her thoughts had done little to strengthen her own marriage. "I guess there's always room for improvement," she conceded quietly.

"Sure is. Nothing on this earth was meant to be perfect. Marriage in particular." He flashed a slanted grin. "I bet even Katharine Hepburn and Spencer Tracy's characters squabbled about one thing or another. Film credits just rolled 'fore they could argue over leaving the fridge open or dirty socks on the rug."

Kate started to smile until she recalled Drew's last message. She pounced on the opportunity to redirect the discussion to something less personal than marriage problems. "So what other jobs did you have before this one?"

"How much time ya got?"

Hopefully not much before his wife arrived. Kate finished the rest of her coffee in lieu of answering.

"Let's see now. I've worked in a warehouse, on the docks...for the railroad, in a battery factory. Did some corn detasseling, and worked as a smithy. Not the most glamorous jobs, but all a means to put food on the table."

An image struck her like a sobering slap: her father, what remained of him, deprived of any nourishment but measly minerals supplied in shavings of frozen water. True, he was far from perfect, but she couldn't say she'd ever gone without a meal, a roof, or clothes on her back.

"I joined the service instead of finishing high school," Mick explained. "So my options for steady work have never been as great as I would've liked. That's why I'm gonna see to it my kids do better than me. I can hardly wait for the day I see them walk across that stage, college diploma in hand. I'll be a proud papa, that's for sure."

A proud papa. That would have been nice. Certainly better than the disappointment her choices had prompted from her father. Disappointment that lingered like the smell of paint thinner on her fingers, invisible yet always present.

"You a college grad yourself?" Mick asked.

"Nope," she said, lowering her hands to her lap. She rubbed her thumb over the dried paint on her nails. "Though my father would've shared your enthusiasm had I gone that way." As her father had told her again and again, she was supposed to be the first in her family line to go past high school. Instead, she'd become the daughter who never lived up to her full potential.

"Well, I'm sure your dad is proud all the same. Dads can't help themselves. Especially when it comes to their little girls."

She nodded weakly, scouring her mind for a topic shifter. "So, you have more than one child?"

"Not yet. But we hope to someday. I'd have a dozen if we could. The second one's taking a tad longer than the first, but I figure we've got plenty of time." He drained his cup, then wiped the back of his hand across his mouth. "Got any of your own?"

She barked a laugh. "No. If I did, I'm pretty sure Super Nanny would have family services whisk them away."

"Super who?"

"Never mind." She shook her head. "My point is, I don't think I'm the mothering type. I can barely take care of my cat."

"Hey, I couldn't keep a plant alive, but that didn't stop us. Sometimes you just gotta jump in feet first."

"You sound like my husband." She immediately chastised herself for volunteering such private information. It was an issue she always did her best to avoid, even with Drew, despite knowing how much he yearned to start a family.

"Your husband must be a lot more confident than I was," Mick said. "When I found out my wife was expecting, I was terrified. Didn't sleep well for months. But then, the doc handed me that sweet baby girl at the hospital…" He sighed, a look of wonder on his face. "She wrapped her tiny hand around my finger, and I knew I was done for."

The warmth in his eyes and voice soothed Kate like hot chocolate on a blustery night. "I'd say your daughter is lucky to have you."

"I don't know about that."

"Really, you sound like a wonderful father."

"Appreciate you saying so. Though I gotta be honest.

Half the time I'm beating myself up for the mistakes I'm sure I'm making."

Kate smiled. "Somehow I doubt anyone else would agree."

"Oh, I think there are a few out there who would."

"Like?"

"Well...my wife, for starters. Then there's the entire nursing staff at the hospital..."

Kate tilted her head. "Why, what happened there?"

"The day our baby was born, I was so excited about being a daddy, I passed out two dozen cigars before realizing they all read *It's a Boy*."

The image gained vividness, feeding Kate with overflowing laughter. It was welcome release from the day's mounting tension.

"I swear," he added, "it'd be a whole lot easier if kids came with goof-proof instructions. Then I'd know for certain which end was up. And when they hit their teenage years, I'd know where to ship 'em back to."

Her laugh faded into a few moments of comfortable silence before she remembered why she was there.

"Mick, would you mind if I checked the phone to see if it's working yet?"

"You stay there and relax," he told her, already scooting out of the booth. "I'd be happy to do that for you."

He picked up their empty mugs and walked toward the black old-fashioned telephone at the bar. There, with his back to Kate, he pressed the receiver against his ear. She did her best not to stare intently, but when she heard him replace the handset, her gaze snapped up to his face expectantly.

He shrugged, frowning.

"No luck?" she asked, trying to hide her disappointment.

"Not yet."

"Thanks for checking."

"You think anyone's started a search party for you?"

It was a natural question, yet she hated it. "Probably not."

In the old days, she and Drew were together so much it would have only taken an hour for him to notice she was missing. More importantly, their connection was so strong, he'd always known what was bothering her without having to ask. She missed those days when they used to finish each others' sentences. Now, most of the time, she had no idea what he was thinking.

"Can I get you a refill?" Mick asked.

"No, thanks. If I have any more, I'll never fall asleep."

"Alrighty then. I'll go toss these in the washer." He held up the mugs by the handles. "Don't you go anywhere now."

Right. Where would she go?

He grinned and pushed through the swinging silver door next to the bar, disappearing into the kitchen.

Kate looked out the window and sighed. It was still black, except for the reflection of her face and the diner's interior. The room took on a two-dimensional image from this view—a sketch in need of vibrant strokes of color. Her gaze floated upward, depositing imaginary paint on the reflected objects deserving attention on the wall behind her: antique roller skates hanging by their knotted laces, a striped hula hoop, a metal poster for malted milk, a montage of framed pictures.

She was about to abandon her mental exercise when a particular photo snagged her attention. The last one on the left.

She turned around.

Something in the picture told her to come closer.

Though not sure why, she scooted out of the booth and headed for the memorabilia display. She moved over the floor tiles as if in a trance, her eyes locked on the grey and white tones of the snapshot.

A few more steps and Kate froze.

"It can't be," she gasped, fearing the floor might give way under the weight of her shock.

Twelve

Drew's eyes were locked on the corner of Brian's coffee table. It had taken him several minutes to render a full explanation. A dissolving martial summation, lacking any disparaging details. "Mind if I crash here for a while?"

"Whatever you need," Brian replied.

"Thanks."

Silence yawned and stretched its arms in slow motion.

As Brian shifted in his chair, Drew glanced at the comical illustration on his friend's sweatshirt: a Keystone cop beside a paddy wagon that read *Bed & Breakfast Shuttle Service.* He still found it hard to believe Brian had abandoned his business degree and investment banking corner office to play dress up and set speed traps for a living.

"So…" Drew said. "Arrest any jaywalkers today?"

"Nah, too dangerous. Rookies are only allowed to shoot people."

"Well, good thing they waived the minimum height requirement. Otherwise you wouldn't be able to help with our overpopulation crisis."

Not that Brian needed a department-issued gun to take out a threat. With the muscles he had packed onto his five-foot-six stocky build, Drew would put money on him in a boxing match any day of the week. His dark Sicilian features, like those of a kid from Hell's Kitchen, were an added advantage.

"Hey, I've been meaning to tell ya," Brian said. "My mom told me to invite you and Kate..." He caught himself. "Well, when you two make up anyway, you're overdue for a Sunday dinner."

"Sounds good." Drew passed over his friend's assumption about reconciliation and instead focused on the thought of Mama DiSanto, a woman whose dedication to her family was equaled only by her ability to cook up a legendary platter of spaghetti and meatballs. He could almost taste the garlic and garden-grown tomatoes from her third-generation secret recipe sauce that took a full day of simmering for the little, rounded woman to prepare. On a dare, he had once tried to peek through the kitchen shutters at the culinary process that Lindsey alone was promised, literally to be passed down via her mother's will. Mr. DiSanto, like a brawny protector of the Corleone family treasure, had appeared out of nowhere, flicked the back of Drew's head, and told him to go play with Brian, as if they were in grade school rather than college.

"How was your parents' trip?" Drew asked, trying to keep the conversation light.

"Are you kidding? They loved it." Brian took a chug of beer. "My mom can talk for hours about going to Easter mass at St. Peter's Basilica. She swears the Pope looked right at her."

Drew smiled as Brian went on, "I'm giving you fair warning, though. You'd better block out a whole evening. She's got two full boxes of photos to show off."

Drew imagined Brian's mother learning of his and Kate's separation. She'd have no qualms about spouting orders at Drew, telling him which flowers to buy for his wife to rekindle their romance.

He wished it were that easy.

"Tell your mom I'd love to go." Drew scraped for a reasonable excuse. "But my work load is pretty heavy right now. When it slows down, we'll try—"

"When it slows down?" Brian snorted. "I've heard that one before." He shook his head and pulled on the last of his bottle. "I tell you, man, if you don't ease up, one of these days you're gonna wake up and realize you missed it."

"Thanks for the tip," Drew muttered. He'd heard a similar lecture from Kate when they had to postpone their weekend getaway in order to attend a last-minute dinner for one of the firm's senior partners. Or when they had to cancel a romantic dinner because an additional case got slapped onto his pile so the "overseers" would look good. Sure, some of their personal plans had been called off. Okay, most. But sacrifice was simply part of life. A lesson that had been ingrained in him since childhood.

"Seriously, Drew." Brian furrowed his brow. "When's the last time you and Kate did anything together?"

He tried to come up with an answer, but honestly couldn't remember. Then again, who was Brian to judge? Up until a year ago, his work schedule had been just as packed.

"I think I've made my point." Smugness thinned Brian's lips.

"Yeah, and that is?" Drew didn't register the bitterness in his own tone until his friend's face hardened.

The room quieted, except for the creaking of moving tenants on the floor above. Phantom eavesdroppers.

"Look, I'm just saying..." Brian's eyes deepened with his voice. "You need to do something for the two of you. Take a vacation, get away for a while."

Vacation is for slackers, that's what Drew's old man used to say. Said it so frequently that part of Drew had come to believe it. Besides, it was a well-known fact that high-profile attorney Marcus Coleman had never in his career taken so much as a sick day from his prestigious Seattle firm. So why should his son's life be any different?

"Brian, I appreciate the advice." Actually, he didn't—not right now. "I've got it under control, though, okay." *Okay* wasn't intended as a question.

"Sure. That's why you're parking on my couch."

Drew gripped his empty glass tighter, tried to settle the emotions mounting inside. But a few more loaded remarks from his old friend and anger could easily shatter the tumbler in Drew's hand. "If you've got a problem with my staying here..."

"Right. That's what I was getting at."

Drew threw his gaze the other way, almost expecting to find ropes squaring them into a boxing ring. Junior high was the last time Drew had been in a fistfight, one that lasted no more than fifteen seconds before a teacher broke it up, but tonight he was ready to come out swinging if pushed hard enough.

Finally Brian leaned forward, set his bottle on the table, and sighed. "Drew, we've been friends a long time."

Here it came. A declaration of what Drew deserved. The formula introduction to nearly every ugly divorce case he had handled. *I've been your selfless wife in a decade-long marriage and bore and raised four children without you lifting a finger...* And let's not forget: *I worked my butt off for eight years to make sure you could buy anything you pleased... blah, blah, blah.* Everyone had earned something from someone else, specifically if it had a sizable receipt.

"I've never said a thing before," Brian went on, each word slow, weighted. "Figured it wasn't my place. But, man, I gotta say it."

An empty room at Motel 6 seemed more and more appealing.

Brian shook his head. "You keep this up, and you're going to end up just like—"

"Who?" he snapped, spearing Brian with his eyes. "My father?"

Drew cringed at the memory of the phone call from his father's secretary, delivering the news during final exam week at the university. Whether it had been a hereditarily fated heart attack or if his father had literally worked himself to death, Drew would never know. What he did know was that this was the last discussion he needed today.

Brian fixed a laser gaze on him. "I was going to say *me*," he corrected, steady as a flat line.

The unexpected response drained Drew instantly. He was ready to battle before confusion stripped his armor. "What are you talking about? You live the way you want to live." He flung his hand to the side. "Look at this place. Your life is set."

Brian huffed. "Drew—wake up. You don't want this, not compared to what you have. Believe me."

What was this? The venting of exaggerated woes over single life?

Granted, divorce was never easy. Drew of all people knew that. It could shred a person into pieces so tiny a light breeze would blow them into oblivion. Despite Mama DiSanto's Catholic objections, he'd helped Brian and his ex draw up the final papers several years ago. As splits went, theirs had been smooth. No shouting matches over divvying up furniture or wedding gifts.

And in a flash, Brian had soared into bachelor utopia. All-night poker parties, a noble job as a city cop, and thanks to his lucrative investments, a condo overlooking the marina. It never occurred to Drew that his buddy had constructed for himself anything other than the ideal life.

Brian leaned forward, his elbows pressed into his navy sweatpants. For several long moments, he stared at his own reflection in the dark television, then said, "About a year and a half after the divorce, I ran into Madison. It was at a Mexican restaurant downtown. I was telling her how good it was to see her, when in comes her husband—some guy she used to work with—pushing their twin baby girls in a stroller." Moisture glossed his eyes. "She looked happy. Real happy."

Drew realized Brian wasn't looking at his own image

on the screen but imagining Madison's.

"It was brief but cordial," Brian added quietly. "We said good-bye. Then I went back to my car, sat behind the wheel. For twenty minutes I couldn't get myself to turn the key. One thought kept running through my head." He turned his solemn gaze to Drew. "That should've been us."

From the subtle hum of the room's neon liquor signs came thoughts of reason. Drew had heard plenty of post-gavel remorse in his career. Clients liked to martyr the marriage they convinced themselves they used to have, particularly after spotting their retired love strolling by with a fresher, younger replacement, or spending too many tear-filled hours flipping through the scrapbooks of their lives together. The feeling was understandable. Nuptials, birthdays, hugs and smiles. Nobody snaps pictures of the bad times.

"Bri," he said, "I know it must've been hard seeing her move on. But you have to remind yourself why you two split up. You were high school sweethearts. It's no surprise you grew apart. I see it every day."

"That wasn't it," Brian argued. "We didn't just grow apart. I left her behind."

For once, Drew didn't have a rebuttal.

Their gazes retreated to opposite corners of the room, making way for silence to sweep back through.

Drew rolled his tumbler between his hands. His view eventually settled on the regatta medal encased in a frame on the wall, a tribute to their varsity crew days as Huskies. What a great feeling he'd had when those shiny medals were placed around their necks. They'd squeezed UCLA into the south wall of the Cut and won by a third of a length. But Brian hadn't truly celebrated until Madison accepted his marriage proposal two nights later.

"She made me promise not to tell anyone," Brian now said at last, looking down at the bottle in his hand. "She didn't want sympathy. But I suppose there's no harm now. Under the circumstances." He took a long breath. "As you know, I wasn't in any hurry for kids. I was grinding out sixty-hour weeks. Part of me was still wondering why we hadn't waited to get married. I wanted to be more established, have something saved up. So when Madison got pregnant, I wasn't exactly thrilled."

Drew didn't move, not even to blink.

"She didn't want to announce the news till she was past the first trimester. She was one week away when she miscarried."

Drew had no idea what to say. "I'm...so sorry, Bri."

"I never said it to her—that I was relieved—but she knew." Brian's neck reddened. "I told myself we weren't ready. But that wasn't it. *I* wasn't ready. I was so...*stupid.*" He spoke through gritted teeth. "I told her we'd just try again, like it was no big deal. Like we were replacing a broken appliance or something. I didn't take a single day off to be there for her. It wasn't till I lost her that I saw how screwed up my priorities were..." He mumbled a few words Drew couldn't make out before his voice returned to a perceptible level.

"Then, when I saw her again, with the family she always wanted—the one she deserved—that's when I realized it's true what they say: life's too short. I decided I wasn't going to waste another day killing myself for a career that deep down I never really cared about."

Drew rubbed his forehead as he digested Brian's tale. He stopped when a revelation found him. "So that's why you decided to be a cop."

Brian gave his nose a swift brush with his sleeve. "It's what I always wanted to do anyway. Just didn't have the balls to step up and do it sooner."

He had exposed himself as vulnerably as a naked man in Times Square on a winter day, making Drew feel like a liar.

"I left Kate." The phrase leapt out.

Brian nodded slowly. If the announcement surprised

him, he hid it well. "You gonna work it out?"

Drew rolled his shoulders. "I don't know if we can."

Silence returned, like the grueling deliberation of a temperamental judge.

Compared to what Brian had shared, Drew and Kate's dilemma seemed trivial. Nonetheless, their issues were just as valid. The air between them was just as cold, their lives just as divided.

"To say Kate's been consumed by her career would be an understatement." Drew pled his case firmly. "She practically lives in her studio. Sleeps there half the time. But supposedly I'm the only one who's working too much. *I'm* the one who gets falsely accused of cheating."

"Cheating?" Brian asked, looking baffled. "You're not talking about the time you and my sister grabbed drinks, are ya?"

"Yeah, can you believe it?" Drew blurted out before revisiting what had transpired only moments before Brian's arrival.

"Ah, well—cut your wife some slack." Brian gave him a semi-smile. "You know how easy it can be to get the wrong idea about those kinda things."

Drew knew exactly what Brian was referring to. He and Kate had been married only a few months when some guy's message on the answering machine sent Drew into a tailspin: *Kate, it's Shane. Jordan is out of town till Tuesday. I should be home all night, but if I happen to run out, let yourself in. The key's under the planter.*

Kate had laughed, though not as heartily as Brian, after she explained that Shane was a customer arranging delivery of a painting he'd commissioned for Jordan, his lifelong *male* partner.

"Thanks for the reminder," Drew said dryly.

The sparks of amusement dimmed in Brian's eyes, replaced by a look of empathy. "I'll back whatever you decide, man. Really. Before you do anything you'll regret though, be sure and ask yourself if you still love her. If the answer's yes, don't give up. Not yet at least."

Drew wanted desperately to say the answer was no. It would be so much easier if he didn't care. But he did. And the thought of seeing Kate in the arms of another man caused a pang in his chest.

"I think we'd have a shot," Drew said, "if she wasn't so...independent."

"Well, Kate was never cut out to be a timid little housewife. I could've told you that the day we first met her."

Drew allowed himself a small smile as he recalled their initial encounter at a popular pizza joint in Seattle. While squeezing past him, she'd accidentally dropped a ten-pound art book on his foot. When he tried to milk his injury for all it was worth, she'd giggled and suggested that Brian get his pal a Smurf Band-Aid and the *My Heart Bleeds for You* CD. Drew had never met anyone like her. He knew right then he'd found the woman he was going to marry. Now he only wished he knew how to find her again.

"Honestly," he said, "I've always loved her independence. But two years ago, when her dad got sick, it's like she closed herself off. I thought things between us would improve when he got better, but they've only gotten worse."

Brian gave a small shrug. "Maybe you guys just need to remember."

"Remember what?"

"What it was like in the beginning. Without your careers. When it was just the two of you."

That sounded simple enough. Yet their worlds that used to complement and overlap each other had diverged into different galaxies. Truthfully, he wasn't a big fan himself of black tie, kissing-up lawyer fests, the demeaning rituals he'd grown accustomed to on his father's golden path to stardom. Still, in spite of his support for her passion, he preferred such evenings over Kate's art receptions. At least at the double-olive martini gatherings he frequented, arrogant good-ole-boys and trophy wives resembled human beings. It seemed the more success Kate's exhibits garnered, the more eccentric the attendees became. It was like a summoning of Seattle's underground city dwellers: clicking tongue rings, spiked dog collars, heavy eyeliner on male and female patrons alike. And, worst of all, the inevitable ineptness he felt struggling to interpret the foreign language of abstract art connoisseurs.

"I'll give it some thought." Drew fiddled with the wedding band on his finger. Then he turned to Brian. "So is this your way of telling me you don't want me to move in?"

Brian yawned while scratching his chest. "Like I said, Drew, we've been friends a long time. But I don't see how we can take our relationship to the next level until you stop stealing all the covers."

Drew laughed. "Hey, at least I don't snore."

"What are you talking about? I don't snore."

"Like a Harley."

"You're full of it." After a pause, genuine concern constricted Brian's face. "Do I really?"

"Not to worry, Bri—I love a manly man." When Drew stuck out his chin and puckered his lips, Brian snagged a Huskies T-shirt from the floor and chucked it at him. Drew tossed the sweaty garment away, but not before the stench resembling a high school gym locker assaulted his nose.

"Man, you're a pig." Drew tried to inhale only through his mouth.

Fittingly, Brian delivered a deep, hollow belch. "Thank you, sir."

"It's truly a wonder you don't have a girlfriend, with those impeccable manners of yours."

"Who needs manners when you wear a chick-magnet uniform for a living?"

"Yep," Drew said. "I should've figured that was your

real reason for becoming a cop."

Brian grinned. "It's not a bad benefit, I tell you that."

Drew laughed again. He had no clue what tomorrow held in store, but for now at least, he was grateful for the mindless distraction.

Thirteen

Kate was afraid to blink, afraid to interrupt her view of the hanging photograph for even a fraction of a second. Her desire for the image to be real was so great that she knew her mind could very well be inserting a vision from her subconscious.

Eventually, her eyelids flashed a blink. Still the picture remained the same.

Amidst the display of nostalgia—ocean scenes, drive-ins, '60s hot-rods—was a black-and-white snapshot of teenage girls in front of the diner beside a classic Chevy. In the center of the Capri pants, plaid skirts, and hair flips, with a smile on her face and small Coke bottle in her hand, was the woman whose departure had changed Kate's life forever.

It was her mother.

Kate knew the photo in her locket by heart, thanks to the countless hours she'd spent studying it since childhood. This woman's features were unmistakably identical. Doe eyes, dimpled cheeks, wavy shoulder-length mane. Time and time again, Kate had wondered how different their lives would have been if only her mom hadn't walked out the door that night.

She slowly reached for the figure in the photo. Her finger made contact with the glass as she traced her mother's hair.

"Why did you have to go?" she whispered. "How could

you leave me all alone?"

Her body suddenly felt too heavy for her legs. She staggered backward, her eyes never leaving the picture, and lowered herself onto the edge of a cushioned booth, a booth where her mom could have very well sat years ago. She'd known her parents had grown up in the area, but finding this photo here was the last thing she'd expected.

Something warm hit Kate's hand. She glanced down. A drop of moisture trailed across her skin and landed on her jeans. The salty culprit had broken the vow she'd made the week after her mother's death.

"You all right, over there?"

She jerked her face toward the voice, remembered she wasn't alone. A second tear slid down her cheek and clung to her chin in a battle against gravity. She swiped her face with her sleeve.

Mick looked concerned. "Is there anything I can do?"

Her mind rummaged for an excuse. "I...there's..." What was the use of lying? "It's my mother."

His expression turned quizzical. "Did something happen to her?"

It had been decades since Iris Flaherty had died. Simply stumbling across a photograph shouldn't have hit Kate so hard. "My mom's in one of those pictures. Up there."

He glanced over his shoulder at the wall, then immediately back at Kate. Thank goodness he hadn't asked Kate to point her mother out, as she didn't have the strength to move.

"Is she...?" He stopped short.

"She was killed," Kate half whispered. The instant the statement left her lips, she felt like a melodramatic guest on a talk show—one of those weepy girls who didn't have the gumption to spill her guts to anyone who gave a rip, preferring to wait until five million viewers were tuned in. "I was eight when it happened. I don't know why I'm getting so emotional about it now."

Mick grabbed the top of the black parlor chair behind him. He flipped it around and took a seat facing her. "Go on," he prodded gently, his eyes impelling her.

Kate dropped her gaze to the table. Her memories charged through her defenses and flowed like a broken water main. "I was in my bed, the covers pulled over my head. Mom was crying and shouting at Dad. I didn't know what was going on. Maybe I didn't want to know. I heard the front door slam and a car speed away. Somehow I...I fell asleep."

She tried to make her voice stop trembling. "The minute I woke up, I knew something was terribly wrong. But I had no idea that I'd never..." A warm tear channeled down her flushed cheek.

"That you'd never see her again." His lips barely moved.

She nodded.

"I'm so sorry," Mick sighed, his eyes glossy. "When you lose someone you love, it can rip your heart right out of your chest. I know." There was deep sincerity in his tone, more than any condolences she'd heard at her mother's funeral. It was as if he truly understood. She doubted, though, that he'd be able to relate to her particular circumstances: those that stole nights and years from her, leaving her numb with fear of accepting the truth.

"My father, he..." She nudged the final words onto the edge of the cliff and waited for them to fall. "He killed my mother." The words plowed over her tongue, through her lips, and into the air where a witness could hear it.

She didn't crumble. Instead, she felt liberated.

But only for a moment.

Raw silence poured in around them, filling every inch of the room like seawater in a sunken ship.

Mick's blanched face and strained expression suggested he might not want to hear more. She certainly didn't favor going into detail, but she knew her accusation verged on a lie. Unlike her father, dishonesty wasn't her best suit.

"I don't mean he actually murdered her," she conceded. "Not directly, anyway."

The tension in Mick's forehead relaxed slightly.

"But if it weren't for him," she pressed on, "my mom would've been home that night. She never would have raced off in a blind rage. And some guy, who left a wedding after downing a dozen beers, wouldn't have hit her car head on."

She could still see her dad's profile as he sat in the rocking chair he'd never finished staining. Tucked around the corner, she had watched him staring at the shed wall, no words, no reaction, while the policemen talked to him about the accident and his right to press charges.

"They settled out of court," Kate said. "It was clear my dad didn't want to discuss that night. For weeks, he didn't leave the house, hardly spoke or ate. Unless he did it behind closed doors, I don't think he cried at all. He didn't even bother to go to her funeral."

Mick leaned forward, the compassion in his eyes drawing her anguish out of hiding. She felt a pinch in her chest as she struggled to hold it in, to keep the pieces of herself from breaking apart once more. Defenses rising, she reached deep down for slivers of anger, shards of resentment for the coldness her father had bestowed in unlimited supply.

"You know anything about morphine, Mick?"

He shrugged and replied as if answering a trick question. "Takes away the pain when you're hurt, I'd guess."

She released a cutting laugh. "Yeah. That's what it's supposed to do. Unfortunately, it doesn't always work that way."

The Top Secret file in her mind began to open, as if Mick, a random guy in a diner, was the one person on earth with security clearance.

"A month ago," she continued, "I was visiting my

father. He's been ill for some time now, and after foregoing another round of treatments, he made the decision to die at home." She still couldn't believe she was about to divulge such a dark family secret, one that should never have been revealed in the first place. A secret that should have been interred six feet under.

Kate's eyes fixed on her mother's face in the framed photo. "He thought I was her that day, because of the morphine. He thought I was my mom."

Another tear fell. And another. Perhaps Kate had said enough.

Then again, the chances of her ever seeing Mick again were slim to none. She had nothing to lose. "He apologized. Actually pled for forgiveness."

Mick tilted his head. "For the last fight they had?"

"For the affair that caused the last fight they had." She dragged her fingers back and forth along the silver edge of the table.

"This affair—had it been going on for quite a while?"

Kate froze. The possibility of a long-term relationship hadn't even occurred to her. She'd automatically assumed it was a one-time thing, but maybe they'd been together for years. Maybe her father had another family out there who had kept him away.

She hugged her arms tight, trying to squelch her thoughts.

"Certainly makes sense," Mick remarked finally.

"What does?"

"Why your dad stayed on the road, and didn't attend the funeral. Probably couldn't face what he'd caused." He shook his head. "All that guilt must've been troublin' him something fierce."

His comment startled her. She'd been so consumed by her father's confession that she hadn't yet linked elements that were obviously and undeniably related.

"I suppose," Kate mumbled, relenting a little as the remnants of her justified fury slipped from her grasp.

The room stilled. And from that stillness came the question she hoped would lead to some sort of understanding, even if she didn't agree.

"But why do they do it?" She pinned Mick with her eyes. "Why do married men feel the need to cheat?"

He reared back in his seat and took a breath. "I don't think *all* men are that way."

"No, of course not." Now she definitely sounded like one of those irritating guests on a talk show—a scorned woman wanting to interrogate the entire male species. "I mean, I know women are just as capable of being unfaithful. What I don't get is why someone would risk everything they had for a stupid fling."

Mick twisted his lips, contemplating. "All kinds of reasons folks make mistakes, I suppose. Just part of being human. Can't go back in time, no matter how much we'd like to. All we *can* do is chalk it up to learnin'." With that, he plucked a napkin out of a tabletop dispenser and placed it tenderly in her hand.

Fourteen

Brian's shower was still running when Drew returned from getting his cell phone from his car. He sank down into the couch, damp from the rain, and stared at the screen. Two missed calls: one unidentified number, one from Kate. Two voicemails.

His thumb hovered over the message retrieval key as he debated whether he was ready to hear what she had to say. What if Kate had agreed to a separation? Was he prepared to hear the finality in her words?

Drew laid his head back onto the cushion. He gazed up at the tan plastered ceiling, and with a here-goes-nothing breath, hit the button and brought the receiver to his ear.

"Hi, Drew, it's Beth. Just confirming your eight a.m. meeting with Mr. Stricklen on Monday."

He hit *Save*, then skipped forward to the next message—the one that really mattered.

Anxiously he listened.

Kate's voice. Explaining she was coming home from her father's...

Her father's?

She never spontaneously visited her dad. If she'd planned to go there, surely she would have mentioned it before his trip to Chicago. Something had obviously happened. That would explain her leaving the house in spite of Drew's message. Maybe there was hope for them after all. Then again, maybe they still needed…

A scream jolted him from his thoughts. *Kate's* scream. Then a monotonic programmed voice: "End of messages."

Wait! What just happened?

He punched the key to replay the message, nervous energy surging through him. Kate's voice again. She was headed home. A detour. Highway sixteen off one-o-six.

Where's one-o-six?

Her panicked cry pierced his ears, then his heart. He immediately dialed Kate's phone number. It went straight to her outgoing message. Either the battery had died or there was an accident and the phone was destroyed.

He noted the time of her call. She could still be there, body mangled, lying in a ditch. The image scorched his brain.

He grabbed his coat off the back of the couch and raced to the bathroom. "Brian!" He pounded on the bathroom door, trying to be heard over the sound of spraying water. Then he jiggled the handle. Locked. "Brian!" he bellowed, fear amplifying his voice. He pounded again, harder.

The shower stopped. "What're you saying?" Brian asked.

"Where does highway sixteen meet one-o-six?" Drew yelled.

A squeak and hustled footsteps followed. Brian cracked open the door. He was dripping wet, holding a towel around his waist. "What's that?"

Anger based in terror chewed away at Drew's insides. "One-o-six," he barked. "Where does it meet sixteen?"

Steam seeped from the bathroom as Brian squinted, thinking hard. At last, he spouted out the directions. The second Drew had gathered enough information to get him in the general vicinity, he took off running toward his car.

"Hold up, man," Brian called out. "Tell me what happened!"

But even if he'd wanted to, Drew couldn't make himself stay long enough to provide details. He was functioning on instinct, propelled by emotion.

Racing outside to his car, he climbed in and sped off into the night. Windshield wipers battled the pelting drizzle. The beams from his headlights ricocheted off car bumpers as he zoomed around them, weaving from lane to lane. An entire police squadron could collect in his wake, sirens blazing; they'd have to set up an impenetrable barricade to stop him before reaching his wife.

Kate has to be okay...please, she has to be...

What was he thinking, threatening to leave? As if their splitting up was what he actually wanted. Truth to told, he'd intended the bluff to be nothing more than a wake-up call, a reminder of what was at stake. And now, here he was, slammed by a terrifying revelation of what he might have already lost.

His cell phone trilled. Kate! She was all right!

He flipped open the phone.

"What's going on?" Brian demanded.

Drew's hope plummeted further. He gunned the accelerator through the tail end of a yellow traffic light.

"I need help," he told Brian. "Call the station. Call the hospitals. See if Kate's been in a car accident."

A breath. "You got it," Brian replied simply and hung up.

Drew's hands shook on the steering wheel as he flew onto the interstate. The wheels of a long-haul truck beside him kicked up water, flooding his windshield and blinding his view. But his only thought was of Kate's safety.

Fifteen

"Well, there you have it." Kate dabbed the coarse white paper below her eyes, mustering a smile to fight her embarrassment. "Women speak sixteen thousand words a day, and I've already used up half my allotment since I walked in the door."

If Mick were in his right mind, he would take her comment as an opportunity to check on his to-do list in the kitchen.

"Who ended up raising you, with your dad on the road?" he asked, his patience monumental. Earnestly his eyes glowed, further drawing her past out of hiding.

"My mom's only sister. She moved into the house and stayed until I graduated from high school. She and my dad never got along, and with my mom gone, they had even less to talk about."

Mick's eyes reflected his smile. "Well, from what I can tell, your aunt did a fine job raising you."

"She definitely ran a tight ship." To say the least.

Aunt Sophie's standards had felt more like a hedge-leaping course than a guiding track throughout Kate's youth. When it came to school report cards, her aunt would question the B's rather than praise the A's. And breaking curfew by a mere twenty minutes had resulted in a month-long grounding, to which Kate had retaliated with a heart-stabbing, "You can't tell me what to do! You're not my mother!"

Kate blew out a breath at the memory and admitted, "I suppose I didn't always make it easy on her."

Just then, the jukebox dropped the needle on another record. The opening notes of "Strangers in the Night" filled the room—the same annoying tune that used to play on Kate's musical toothbrush when she was a kid. She couldn't help but laugh. "Mick, you have an uncanny way of picking music I grew up hating."

He grinned. "Hey, I said you could choose, but you weren't interested."

A humorous moment was precisely what she needed. "I bet you're wishing right about now, that you'd bolted the doors shut before I ever showed up."

"Why would I wish that?"

"Giving a free counseling session to some crazy woman couldn't have been the kind of evening you had in mind." She wiped her nose with the napkin.

"Well, I really should've warned you," he pointed out, "the first hour was complimentary. After that, I charge by the minute."

As they both laughed, Kate wondered how late it was. It felt like an eternity since Mick had assured her his wife would be arriving at any time. "So is your wife out running errands?"

"Nah, she's been home working on a family trip we're planning to take. Some place in Canada called...the Twirl Center...or Twirl-a-World..."

"Oh my gosh. Is that still around?"

"Have you been there?"

"Sort of."

His eyes filled with question marks.

"My parents took me there for my birthday, ages ago." A smile touched her lips. "The whole ferry-and-car ride up, my dad raved about that place having the world's highest roller coaster, the funniest clowns, and on and on. We finally make it, and there's a sign at the entrance: *Closed for renovations.*" She shook her head. "We were just like the Griswold family."

"Oh, that's terrible." He laughed again.

"Well, *some* good came out of it. My dad felt so bad, he checked us into the nicest hotel we'd ever stayed in. We spent the whole evening in the swimming pool, in our shorts and T-shirts, since we hadn't packed bathing suits. Then, before bed, he went on a mission for a cake and candles, insisting it wasn't a real birthday unless I made an official wish."

Warmth spread through Kate's chest as she recalled the scene that followed. "An hour later, he came back with the best substitutes he could scrounge up: a Twinkie from the vending machine, a tea candle he found in the hotel lobby, and three linen napkins he borrowed from the bar to use as birthday hats. It was actually the best party I'd ever had."

Mick nodded as he laced his fingers behind his neck. "Your father sounds like quite a character."

"Oh, he is that, all right." Her smile dropped as she recalled that soon she would be speaking of him in the past tense. As that grim thought arrived, her stomach growled like a mountain lion. She wrapped her arms around her waist to stifle the sound.

"Can I get you something to eat?" Mick's question confirmed he'd heard it too.

"No, it's okay. I'm fine." The lion roared again in protest.

"C'mon, it's no trouble."

She glanced at the pass-through separating the bar area from what appeared to be a spotless kitchen. "I can wait till I get home. Really, I wouldn't want you to make a mess on my account."

He lifted an eyebrow. "Well, I wasn't about to fire up the grill for ya, if that's what you're thinkin'." He rose. "Pretty sure I could manage a sandwich, though. Maybe a few cookies?"

A scrumptious image popped into her head.

She gnawed on her lip like a five-year-old, mouth watering, chin tucked. "Any chance of an ice cream sundae?"

Mick chuckled. "I shoulda guessed. Comin' right up." He spun around and headed for the kitchen.

Kate smoothed her hair behind her ears and took a deep breath. Who would have thought this was where her day would take her? She'd definitely have to bring Drew here sometime.

Drew...

The man she'd envisioned growing old with, sharing stories about their adventures together until they couldn't remember anymore.

When was the last time they'd laughed like this together? The laughs that went on so long she couldn't recall what it was they'd originally found so funny. Days when he supported her career more than anyone else. When he would lie in bed holding her, in no hurry to leave for a meeting or an uppity cocktail party. When they marveled at never running out of things to say to one another.

It didn't make sense. Already, she'd shared more about her past with a stranger than she'd ever done with her own husband. Maybe it wasn't all Drew's fault. Maybe she could have tried harder. Maybe she'd been too tough on him.

Maybe a lot of things.

The only thing she was sure of was that she needed to hear Drew's voice. She needed to confirm they still had a chance.

"Mick," she hollered, "would you mind if I tried the phone?"

No response. Just the tune he was whistling over the sound of running water in the back.

"Mick?"

Still no answer.

There didn't seem to be any harm in helping herself. She walked over to the bar and reached for the telephone. A rotary dial. She hated those. Mess up the very last digit and you'd have to spend five minutes dialing all over again.

"Please, please, please," she uttered as she lifted the handset off the cradle. She pressed the receiver to her ear.

No static. No dial tone.

Ah, well. One way or another, she'd make it home tonight.

Her stomach released a desperate cry.

Oh how she hoped the chocolate syrup on her sundae would be just as rich and thick as she remembered from her childhood. She replaced the handset and began to walk away when a thought stopped her in her tracks. Something was off.

She turned her head as slowly as a mechanical Santa in a department store window display. She picked up the entire telephone to verify she wasn't mistaken, and immediately set it back down.

A gasp slipped from her lips. Sealing her mouth closed with both hands, she took two steps back, terror combusting inside.

The phone line cord for the wall jack was…gone.

Sixteen

"Whaddya thinkin'?"

Kate whipped around as Mick's voice boomed from the kitchen. The back of his dark head moved in and out of view through the rectangular opening in the wall behind her.

"You just want chocolate?" he called.

She snapped her gaze back to the phone.

Why would he lie about the lines being down? How long had she been there before he'd removed the cord?

"Well...?" he asked.

Answer him. Answer him.

Her neck muscles twitched in fear.

"That's fine," she got out around the lump in her throat, then realized it was only a rusty whisper. With the tiny bit of saliva in her mouth she was able to gather, she swallowed and forced a more discernible response. "Just chocolate's fine."

This couldn't be happening. He seemed to be such a nice guy. Attractive. Personable. Charming. Just like...Ted Bundy.

Her eyes shifted to the wall of windows, the panes in which she'd anticipated seeing his wife's headlights. And it hit her like a ruthless semi: no one was coming to take her home.

"Anything else you want on your sundae, darlin'?"

She stared at the handle of the front door. Would she have noticed if he'd locked it? She tried to get a grip on herself, hold down the quiver that threatened to give her away. "Nothing else. Just chocolate." Her answer sounded so calm, she wondered where the voice had originated.

But wait…to escape, she needed to stall him.

"Actually, Mick, on second thought—let's load it up. Whipped cream, chopped nuts, the works."

"That's my kind of woman."

A chuckle echoed from the kitchen, but one that now seemed maniacal and dark. Like that of a murderer heckling his prey.

She darted her gaze around, seeking a sharp object. A knife, a fork—anything that could be used as a weapon. But there was nothing. Only meticulously folded napkins and condiments aligned in a perfect row, as if set for a military inspection.

A thought shot into her mind: *the pepper spray!*

A few weeks ago, she'd thought a man in the parking lot was following her to her car. The protective mini-tube of pepper spray Drew insisted she carry had been her one source of comfort on that long, lonely walk. She'd held it tightly until the man disappeared into the shadows. And now, once again, it would serve as her saving grace. All she had to do was get back to the booth and discreetly reach into her…

Crud! Her purse was in the 4Runner.

She wracked her brain for another option.

Silently, she crept away from the bar on her tiptoes. Then came a familiar sound. A metal whoosh. Like a cleaver being whisked out of a knife block.

Her breathing intensified.

"Mick, I just remembered that I left my purse in my car. While you're finishing up, I'll go get it really quick."

His face appeared in the pass-through. His eyes widened and deep lines creased his forehead. "You think I'm crazy?"

"Wh-what?" She shoved her lips into a smile, her cheek

muscles resisting.

"What gentlemen in his right mind would allow a pretty thing like you to venture out there all alone? Especially with it being so wet."

She risked a glance at the windows entrapping her. A human aquarium on a deserted road. Tiny drops dotted the panes. She turned back to Mick.

"Are you kidding?" She waved her hand airily. "I was raised here. I'd wilt if it weren't raining."

"Yeah, but I don't see why we can't swing by and grab it on our way to Auburn."

Come on, Kate. Give him a reason!

"Mick, I refuse to take advantage of your generosity any more than I already have. Besides, it'll only take me a few minutes. My car's right around the corner."

He wiped his hands on his shouldered bar towel. "Give me a sec and I'll walk you there."

"No," she protested brusquely, then cushioned her tone with another smile. "No, really—I'll be okay. And someone needs to stay here for when your wife arrives. Wouldn't want her to think you ran off with some other gal."

Mick winked at her, chilling her blood. "I suppose it's not my place to tell ya that you can't go."

"Not to worry. I'll be right back for my sundae."

After steps she couldn't remember taking, she arrived at the door. She grabbed the metal handle and yanked. The door didn't clink against a lock; it swung open so fast and hard it tugged at her pectoral muscle.

"I'll be timing you now." A smirk reverberated in his voice. "Don't make me come looking for ya." Those were the last words she heard as she entered the black sea of gravel, blinking off the raindrops attacking her eyelashes.

Ten. She'd take ten steps, then her walk of terror would become a sprint for her life.

Seventeen

Kate's lungs burned as her boots pounded the bumpy dirt road. Musty dampness condensed the air. It hurt to breathe, yet she couldn't stop. She had to run. Far and fast. Before Mick realized she wasn't coming back.

Where could she go?

She needed a guide now more than ever. She glanced up and searched for the moon. Clouds had eclipsed the light, and the drizzle was nearly blinding her. Moisture filled her eyes. Raindrops, tears—she wasn't sure which.

Suddenly something latched onto her toe. She screamed as she flew forward. The heels of her hands hit first, bulldozing two paths in the mud like fleshy garden hoes. The mystery trap released her foot and her knee slammed against material more unforgiving than dirt. The pain burst through her adrenaline wall, curled her body into a cannonball with no swimming pool to catch her landing. The rain pelted down, faster and faster, streaking over her face. She was drowning with fear, drowning like that day at the lake. But now her father wasn't here to save her.

A tree branch cracked behind her. She snapped her head up from the mud and dared to look back. Patches of fog. Tar-black darkness. The shadow of the Reaper reaching for her soul.

Don't make me come lookin' for ya.

Mick's words clawed at her mind. With the ball of her foot, she pushed against the railroad track that had taken her down and scrambled to her feet. A nauseating headache erupted, beating into her neck and grating on the backs of her eyes. Inside, she was screaming for help. The muted screaming of Edward Munch's terrifying painting.

She had reached the highway. Now where to?

Her window of opportunity was slipping away.

To her left, only a wall of blackness. She'd have to take her chances with the lit house she'd passed a few miles back and just hope someone was home.

She turned right and made her way down the middle of the slick pavement, hindered by her limp. Strands of her wet hair swung at her eyes and adhered to her cheeks with mud as thick as rubber cement.

The bridge was no more than thirty feet away when she spotted a light flickering through the trees. She increased her speed, ignoring the flare in her lungs. With every aching step, she hoped the glow wasn't merely a street lamp.

Please...please be a house...

She heard the hum of a motor growing louder and nearer. She grabbed her knee and wheeled about. The approaching headlights blinded her. She raised her hand to flag the vehicle down, its white orbs prancing on her pupils. As the car slowed, she exhaled her greatest thoughts of doom.

She squinted against the glare, thankful to be saved from a lunatic's grasp. Yet no sooner had her mind found relief than a ghastly theory pillaged her hope. She knew he'd been lying to her, keeping her there deliberately. What if Mick's truck had been parked in back all the time?

A newfound horror streaked through her, riding her veins as her heart pumped painfully. She spun around, begging for her feet to cooperate. Yet her pleas failed to reach her legs, which softened like jelly.

Somehow she pushed on. *Head for the bridge. Cross*

the river. Get to safety on the other side.

Tires crunched over gravel. The engine quieted.

"Kate!"

A man's voice. She knew it was him.

"Kate, stop!"

She stumbled, her feet searching for traction on pebbles as round as marbles.

A door smacked closed.

Her footing regained, she stumbled along the shoulder of the road. Away from his car. Away from *him*.

"Kate! Hold on!"

She forced a glance over her shoulder. Just as the outline of his body took shape, the ground below her gave way. Down she slid, the muddy bank taking her. Her arms flailed as she reached for a rope that wasn't there.

Her arms yanked, and she stopped. She'd found a tree root. She held on with both hands, as the relentless rain pelted her face. Fear was everywhere: above her, below her, behind her. She looked down, white spots still blocking her vision, and heard the sound of water. The river. If only she could see how far the drop was.

"Oh, God," she implored, "please, please help me."

A hand clamped over her forearm. "I've got you!"

"No!" she shrieked.

He was going to kill her. Right here. Right now. She tried to pry his fingers loose, but mud coated her hands like oil.

"Kate, stop it! It's *me*!"

She pounded on his wrist twice before registering the voice. "Drew?"

"It's okay," he said. "Give me your hand."

She raised her gaze. Indeed it was her husband, silhouetted by shining headlights, an angel coming to her rescue.

Eighteen

The nightmare fell away as Kate closed her eyes. Standing safely on the shoulder of the road, she cocooned herself in her husband's embrace.

"Shhh...it's all right, baby—I'm here," he said, gently pushing her hair away from her face.

She registered a trembling, but wasn't sure if it was coming from her body or Drew's.

He exhaled heavily. "When I heard your message on my cell, when I heard you scream..." Fear resonated in his deep voice.

He held her tighter.

She couldn't remember the last time she'd felt so protected, so loved. She relaxed her grip on his shirt, savoring the warmth from his body and the lining of his open suit jacket. As she inhaled the faint scent of his musky cologne, the feel and sound of his heartbeat soothed her like a lullaby.

His palm cupped her cheek, her chilled skin warming from his touch. "Are you all right?" he asked.

She took a step back and looked up at him. She wanted to assure him she was fine. As long as they were together, she'd always be fine. However, as soon as she nodded, a sharp pain seared her forehead. The image of Drew's face blurred in her narrow vision. As she swayed onto her heels, he gathered her back into his arms.

"Come on, Kate, let's get you out of the rain."

He removed his coat and laid it over her shoulders. Then he walked her toward the headlights, supporting her wobbly legs by gripping her waist. Glowing white fog surrounded them, a portal to another universe. Salvador Dali's world of melting images. Everything about her day was too surreal to have happened.

As they approached the vehicle, she turned her face from the piercing beams. Drew shaded her eyes by blocking the rays with his hand until they reached the passenger side of the car. Holding her elbow, he carefully guided her inside.

Once seated, she braced herself for the slam of the door, but only a faint click projected from Drew's guarded closing. While he circled around the front, Kate threw a glance over one shoulder, then the other, making sure Mick wasn't lurking behind.

No movement but the weave of branches. Still, she felt a pressing need to reclaim the safety of their house as soon as possible.

Drew opened his door. The interior lights reinvaded her senses, along with a torturous ping that penetrated her eardrums. He slid into his seat. This time, the click wasn't quite as soft. In the dimness, he gripped the steering wheel. He directed his rain-glistened face to the frantically swishing windshield wipers. The car was already idling. Why wasn't he shifting into gear?

"Drew, please. Let's go."

He didn't move.

"Drew?"

He shuddered as he pulled an audible breath. "Baby, I'm so sorry." His volume bordered on a whisper. He turned toward her. Tears pooled in the corners of his sea green eyes, his expression grave.

She didn't understand. He had saved her. What did he need to apologize for? She stared at him, perplexed.

"My phone was in the car," he explained. "I should have checked my messages sooner." He reached out and tenderly ran his thumb over the sore spot on her forehead where a bump had already formed. From the concern in his eyes, she must have banged her head against the steering wheel harder than she remembered.

"I thought I'd never find you. I thought..." The words died on his lips.

She wanted to suggest they head out and continue their conversation on the drive home. Yet her heart fought to extend this moment, fearing that the adoration and worry emanating from her husband would vanish if the car moved even an inch.

"Kate, what happened to you tonight?"

The question was inevitable. Of course he would ask. But she hadn't had a chance to sort through the harrowing events. She would have to make a decision on the spot: how much to share, how much to deposit for safekeeping, like an investor in emotional currency.

"I was coming back from my dad's," she began, gauging her words, "when I swerved around a deer and ended up in a ditch. I couldn't get a signal on my cell. So I went looking for a landline." Her mind skimmed through her recollections of the night, a movie in fast forward. No sound, only scenes jumping from one to the next.

How much should she risk telling him about her run-in with Mick? That she'd put her soul on display for some guy she'd just met, and even accepted his offer of a ride home? A guy who had then scared her senseless by disconnecting and hiding the phone cord before going to the kitchen to make her an ice cream sundae?

She didn't have to relate the details to determine how naive and ridiculous it all sounded. Besides, what could Drew do about it? Drive up to a now-closed, empty diner to investigate a telephone cord that had now undoubtedly been replaced?

She took a furtive glimpse at her side-view mirror.

No one there.

Maybe the bump on her head had made it all seem more dramatic than it was, or at least that's what she would tell herself from here on out. So long as she never had to talk about Gordy's Diner, life could return to normal. Whatever normal was.

She shrugged. "With the dark woods and rain, I guess I just got spooked."

"Are you hurt? Do you want me to take you to the hospital?"

"No, no, I'm alright." Her gaze fell on the mud on his white shirt that had rubbed off from her hair and clothes. "I slipped on the train tracks, but otherwise I'm good. Really." She gave him a forced smile, like tossing a log onto the flames to maintain a steady campfire of near-truths.

He studied her face as if deciding whether to solicit a more qualified medical opinion.

"Please, Drew," she pleaded, "I just want to go home and forget this night ever happened."

Reluctantly he nodded.

After helping with her seatbelt, he eased onto the highway. With her head laid back, Kate focused on the long shower she yearned to take, hoping that along with the grime, the hot spray would wash away any petrifying memories of Mick.

Nineteen

Kate swept her bathrobe sleeve in an arc across the foggy mirror, producing a light screech. A layer of steam immediately recoated the surface. She wiped at it again, more aggressively, intent on inspecting her battle wounds, then grimaced at what she saw. With mascara smeared down to her cheekbones, she needed only a black numerical slate below her chin to pass for a prostitute being booked. That or a handheld microphone to pass as the newest member of KISS.

She grumbled. If it weren't for knowing how much harder the streaks would be to wash off in the morning, she'd beeline it to bed this instant—even skip the tomato soup Drew was preparing downstairs. She wanted nothing more than to burrow her face in a fluffy pillow and submerge her clean, exhausted body into the goose down bedding. She would need all the strength she could gather for her return trip to her father's cabin in the morning.

From a gold tray on the marble counter, she snatched her makeup remover and poured a generous amount onto a cotton square. Her nose twitched at its rubbing alcohol-like smell. Sliding the dampened wipe under her eyes—back and forth, back and forth—her frustration bloomed along with her complexion. Why did waterproof mascara only work when you actually wanted to take it off?

A little more scrubbing and her skin approached

normalcy. Now she just looked spent. She pulled her damp hair back off her forehead to examine the knot, which she could already tell was going to be a beauty. By morning the purple-tinted, quarter-sized spot was destined to become a dark brown, half-dollar-sized bruise. A delicate inspection of the marks on her hips and shoulder revealed the same progression.

She sighed as she ran a finger over one scraped palm, then suddenly felt dizzy. As the room tilted, she planted her hands on the emerald counter to regain her center. She closed her eyes and inhaled deeply. The faint scent of rosemary and mint conditioner had just begun to calm her when the phone rang, only to be cut off in the middle of the third ring.

She secured her burgundy towel and strode into the master bedroom. Out of her dresser, she snagged her flannel tie-waist pants and a Picasso T-shirt reading, *A Spaniard's brain on drugs. Any questions?* Her favorite pajamas never looked so comfortable. A few more minutes and those PJs would be on her body, snuggled between the sheets.

As she closed the drawer, she heard footsteps ascending the stairs. A creak let her know Drew was two steps from the top. The call was obviously for her. But who would be phoning after ten o'clock at night?

Then she knew.

When Drew nudged the door open, Kate froze, dreading what was coming.

"It's for you." He held out the cordless phone. "It's a woman calling about your dad."

She stared at the handset as though it were a loaded handgun that might go off if she dared to touch it.

"Kate?"

She tried to analyze his expression. She wanted a hint, a sneak preview, a cheat sheet. Depending on what she saw in his face, there wouldn't be any need to take the phone.

But it wasn't grief or sympathy in his eyes, it was puzzlement. He was wondering why she was hesitating.

Maybe there was nothing to be scared of. Maybe Doris was calling simply to keep her updated, or confirm her expected arrival time. Of course—that's what she was doing. After everything Kate had been through with her accident and her flight from the diner, this couldn't possibly be the night her father left her permanently, not before she had a chance to forgive him. Even God, if there was a God, couldn't be that cruel.

She cleared her throat and accepted the phone. Calm was in charge, not panic, not fear.

"This is Kate."

"Hello, dear, it's Doris. I apologize for calling so late."

"No problem at all." Kate smiled casually, hoping to relax Drew's pinched brow. "We were still up."

She waited for Doris to continue. But she didn't.

Why? Why was she pausing? Kate swallowed hard.

"Doris?"

"Yes, dear," Doris replied. "I'm here. I'm sorry—I never get used to making these calls."

The words Doris chose, the regretful tone, made her stomach contract.

"Kate, your father passed away shortly after you left. I phoned the numbers I had for you several times, but kept getting a recording on both. I hope you don't mind the delay. I just never leave this type of news on an answering machine…"

Kate didn't realize the telephone had slipped from her fingers and onto the carpet until Drew bent over to pick it up.

"Yeah, we're still here," she vaguely heard him say.

Kate turned back to her dresser, squeezing the pajamas that were still in her hand. She stared at her painting on the wall, the first one she had ever framed. The streaks of blue paint—indigo, aqua, cerulean—seemed to lift right off the canvas and swarm around her, picking up speed with every rotation.

"What?" Drew's voice echoed. "I had no idea…"

Bile rose in Kate's throat. Her eyelids became as heavy as velvet curtains preparing to drop at the end of a show. Holding the edge of her dresser to steady her balance, she focused on the necklace she'd laid out before showering. She picked up the thin gold chain and clasped the locket in her hand, tighter and tighter, as if meshing the keepsake into her skin could bring her mother back to help her through this.

"Kate?"

She heard Drew calling, his voice distant, searching for her in a deep mineshaft. Her mouth opened to answer, but no sound followed. Perhaps she didn't want to be found.

She tried again to speak, but the sensation of hot tears streaking her face intruded on her effort. The protective wall surrounding her soul had split in two. A lifetime of denied emotion had broken through the dam, and there was no holding back the flood.

"Daddy, please, not yet," she whispered, then crumpled to the floor, wilting like a rose in her mother's forsaken garden.

Twenty

Spiraled candelabras cast an eerie glow over the dark cathedral. The reflection of flames stroked empty pews like soft yellow hands, waiting to pull Kate onward, to the place where she at last would say good-bye.

She stood at the back of the aisle, gloved fingers grasping a black clutch purse. She gazed down the narrow runway of tiles. At the end, glimmers of light bounced off the half-open casket.

Boom!

Her heart seized as she spun around. The Gothic wooden doors had closed, their circular handles resembling those from a medieval castle. She gulped a breath and turned back to embark upon her journey. Her heels clicked guilty echoes in the stone-walled room. The scent of lemon oil mingled with the fragrance of roses in the arrangements flanking the altar.

She averted her focus from her father's mortal encasement to the monstrous pipe organ in front, an instrument right out of *Phantom of the Opera*. The entire setting, in fact, resembled a theatrical stage.

Suddenly a shimmer of red light appeared. It danced over the organ's splayed white keys and drew her eyes to its source above. There, she found three arched stained glass windows, almost too large for the building. Moonlight streamed through the vibrant collages of biblical scenes, each window captioned with a single word: *LOVE...FAITH...FORGIVENESS*. Their crimson letters blared like those on a neon sign.

She lowered her gaze and was startled to find she was less than ten feet away from the coffin, shiny and black, embellished in ornate gold. Soon to be buried in the heart of the earth.

Her mouth went dry, too dry to swallow. She wanted to run. But like viewing the aftermath of a freeway accident, morbid curiosity summoned her attention. She leaned forward slightly, but could see only tucked ivory satin on the interior wall of the casket. And so she proceeded with the tiny, bashful steps of a flower girl.

Forward, forward, inching forward...until she looked down, in shock.

Empty. The coffin was empty!

What did they do with her father?

Confusion and fright closed in on her. The ceiling bore down. The walls narrowed.

"Katie." The man's gruff voice from behind swung her around, her feet all but tripping over themselves.

She gasped at her dad standing in front her. Woven into his thick white hair were the last of his brown strands, the same as his neatly-trimmed mustache. His cheeks were clean shaven, lacking the stubble she had rarely seen him without. He had a hazy, dreamlike appearance, the age lines on his rounded face had vanished.

"You still have a choice, Katie."

A choice? What choice? "What are you talking about?"

"Forget all the expenses. If you want to change your mind, it's not too late."

"Dad, what are you saying?"

He tugged his black bowtie away from his stout neck. It was then she realized he was wearing a tuxedo. A red carnation entwined with baby's breath adorned his lapel. The button on his jacket pulled a crease across the fabric, taut around the full belly of a man who'd spent his life in the cab of an eighteen-wheeler. It was the mountainous version of her father that had disappeared after chemotherapy treatments had filled his body with equal doses of hope and poison.

"I know I gave Drew my blessing," he explained, his eyes intense behind his dark-rimmed glasses. "That's why I tossed and turned last night, debating whether or not to speak up."

She tightened her grip, only to discover that a bouquet of lilies had replaced her purse. Her black pantsuit had morphed into a white wedding gown. It was the lacy sweetheart neckline she'd sewn herself, trimmed with the pearls Aunt Sophie spent a week attaching by hand.

Kate knew she was dreaming. But she didn't want to wake up. Not yet.

Just then, chords blasted through the organ pipes. Wincing, she covered her ears until the notes fell distant and flowed into a familiar hymn. She raised her eyes. Her father was still there, but they were no longer in the cathedral.

Pastel paisley wallpaper, a framed portrait of Jesus, a full-length mirror. She and her dad were in her bridal dressing room.

"Not in good conscience," her father continued, "could I walk you down that aisle today without saying my peace."

Wait. She knew this talk. It was the one they'd had minutes before the ceremony began.

"Katie, I'm sure you think you've got life all figured out, believing you two are gonna live happily ever after. With his rich family, clearly you'll never have to worry about a dime. But at the end of the day, five months of wining and dining doesn't mean you truly know each other. So you may disagree, but as your father, I think you're making a big mistake."

Kate was speechless—just as she'd been when he'd actually spoken those precise words.

"It's not too late," he said. "Forget about the cost of this wedding. If you have any doubts, any at all, you just say so, and we'll march out of this church right now."

She reached for the locket around her neck, unsure which statement astonished her more: that he was willing to waste the funds he'd spent despite Mrs. Coleman's offer to contribute, or that he believed she'd willingly abandon Drew, the man she loved more than life itself. Her throat tightened at the very suggestion, preventing her from voicing any argument in support of her unwavering decision.

Silence engulfed the room until the distant organ notes of the processional song drifted through the gap beneath the door: "Hymne" by Vangelis. The congregation, with ten times as many guests on the groom's side, would soon be growing restless. The minister would be checking his watch, her fiancé would start fidgeting.

She reminded herself this was only a dream, the memory of a moment she'd already survived. There was no reason for her to be so affected by the reenactment. Still, tears welled in her eyes.

"We need to go, Dad," she managed, the same response she'd given before, the cowardly exit that had haunted her ever since. She squared her shoulders and turned toward the door. But after two steps forward, she stopped. Now was her chance to say what she'd always wished she had, to stand up for herself, her marriage, her choices.

She wheeled about and looked him in the eye. "Dad, I know I'm not the daughter you wanted."

His expression fell. "Katie, that's not—"

"Please, let me finish."

He dropped his shoulders before issuing a nod.

She could do this. She *had* to do this.

"It's no secret you wanted me to go to college and

study business. Or whatever would earn me a cushy office job. I know I've disappointed you by putting all my efforts into something you see as a silly hobby." She fed her mounting strength with a heavy breath. "You may not understand my passion for painting, and that's okay. But I'm not a little girl anymore. And at some point, I'd hoped you'd respect my decisions. Even if you don't agree with them."

Keep going. She couldn't back off now.

"As for Drew, I love him more than anything in the world. I can't imagine my life without him." She felt tears tumbling down her cheeks and wondered if she were really crying in her sleep, depositing salty drops of pain onto her pillow. "He's so excited about the idea of starting a family and watching our kids grow up. But I told him I wanted to hold off because of my career, and he's never once argued with me about it. He's willing to give me the time I need. He loves me that much."

The sharp lines on her father's face softened, as if ironed away with the digestion of each of her assertions. "I'm just concerned," he said, "that your differences are going to get in the way."

She knew exactly where he was going. She'd had the same worry when Drew first took her home to meet his parents. In a pillared house that could store a 747, they'd dined on imported caviar and collectable wines certified by Sotheby's, all while being served at a table covered with so many pieces of polished silverware Kate almost had to ask for instructions. However, on the way back to her apartment, Drew had insisted they wash down the "overpriced fish bait" with Coke and a pepperoni pizza with extra cheese. It was then she realized they were more alike than she ever expected.

"You're right," she told her father, "we weren't raised the same. But that doesn't matter." Exhilaration rose within her, as did her conviction they would defy his prophecy that their marriage would fail. "The fancy houses and cars he grew up with, they're just things. Being together is all that's important to us."

Her dad's eyes glistened as he lowered his chin. "I'm sorry, Katie. I am truly sorry I wasn't able to provide for you better."

Did Collin Flaherty just apologize? Were those tears in his eyes?

"I had hoped you'd go on to college," he said, "so you'd have opportunities I didn't have. I wanted to give you so much more, but I couldn't."

"Dad..." Her voice quaked. "I never wanted anything but to be with you. And to hear that I wasn't a disappointment to you."

He edged his head up and his somber eyes met hers. "Oh, Katie—not in a million years could you ever be a disappointment to me." He extended his arms. Dropping her bouquet, she embraced him as more teardrops cascaded down her face.

"I know I wasn't there like I should've been," he whispered. "But I do love you, Kathryn Grace. Always have, and always will."

Squeezing her eyes tight, she wished this feeling would last forever. But only moments passed before he pulled his head back and wiped her cheek with his thumb. "It's time to go, pumpkin. I don't want to keep your mother waiting."

His words doused Kate's soul like a bucket of ice water. Her mother hadn't lived to see her wedding day, and now he was leaving her as well.

Before she could speak, a light knock sounded on the door. Aunt Sophie poked her head in, her cheeks a few shades lighter than her long plum dress. Sophie's enthusiasm hadn't diminished a single degree since the day Kate announced their engagement. "Are you ready?" she asked in a loving tone, her eyes shining like the ribbons of silver hair entwined in her blond mane.

"I believe we are," her father replied, and started to follow Sophie out.

"Wait." Kate felt the panic rise. "You can't go yet. I have so many questions. How can I forgive you if I don't understand?"

He kept walking, unaffected by her words.

"Daddy, stop! You can't leave." She tried to grab his sleeve, but her hands passed right through his arm as if he were a mirage.

In the doorway, he turned sideways facing her. "No matter how old you are, you'll always be my little girl. Don't you ever forget that." Then, pulled into another dimension, he faded into a translucent figure.

She wanted to go with him, wherever he was going, wherever her mother was waiting. She lunged but the door slammed shut, trapping her in the sealed-off room.

Once again, they were divided.

"Daddy!" Her hand scrounged for a handle that wasn't there. She beat on the door. "Come back!"

Over and over she hit the solid wood. The strikes should have pained her hands to the bone, yet she felt nothing but sorrow. The only chance they had to share their feelings and speak about things that really mattered was gone.

"Shhhh." A man's voice startled her.

She whirled around. No one else was there.

"Kate, it's all right," the soothing voice whispered.

She'd forgotten she was asleep. She felt someone's hand on her face, stroking her cheek. And from the muddled solitude of the in-between world, her spirit reentered the land of the living.

Twenty One

Kate opened her swollen eyelids and squinted at the room's overwhelming brightness. As her vision adjusted, she could see Drew seated beside her on the bed.

"What time is it?" she asked.

"About eleven-thirty."

"Eleven-thirty?" She never slept past eight. A restless sleeper for years, she'd painted the finishing touches on a few of her bestsellers at four or five in the morning.

"It was a long night," he assured her. "You definitely needed the rest."

"I suppose," she said quietly. She didn't want her mind to wander over the well-covered emotional path. "My car, do we need to—"

"It's taken care of. A repair shop's waiting for the tow truck to bring it to them. They'll call when it gets there."

How had Drew managed to do all of that already? Oh, yeah—it was almost noon.

She rubbed the sleep from her eyes. Not until then did she notice the aroma of percolating coffee wafting from downstairs. One good inhale and the caffeine fumes aroused her from her drowsy state.

"Doris called earlier," he said, his expression indecipherable. "She wanted me to tell you everything at your dad's house has been taken care of."

Silence overtook the room. The hum of Drew's alarm clock and the whooshing of air through the heater vents provided the only reprieve from their stilted conversation.

"How are you feeling?" he asked finally.

Tired. Confused. Sore. Her whole body hurt.

She proffered a smile. "I'll be fine, thanks." The Flaherty stock response.

"If you want to talk about your dad, I'm here. Okay?"

She nodded, though she could see in his eyes he didn't expect her to follow through. He had been around too long to be that credulous.

She nestled her cheek back into the pillow. The cool, damp spot confirmed she'd spent half the night awake and weeping, grieving over her father's death interspersed with a mental replay of her encounter at the diner. She'd only dozed off after feeling confident she hadn't given Mick enough personal information to find her, assuming he was that demented. Why hadn't she trusted her instincts that told her to run away when they first shook hands?

Drew moved the tangled strands of hair off her forehead. He lovingly stroked her locks until she closed her eyes. She recalled now the way she'd fallen asleep: curled up beside him, her face tucked into his neck, his arms wrapped around her. Safe arms that told her there was no other place she'd rather be.

"You've got to be hungry." He rose, leaving her to salvage warmth from the comforter covering all but her head. "I'll bring up some breakfast."

"Don't you have to be at work?"

It was noon on Monday. Aside from taking time off for a violent flu bug and wisdom teeth extraction, her husband had never missed a day at the firm.

"I called in. Said I'd be out for a couple days."

Great. He'd probably told them she was having a nervous breakdown. In all their years together, she'd never shed a tear, only to rock his world with a night of sobbing over a father she'd hardly spared two words about.

"Drew, really, I'll be okay. You're overloaded with cases as it is."

He grabbed a T-shirt out of his dresser. "They can wait." His tone made it clear the subject wasn't up for debate.

Warmth embraced her heart. From behind, she watched him pull the garment over his close-cropped, sandy-blond hair. His broad shoulders and back muscles shifted as the fabric slid down the smooth fair skin she used to relish. For hours they would hold each other, their bodies glistening from sweat on nights when their love felt so strong it seemed impossible for them to be close enough.

Yet somehow, when no one was paying attention, those intimate sessions became obligatory exchanges. Scheduled meetings. Monthly dues of marriage.

And why?

It wasn't for lack of attraction. He was just as handsome to her as he'd ever been, with those dreamy jade eyes, chiseled jaw line, and GQ model smile. His body, though slightly thickened from maturity, still had a natural athlete's definition. So when had she stopped noticing it? When did it become so easy to take each other for granted, to focus on the negative, to live such separated existences?

She'd refrained from telling him about her father's confession, seeing little chance of gaining support from someone who appeared to be traveling down the same adulterous road. But why didn't she bother to at least inform him of her father's relapse?

She didn't have to search far to find the reason. Inside, she knew why.

Drew closed the drawer with his knee. "I'll whip up some eggs and toast." He turned to her, his hands resting on his hips. "Then we'll go through what needs to be done for the funeral, all right?"

He was demanding she accept his help, whether she liked it or not.

Kate nodded. As usual, the artist inside wanted her to flee from any hardships peeking over the horizon. To brush the colors of her emotions onto a fresh linen canvas until all the bad things went away. To escape…like her father used to do.

Had she become the very thing she hated?

She glanced across the hall at her studio. Never before had she noticed how similar the room was to the cab of her father's semi, complete with its small bed, pile of clothes, and guarantee of seclusion from the world.

How foolish she'd been, thinking her husband was like her father. Drew wasn't the type to cheat or to leave her. In fact, he'd sped to her rescue. Now it was her turn to reach out, to appreciate his efforts.

Drew was only a few steps from the doorway. Her confidence might exit with him if she didn't act now. "Wait," she blurted. "I can explain."

He turned back around. Curiosity brightening his eyes, he nodded for her to go on.

At last she had launched the javelin, and now it was too late to question whether throwing it into the air had been a wise decision. Where would she begin?

She edged herself up and sat against the leather-tucked headboard, arms lassoing her knees. "My parents used to call me a 'water baby.' Said that once I got in, I wouldn't come out. Not till I was as shriveled as a raisin."

Drew leaned on the doorjamb and folded his arms, listening intently.

She increased her pace, pushing the tale out before it had a chance to dig its heels in. "I was seven years old, and my dad was stowing gear on his Bayliner. We were tied to the dock. I was on the bow of the boat, getting in a few more tries at a back dive before heading home. I remember being underwater, so excited that I'd finally landed in the water the right way."

She dropped her gaze to the copper comforter and rolled a loose thread between her fingers. "Next thing I knew I was lying on the dock, coughing up water and crying. A paramedic was kneeling over me. He was a family friend who just happened to be there."

"Was the water too shallow?" Drew asked.

She shook her head. "I came up under the boat and hit the top of my head. Came pretty close to drowning."

"So your dad saved you then?"

She hesitated, hating her answer. "I don't know. My father's clothes were soaked, so I assumed he'd pulled me out. But we never talked about it." Shame prevented her from raising her eyes. "At first, I thought he was angry for the trouble I'd caused. Later, I figured he was just as shaken as I was. He said that telling my mom would only worry her, so we kept it our secret. A few months later, she was killed. And after that…well, he and I really didn't discuss much of anything."

Drew crossed the room and sat on the bed next to her.

She forced her gaze to meet his. To her relief, genuine caring shone through, inviting her to continue.

"I didn't tell you my dad's cancer came back for the same reason he and I never talked about that day on the lake." She released the snippet of a nervous laugh. "It's the Flaherty way."

Drew narrowed his eyes.

"See, if you don't talk about things that upset you, pretend they didn't happen, then they're not real. And, if you do a really good job keeping your emotions tucked inside, nothing can ever hurt you. Right?" She flashed a tight-lipped smile in acknowledgment of the absurd notion before realizing the theory applied to her father's indiscretion as well.

"I understand, Kate, I do," her husband said warmly. "I lost my father too, remember?"

She nodded. It had been either a heart attack or stroke,

before she and Drew first met.

"If you'd let me, I could've helped you through this," he added. "Sometimes, admitting you don't have it all figured out takes more courage than anything else." As he brushed her hair off her shoulder, his fingers swept across her neck. A tantalizing current shot straight to her heart. "All I ask is that you don't shut me out. If you love me, you're going to have to trust me."

He was right. She knew he was right. And his expression now was no different from the one he'd had when he avowed his love and commitment all those years ago. The sincerity in his eyes insisted those same feelings remained. There was no reason to doubt him, save her own insecurities and expectations of being let down.

What she wouldn't do to take back her harsh accusations and their senseless arguments.

Drew swiped two tissues from the box on the nightstand and handed them over.

"Look at me." She wiped her nose. "I'm a blubbering mess."

"That's okay. I prefer to be married to a human being." He released a soft chuckle. "Maybe now I won't be the only one who wells up when Leo sinks at the end of *Titanic*."

Man, she loved his laugh.

More than that, she loved him.

"So how about that gourmet breakfast?" she asked, wanting desperately to shift the focus.

"Oh, I think I can scramble a few eggs for you." He smiled, then tipped her chin up with his hand and leaned in until their lips met. The kiss was gentle, his breath warm, his lips soft. Just like the finale of their first date. Outside her apartment door they'd stood, her feet seeming to hover over the ground.

Now, with her eyes closed, the masculine scent of him took her back to that night. She laid her palms on the sides of his neck and moved them downward, her fingers rediscovering the contours of his body. She'd just reached his chest when an electronic ring shattered the moment, like a crystal glass destroyed by an operatic note.

Drew pulled away, crawled across the bed, and snatched the handset. "Hello." A pause. "This is he."

And with that, their journey through reminiscences came to an abrupt end.

"Are you positive?" Drew's voice was low and direct, an attorney's truth-seeking tone polished for cross-examinations. "All right," he sighed. "I'll be there soon." He hung up, then turned to Kate. "A few dents in the bumper and dirt in the grill, but otherwise your car's running smoothly."

She waited, hoping he wasn't about to balance his good news with bad.

"They found your keys and cell phone inside," he continued. "Unfortunately, though…" He hesitated.

"Unfortunately *what*?"

"I guess somebody got into the car. Your purse had been dumped out onto your seat."

Fear stole her breath. She gripped the edge of the mattress and looked up at Drew. "My wallet?" The wallet containing her full name. Her address. Her life.

He shook his head. "It's gone."

"Are you sure?" The words came out automatically, her mind whirling with the implications for her safety.

"I know this is the last thing you needed to hear today. But don't worry, I'll take a taxi over to pick up your car. Then I'll help you sort things out with the insurance company. We'll take care of it together."

No doubt his efforts were well intended, but vehicle damages were the least of her concerns. And admitting the naivety she had illustrated, all for the sake of a free ride home, was the last thing she wanted to share.

Twenty Two

Bells of Ireland: the perfect selection for floral arrangements at her father's graveside service. Surrounding the green stalks of bell-shaped flowers would be Casablanca lilies and white gladiolus. And of course, roses, a funeral standard. The florist recommended yellow, but Kate chose Sterling, purple-silver buds with thornless stems.

The Flahertys had had enough thorns in their lives.

Kate reclined in the kitchen chair, sipped her chai tea and thought of Doris, wondering if the caregiver took a few days off after a patient passed on, or if her boss immediately handed over a new client's file. Kate envisioned a roomful of hospice workers staring up at a chalkboard, like gamblers in the '40s waiting to see which prizefighter's name would next be added or erased.

Waving off the image, Kate placed her pen on the page and pulled a steady line through *Order flowers* and *Funeral home appt.*

The cube she'd drawn at the bottom corner of the notepad caught her eye. Each side of the three-dimensional shape was thick from repeated tracing. A strange sensation filled her as she realized she'd been unconsciously doodling on the paper as if it were a grocery list. A check-off sheet of crime and death.

She scanned the page of duties.

Stolen wallet. Already she'd waded through a series of annoying transfers and "please holds" to make an official police report. She'd then canceled and reordered her debit and credit cards. Shortly after the tow service had called, she'd decided to share her concerns with her husband about a possible link between the theft and Mick. But persistent phone interruptions and the untimely arrival of Drew's taxi had thwarted her plans.

And so, she had busied herself with things like:

Insurance. Drew had planned to contact their agent when he got home, but she went ahead and made the call solo. Any mission to occupy her thoughts. She would, however, take him up on his offer to write the obituary for the *Seattle Times.* Composing the eulogy was going to be enough of a challenge for her as it was.

Announce the funeral. Surprisingly, Aunt Sophie had volunteered to spread word of the Thursday service. She was hardly enthusiastic about it, but Kate had no inkling who to contact or how to reach them.

Last but not least: *Dad's documents and suit.*

She dreaded the thought of revisiting her father's empty cabin where every step risked the disturbance of a dust-covered memory. Still, her heart told her that for more reasons than mere obligation, she was the only one who should be rummaging through his belongings.

The phone rang. She picked up the cordless handset from the table and read the caller ID screen.

PRIVATE CALLER.

It had to be Drew on his cell, one of the few people who phoned their house from a blocked number. A defense against potentially irate clients.

She pressed the *Talk* button and cleverly responded as if she were psychic. "So how's my car?"

She waited. No answer.

Shoot, maybe it wasn't Drew. She cringed slightly and

said, "Hello?"

Still no reply.

Probably just a wrong number.

She hung up and returned to her notepad. After a few moments of silence, the phone rang again.

PRIVATE CALLER.

Who on earth...?

Wait. Could it be him? *Mick*? Or whatever his real name was?

No. No, it wasn't. Still, she hesitated before picking it up. "Hello."

Nothing.

"Hello?"

A subtle noise, but no voice.

"Is someone there?" She was about to pull the receiver from her ear when she heard another sound. A wisp of a breath.

Someone was listening.

Her heart pumped faster.

"Who is this?" she demanded. "I said who is this?"

Another faint breath in her ear. Her skin turned to goose bumps.

It was him! It had to be him. She yanked the phone downward to press *Off*, but the horror of the previous night suddenly slammed back, paralyzing her body. She dropped the handset onto the slate floor. The timer on the electronic screen was running. The call was still connected.

She was too frightened to touch the phone, as though his hand might reach through the line and strangle her. But then she realized the private sounds of her home were flowing into his ears like his beloved jukebox songs.

Scrambling for the device, she fell to her knees. She shut off the handset and held it to her hammering chest.

It rang again. An unrelenting, strident ring.

Her muscles jumped inside her skin. She pressed the phone tighter into her body, muffling the trill.

Third ring…fourth…fifth.

Drew must have turned the answering machine off.

Ringing…ringing… Would it ring all day?

She dragged the phone from her chest with as much resistance as pulling a magnet from a magnetic block. Without tipping her chin, she peered down at the screen.

BLAKELY GALLERY.

Relief shot from her gut.

She was being ridiculous. Kids were merely making prank calls.

She took a calming breath, then another, before answering. "Hi," she rasped.

"Kate, love, there you are." As always, Christine Blakely's tone was sultry and deep. Her words, spoken with a hint of a British accent, portrayed the refinement of a woman who'd been born and raised somewhere more exotic than her small hometown of Troutdale, Oregon. Or so the staff had gossiped at last year's Christmas party.

"Hi, Christine."

"I've been trying to reach you all day. Don't you ever check your calls?"

Kate never understood why Christine liked to leave multiple messages with no specifics except that it was vital she be called back. After all, listening to identical directives only slowed the response process. But then, it was hard to complain when the gallery owner's typical announcements involved significant sales or raving critic reviews.

"My cell phone broke last night," Kate told her.

"Well, that explains it. I was beginning to think you weren't interested in hearing my exciting news."

Kate sat completely still, encouraging her nerves to settle like drifting flakes in a shaken snow globe.

"Darling, aren't you dying to know why I'm calling?"

"Please tell me." The cold slate beneath Kate's shins sent an added chill through her body. Or had the temperature of the whole room dropped?

"I do hope you're sitting down..." Christine drew out her words, building the suspense.

Kate nodded to no one.

"We received confirmation this morning." The woman's controlled enthusiasm linked each syllable to the next. "The Montevino—the new hotel downtown I told you about—well, they're putting in a hoity-toity restaurant on the fifteenth floor. And your art is going to be showcased on virtually *every* wall there. The owner's commissioning eight large paintings. Can you believe it, love? *Eight!*"

Kate tried her best to project the excitement Christine rightfully expected to ignite. "Wow, that's...wonderful."

"And that's not all." Kate could almost see the middle-aged woman wagging her index finger and puckering her red Botox-pumped lips. "A handsome chap came in today specifically to ask about you and your work. Apparently, he'd viewed one of your paintings in a newspaper article, and finds everything about you absolutely fascinating."

In an instant, Kate's fear devoured oxygen like a backdraft in a blazing fire.

She choked out the question, "His name—did he give his name?"

"No, I'm afraid not." Christine clucked. "I suppose he preferred his privacy. But he did take all of your biographical information with him."

All her information?

"What did he look like?"

"Pardon me?"

A few contradicting details and Kate could rule Mick out. "Tall? Slim? Dark hair?"

"Why, yes," Christine replied. "Do you know him?"

Kate battled a shiver. "Is there anything else you remember about him?"

"Mmm, let's see. He was a shade mysterious, but

extremely polite. Average clothes, and the little truck he drove was average too. But with as much as he seemed to know about you, I got the clear impression he was a qualified buyer."

The handset nearly slipped from Kate's hand. Her knotted stomach flipped over like pretzel dough. She wet her lips and slowly said, "Thank you for letting me know."

"Darling?" Christine's tone didn't shield her befuddlement. "Are you all right? I just delivered the most glorious news, and you act as though someone died."

Kate knew the comment was intended as a meaningless idiom, but without giving away more details about her new fan, she had no other way to explain her lackluster reaction. "Actually, it was my dad. He died. Last night."

A gasp. Then silence. Obviously, Christine realized she'd inserted her pedicured foot into her mouth. "I'm so sorry," she said at last. "I didn't mean…"

When her voice dwindled off, Kate jumped on the opportunity to exit. "Don't worry. You couldn't possibly have known." Kate's assurances were genuine. She would have offered more if she had the energy. "Listen, I should get going, but I'll be in touch about the commissions, okay?"

"Uh, yes, absolutely. And take all the time you need. You just let us know when you're ready to meet."

"Thanks. I'll talk to you soon." Kate hung up without waiting for a return valediction.

Could this tall, dark man with a truck really be Mick? Was he studying her on the Internet, visiting galleries that carried her work, tracking the footprints of her life?

Then it hit her, the reason she'd opened up to a random stranger on a lonely night in a diner: it wasn't random at all. His presence hadn't simply felt comfortable to her—it had been familiar.

She ransacked her brain, mining for recollections from her last reception at the Blakely Gallery. A cyclone of shaking hands, posing for photographs, supplying quotes to reporters.

Rarely a second to breathe, much less memorize the features of guests she met only in passing. A chance meeting could have very well transformed a silent fan's interest into obsession. Perhaps that was why Mick hadn't wanted her to leave. Perhaps he was another Annie Wilkes, the crazed fan in the Stephen King novel who held her favorite writer captive after he happened to crash his car near her remote cabin. The uncanny similarities ripened Kate's fear.

Her mind scrolled through the conversations she'd had with Mick until pinpointing the moment he'd revealed he knew she was a painter. She'd presumed the splatters on her sweatshirt or fingernails had given her away. But what if he'd already known?

Bam, bam, bam.

Hard knocks at the door stiffened her body.

For the first time in her life, Kate wished she had a gun in the house.

Twenty Three

Light from the overcast sky spilled into the kitchen, glinting on the butcher knife in Kate's hand.

Boom, boom, boom.

The knocks grew louder, more demanding. An insistent fist pounding on her front door.

Her mind suggested it was merely a Girl Scout determined to sell her last box of Do-Si-Dos. One look through the peephole would confirm that indeed it was a sprightly youngster perched on her doormat rather than a stalker.

Steeling herself, she focused on the brass deadbolt switch. Its vertical position assured her no one could enter without her permission. As she moved forward, she looked down at the round doorknob. It would jiggle if someone tried to invite himself in.

The shadowy shape of an arm suddenly appeared behind the door's frosted-glass panel. When the caller's whole body swayed into the narrow frame, Kate halted. The silhouette's height indicated an adult, with a man's bulkiness. Elbow in the air, he shielded his eyes with a hand on his forehead and pressed into the glass.

He was trying to see inside. Trying to find her!

She knew visibility from outside through the foggy pane was zero, but still she remained motionless. Her nose registered something in the air. A masculine, earthy smell. Was it him? Or an illusion born out of fear?

She should have told Drew everything. She never should have let him leave.

Peep.

The high-pitched sound jarred her nerves. It was the phone in her hand. It peeped again, causing sweat to bead on her scalp. The phone's cries were giving her away. She had to stop them.

She pressed buttons with her thumb, producing a jumble of beeps.

Her gaze cut to the screen. *RECHARGE BATTERY.*

"Not now," she whispered through clenched teeth. A rectangular graphic flashed incessantly before the screen went blank. The peeps were cut off, just as she was from the outside world.

Her thoughts raced to the telephone upstairs—the cordless one. Which meant it could be anywhere in the house.

She snapped her eyes back to the window. The shadowy form had disappeared.

On the balls of her feet, she crept toward the door, taking care to avoid the spot on the hardwood floor that invariably creaked. A few more steps and the peephole would give her a fishbowl view of the caller. Perhaps a neighbor was strolling off, his harmless figure already halfway down the driveway.

She was nearly even with the base of the staircase when a wooden thud came from the kitchen.

Someone was at the back door!

She tightened her grip on the knife and sprinted barefoot up the stairs, pulse hammering. Midway to the top, she caught herself from stumbling, but dropped the handset. It clanked, providing proof of her presence all the way down the steps.

Once in her bedroom, she slammed and locked the door. She tore across the room to reach Drew's nightstand where the backup phone stood on its charger.

Thank God.

She snagged the electronic lifeline and aimed her thumb at what could possibly be the last three numbers she would ever dial.

"Come on," she said, stilling her quavering finger that had uselessly pressed *9-1-2*. She reset the dial tone and tried again. The call was ringing through. Her mind was scrambling to recall her address when she heard a sound—a man's familiar whistle. The tune sailed through the screen of her half-open window and drew her gaze to the glass...to the sight of a uniformed figure striding back to his police car.

Brian.

"Nine-one-one. What is your emergency?" The twangy female voice reminded Kate of the phone in her hand. "Hello, is someone there?"

"Yes, I..." How could Kate explain that she'd mistaken her husband's best friend for a threatening intruder? A friend who also happened to be a cop? "My toddler...he was playing with the handset." As if admonishing a child across the room, Kate threw her voice to the side. "Honey, this is Mommy's. This is a no-no." She redirected her attention to the emergency responder. "It won't happen again. I promise." She hung up and rushed to the window.

Brian was opening his car door. "Wait! Brian!" she belted out through the black-netted screen. "I'm home!"

He lifted his head. Kate rapped a knuckle on the raised glass pane and waved. He flicked an acknowledging hand and walked back toward the house.

Besides her husband, there was no one else she would rather see.

She tossed the phone onto the bed and jogged downstairs. After unbolting the lock, she flung the front door wide open.

"Hi, Kate." He smiled his usual glowing smile

sprinkled with charming arrogance. In the authoritative stance that the uniform garnered—legs cowboy distance apart, hands hitched on his gun belt—Brian exuded the image of a veteran officer. A man who'd found his comfort zone.

"I'm so glad you're here," Kate said.

"Everything okay?"

Her lips parted to answer just as his pleasant expression vanished. She traced his downward gaze. Directly to the forgotten knife in her hand.

"Oh, yeah, yeah," she stammered. "I was just... trimming some steaks. For the grill."

"Easy there, killer." Chuckling, he leaned back, holding up a cautionary hand.

That's when Kate realized she'd been flailing the knife around as she spoke. Talking with her hands was an old habit she could never break. In fact, Drew used to tease that if he ever wanted to silence her, all he had to do was tie her wrists behind her back.

"Guess I'm a little jumpy today." Bowing her head, she released the weapon from her stiff grip and let it fall onto the entry table with a clank.

Weapon—what a joke. Hadn't she watched enough B-movies at two in the morning to know that only homicidal maniacs were successful at turning kitchen utensils into deadly objects? She'd be embarrassed if Brian knew what she'd been thinking just minutes ago. Clearly, the car wreck had rattled her brain, cranking up her imagination three ticks past sane.

"What can I say?" Kate shrugged. "Too much caffeine, not enough sleep."

Brian nodded before his smile slipped away again. He rubbed the back of his neck, looking at her with consoling eyes. "I'm so sorry to hear about your dad."

It hadn't occurred to her until then to question the reason for his visit.

"You heard?" she asked rhetorically.

"Beth told me when I called Drew's office."

Beth was a twenty-something law student, as perky as she was curvy, and smart to boot. When the girl's uncle, a senior partner at the firm, first assigned her to be Drew's legal assistant, Kate had joked about stealing a lock of her long golden mane to create a voodoo doll. Fortunately, Beth's outward crush on Brian had quickly put any of Kate's jealous notions to rest. Well, at least when it came to Beth anyway.

"If there's anything I can do," Brian told Kate, "you be sure and let me know, all right?"

"I will."

"I mean that, now."

"Thanks. I appreciate it."

A light breeze disturbed the awkward silence between them. Kate knew this was when almost every well-wisher found himself at a loss for words but felt rude simply bidding farewell.

"Would you like to stay for dinner?" she asked, before remembering she had no steaks in the fridge to support the excuse she'd given.

Brian was about to respond when the police radio attached to the shoulder of his navy blue uniform crackled. Through the static, a woman's voice rattled off numbers. He pressed a button on the device and provided his location. From the exchange that followed, Kate gathered there'd been an incident at a nearby mini-mart.

"Copy that," he replied to the dispatcher. Then he said to Kate, "Afraid I'll have to take a rain check." He jerked his thumb toward his patrol car. "There's a shoplifting call I've gotta see to."

"No problem." She smiled, internally sighing, before his word sunk in.

Shoplifting. A theft.

As in, her wallet.

There had to be options for protecting herself. Who

better to ask?

"Hey, Brian, before you go...I need to talk to you about—" How could she put this? "A possible male stalker."

"A stalker? Is this for *you*?" Concern darkened his face. She nodded.

"Have you filed a complaint?"

"No, not yet. I actually don't know if there's enough evidence to support one."

"Has he been coming to your residence? Bothering you at work?"

A confident *yes* was about to leap out of her mouth, but her conscience drew it back in. Truthfully, she had no idea whether Mick was the guy who'd expressed interest in her at the gallery. A tall, slim, dark-haired man? He could be nothing more than a potential art collector.

"Not really," Kate replied.

"So you've seen him following you, then?"

"No...not that I know of."

Brian straightened and crossed his arms, his chest bulky from his bulletproof vest. His eyes betrayed his confusion. "I'm not sure I follow you. What has this guy been doing exactly?"

"Well," she said, "there were a couple phone calls...although he didn't talk." She stopped herself. A few light breaths over the line and no caller ID didn't warrant unease without adding in the elements she'd yet to share. Now to keep Brian from thinking she was suffering from posttraumatic stress from her father's death, she'd have to enlighten him with the details of her ill-fated encounter at Gordy's.

Alas, here went nothin'.

As she briefly recounted her tale, emphasizing the obvious connection to her stolen wallet, Brian reached into his shirt pocket and produced a small notepad and pen. His expression intense, he jotted a few scribbles before pausing, considering her claims. "And you say his name is Mick?"

"That's what he said."

"I could check to see if he's got any priors, but I'd need a last name. You didn't happen to catch it, did you?"

She shook her head.

Another scribble. "And you're sure you saw him try to use that same phone?"

"I...don't understand."

"The one without the cord. You said it was one of those antique-looking phones."

"That's right."

"I just want to make sure there's no misunderstanding," he explained. "Is there any possibility he used another phone? That the one you picked up was just a prop? You know, like the kind those old greasy spoons usually have."

She replayed the moment Mick had volunteered to check the phone lines. His back had been to her, and she'd looked away from him for a second or two, but she'd definitely seen him hold a black handset to his ear. The same handset she'd held herself.

Or was it?

It appeared to be, but that was from a distance.

Oh no—the alternative hadn't even occurred to her. What if there was another telephone behind the bar, one that had escaped her attention? Was the rotary dial simply a gadget on display for nostalgic ambiance? Like the striped hula-hoop and metal-wheeled roller skates on the wall?

Perhaps it was she who'd come off as a lunatic, leaving to get her purse yet never returning, rather than the other way around. And her unlocked car would certainly have been an open invitation to any driver lacking morals who'd happened along the highway.

Kate recoiled at the revelation, feeling as tiny as a leprechaun from one of her father's mythical tales. "Brian, I think you've solved your first big case."

"Now, hold on—I'm not saying we should dismiss anything yet. Just that we need more to go on." He adjusted his gun belt on his hips. "You did mention some phone calls. If those continue, it could constitute telephonic harassment. Or if you can prove he poses a physical threat—even just a pattern of behavior that causes you to fear for your safety—we could definitely talk about a restraining order."

"Really, I think we can chalk this one up to late night jitters, especially with the accident and everything." She flashed a smile, hoping to squash further investigation into her neurotic display. Thank goodness she hadn't told Drew about her unfounded suspicions. He might very well have stormed back to that diner and ended up getting arrested himself for harassing a guy whose only crime was being a good Samaritan.

"Look," she told Brian, "I shouldn't hold you up any longer. Sounds like you've got a busy night ahead."

Drawing his lips in, he audibly inhaled through his teeth and shook his head. "All right. But if anything else develops…"

"You'll be the first person I call. Now, you'd better get going."

"Yeah, okay." He put the notepad away, taking a step back. "Tell Drew I stopped by, will ya?"

"Of course."

"Ah, shoot—I almost forgot why I came."

Wasn't it to offer condolences? Tilting her head, she waited for him to go on.

"When you didn't answer, I figured you weren't home. So I left Drew's bag on the back porch against the door."

She'd almost forgotten about the terrifying noises from outside the kitchen. Once again, a logical explanation for everything. Except for which bag Brian was referring to.

"You had his bag?" she asked.

"Your message on his phone gave him a pretty good scare. Took off like a bat outta hell. Anyway, when he called to let me know that you'd made it home okay, I forgot to mention his suitcase."

Kate struggled to comprehend this account, as if she were translating a foreign language. She casually attempted to clarify. "He was at *your* place when he got my message?"

"Guess he figured it was cheaper than a hotel." Brian bit off a chuckle. "I'm just glad you two are working things out. Sometimes guys just need a good kick in the pants to wake us up."

The final pieces snapped together. The words on the puzzle read clear: *Drew left me.*

Without giving her so much as an opportunity to defend herself, or the decency to tell her in person, he had moved in with Brian. The argument they'd had the night before his trip had sealed the deal. He hadn't planned to stay with her until he thought she'd been injured in a car crash.

Now she was forced to ask: Would he have left if Dad hadn't died?

The realization that the answer could be yes stunned her. She was more alone than ever. She just hadn't known it until now.

"Kate?" Worry saturated Brian's voice. "You *are* working things out, right? I mean—you knew he was at my place, right?"

Her lips curved up, perhaps only half their range, but far enough to cloak her pain. "Of course. I just have a lot on my mind."

"Oh, sure." He looked relieved. "Well, I'll see you both soon. Have a good night."

"You too. Thanks."

With that, he wheeled and marched back to his car, waving as he pulled away.

"Yeah, thanks," she muttered under her breath, "for opening my eyes."

As Brian's taillights faded around the corner, Kate

reentered the house that no longer held the warmth of a home, and prepared for Drew's arrival.

Twenty Four

Seated on the sable leather couch, fingers steepled at her chin, Kate stared at the black case. There it stood in the center of the living room like a spotlighted showpiece in a travel accessory store. The wheels had seen plenty of miles over the years, though all of them from Drew's innumerable business trips, not one from the romantic excursions for which they'd been intended. Ironically, the wedding gift meant to commemorate the start of their lives eternally joined was now a symbol of their division. In every sense.

Her insides ached as she reviewed their most recent exchanges. His apology when he found her on the highway took on a new meaning. And she wondered how much of their heartfelt talk this morning had been sincere. She only hoped Brian had actually believed her when she'd pretended to know about Drew's furlough. The alternative would burden her with a layer of humiliation she wasn't sure she could take today.

Tap, tap, tap. Tap, tap, tap.

The fresh knocks on the door, though irksome, didn't alarm her. She was sticking with reason. Or perhaps she was too resigned to care even if Charles Manson was paying a visit.

She huffed as she followed the rhythmic raps that promised to be as unyielding as a woodpecker's mating call and snapped out, "I'm coming!" But the knocks continued. The way her day was spiraling downward, she wouldn't be surprised if a missionary had come to preach about the virtues of love everlasting.

When she opened the door, no pamphlets were thrust in her direction. But still, she regretted not using the peephole.

"Well, heavens to Betsy, how have you been?" Wanda gushed in her nasally drawl.

Kate didn't bother answering. Wanda Finch's questions were rarely intended to elicit a response. Not unless she was sniffing around for clues to compile her local reports. The state of national security seemed to depend on the general public knowing which husband on the block was sleeping with the nanny or who'd gotten drunk at the annual company party and ended up telling off their boss before passing out in the restroom. And then there was the ever-important identity of the man who'd been seen picking up Viagra at the pharmacy down the street. No one needed grocery stand tabloids when Auburn had such a devoted investigator.

"Hope I didn't catch you at a bad time." Wanda's mouth moved as fast as a chattering teeth toy. "I was just lookin' to borrow a cup of flour. Wouldn't ya know, I didn't realize I was out till I was smack dab in the middle of mixing up a batch of zucchini nut bread for Amber Pederson—you remember Amber, the sweet gal from my Bunko group? I tell ya, it's nothing short of a miracle she walked away from that accident in one piece. Of course the police are keeping the whole case under wraps for now. But if you ask me, that bus driver shoulda been forced to take a breath test."

Kate's eardrums instinctively transformed the woman's pause-less rambling into nonsensical cartoon sounds from Charlie Brown's teacher: *Wawa-wawa, wawa-wawa.* Meanwhile, Kate swept a glance over the squatty neighbor's unnatural new hair color. Her tight perm bore a pink sheen that had most likely been advertised as strawberry-blonde on a discounted box of dye. Almost as mind-boggling was the brooch on her snug crocheted sweater, a gaudy trinket with turquoise jewels in the form of an unidentifiable animal begging for a compliment.

When her gaze flashed back to Wanda's lips, flittering over slightly crowded teeth, Kate decided she wasn't in the mood for Chatty Cathy to run out of batteries today. "Did you say you needed some flour?" she broke in.

"Huh, what?" Wanda looked stunned. "Oh, dear me. I did get on a roll, didn't I?" She giggled until her eyes lit on Kate's forehead. "My, my, girl. What in tarnation happened to you?"

Kate's fingers instantly rose, shielding her injury. "It's nothing, really. Just wasn't watching where I was going."

"You know, I did the same silly thing a few weeks back," she said. "Was bending down over my mixing bowl and lifted my head right into my open cabinet door."

"Really? Let me get you that scoop you needed." Kate snatched the large glass measuring cup from the woman's pudgy fingers which were now swollen from menopause, according to Wanda in one of her recent too-much-information passings. Then Kate spun around and hurried into the kitchen. She'd just pulled the flour canister out of the cupboard when Wanda's voice alerted her that she'd been followed.

"I do so appreciate this, Kate. You can imagine how embarrassed I am havin' to ask. But you can't make decent zucchini bread without the right amount of flour, now can you?"

"No, I wouldn't think so," Kate replied absently, scooping up the powder as fast as possible.

"Oh my, what was I thinkin'? I always forget you're not much of the cooking type." Wanda chuckled, her hand waving airily. "Down south, of course, no proper married woman would serve dinner out of a box. I tell ya right now, if I so much as told my mama I was fixin' to heat up one of those little Lean Cuisines for Carl, she'd bolt out of her nursing home and hang me upside-down from a clothesline. At least till the sense flowed back into my head."

No wonder that even when Wanda's husband made one of his rare public appearances, he never spoke. Without a chance to squeak out more than a dozen words, his vocal cords had probably stopped working years ago.

"Here you go." Kate handed over the measuring cup.

Wanda jerked her gaze away from the pile of junk mail on the kitchen island. Her cheeks blushed as she accepted the donation.

"Thank you much." She gave the container a gentle shake, leveling the flour. "Oh no, lookee here. You've given me three whole cups, and all I needed was one."

"That's fine—you keep it. You might need it for another batch."

"You sure?"

"Absolutely."

Wanda's eyes widened as she beamed. "Hey, I know what I'll do!"

Kate already knew she didn't want to hear the rest.

"I'll bake a nice hot loaf for you, too. Y'all aren't allergic to nuts, are you?"

If there was the slimmest chance Wanda would simply leave the bread on their doorstep, Kate might have considered her offer. "That's okay, Wanda. I wouldn't want you to—"

"It'd rightly be my pleasure. I remember how much your husband loved my cinnamon peach cobbler at last summer's block party. Helped himself to at least three servings if I recall."

Wanda's mention of Drew reminded Kate of the imminent confrontation she'd been stewing over.

"Besides," Wanda added, "doubling a batch is a cinch when I got the ingredients layin' out already. And there's nothin' like a recipe from my dear Grandma to sweeten up a hard day."

Hard day? Wait...what did she know?

Kate was about to ask, but then assured herself Wanda was only making conversation. The woman was good at ferreting out gossip, but she couldn't be *that* good.

"Really," Kate insisted, "that's very kind of you, but we're...cutting back on sweets."

Wanda pressed her hand to her chest. "Now, that's crazy talk if I ever heard it. If I had a figure like yours, like the one I had in my pageant days, I'd be devouring every dessert in sight."

Somehow, no matter the subject, the southern belle always managed to drop hints about the Miss Congeniality title she'd won at the Miss Alabama contest four hundred years ago. "Don't waste your youth, I say." Wanda punctuated her statement with a sharp nod. "Enjoy life while you can. It all goes by too quick."

Familiar words...where had Kate just heard them?

At the diner. *Mick's words.*

"Wanda, I wish I had time to talk today, but—"

"Say no more." Wanda raised her hand. "I'd best be getting back anyway, before Carl starts to worry. Besides, my daughter, Jenny—the one with the preemie—she's due to be callin' the next hour or so." Wanda turned around leisurely, her eyes undoubtedly scanning the room for fresh leads.

Kate followed on the woman's thick rubber heels. But only a few steps into her departure, Wanda halted and whirled back with a pinched brow.

"Sugar, listen..." Wanda's premeditated words added weight to Kate's cloaked fear. "If y'all are havin' trouble with anything, you know you can come to me."

Kate spotted Drew's suitcase out of the corner of her eye. Did Wanda know he was planning to leave? Was Kate the last one to find out?

Guardedly, Kate said, "I'm not sure what you mean."

"Now, I know it's none of my business..."

If Kate had been in the midst of swallowing milk, she

would have blown white bubbles through her nose.

"But, well...I think you did the right thing asking that officer over. I'd a done it myself, if it weren't for the darn cataract in my left eye."

Mental whiplash. "Excuse me?"

"I just mean I would've jotted down the license plate number if I'd had a better view from my sewing room."

"What license plate?"

Wanda's eyes lit up like she'd just hit the jackpot. "Oh, my—I assumed that's what the officer was here about. I reckoned you must've gotten the heebie-jeebies like I did from that man parked out front."

Kate's stomach went hollow. "Someone was parked in front of my house?"

Wanda nodded briskly. "For a good half hour. I know it was roughly that long 'cause I first saw him sitting there at the start of *Judge Judy*, and he left during the opening of *Young and the Restless*." She displayed her forearms. "Would you look at that? I'm gettin' chicken skin just thinking about it."

Kate pressed on. "Did he ever get out of the car?"

"No," Wanda nearly whispered, shaking her head. "That's why he struck me as not being right. He just sat there, gawking at your house. I know that's what he was doing 'cause all I could see was the back of his head."

"His hair—what color was it?"

"Wish I could tell ya, but his windows were too dark to make him out clear."

Kate spoke slowly in a subliminal attempt to lead Wanda to a desirable answer. "So the car was...a sedan? Or sports coupe?"

"Oh, no, nothing that fancy. It was a truck. A black one. Had a dusty tarp in back coverin' Lord knows what. Didn't catch the make or model, but I'm sure it was American made."

A pickup truck. Dusty from a dirt road. But so what? This was Washington. Here, dust-covered pickups were as abundant as Seattle's Best coffee shops.

Wanda sighed dramatically. "It's a shame he didn't hang around for a minute or two more. I was fixin' to slip on my shoes and take a closer look. You know, so I could get the plate number for you, discreet-like. I just knew there was something fishy about the whole thing. Felt it in my knees. That's where I feel it when things are off. My mama and Aunt Bessie used to get the shakes in their pinkies, but me, well, I get sort of a pulsin' in the joints." She paused and placed a hand on Kate's shoulder. "Do you need to sit down, sugar? You look a bit peaked."

Kate ordered herself to regroup. "No, I'll be fine." Her voice was hoarse but calm. "Thank you for telling me."

"I'm just glad I could be of service. One neighbor helping out another, that's what it's all about." Wanda grinned. "Now, would you like me to tell that officer what I saw? I'd be more than willing to go down to the station and fill him in on the details if that'd be helpful." Her enthusiasm was overflowing. Oddly, Kate's nightmare of a day was shaping into a fantasy for Wanda.

"I don't think involving the police will be necessary," Kate said. "Not until we know there's really something to be concerned about." Brian had already laid it all out for her. She would need solid proof before anyone could legally lift a finger. Yet with this recent development, she was tempted to place a call herself.

"Suit yourself." Wanda pouted, Kate's refusal sprinkling on her parade.

"However—" Kate couldn't believe what she was about to ask. "If you do happen to get that…feeling in your knees again, about anyone suspicious…"

Pride raised Wanda's stature half an inch. "Oh, you rest assured, if I spot that truck creepin' around a second time, I'll call the proper authorities lickety-split. By the way, what *was* that officer doing here, if you don't mind my askin'?"

If Kate didn't supply a believable explanation, her neighbor just might spin a more intriguing tale herself. Still, Kate had no plans to broadcast her marital or parental woes through the living-breathing community loudspeaker.

"My wallet," she answered. "It was stolen out of my car."

Wanda gasped. "You poor thing. I couldn't imagine some stranger rifling through all my pictures and personal information. You must feel so *violated*."

Yeah, this was helpful.

"Mercy, that reminds me," Wanda said, perking. "The other mornin' I was at the Oriental nail salon and overheard two gals chattin' about the wildest story. Apparently, some waitress working at a bar asks a gal for I.D.—"

"Sorry, Wanda, I'd love to hear the rest, but—"

"Oh, right, right." Wanda giggled. "Me and my tangents, I tell ya. If my head wasn't screwed on, I'd lose track of that too." She turned and shuffled toward the entry, finally taking her cue to exit.

As Wanda stepped through the door, she angled her head back and added, "If there's one thing I've learned, it's that criminals love breaking into those foreign cars. That's why I won't let Carl buy anything but a Dodge."

"Thanks, I'll remember that."

"You have a good day, now. And thanks again for the flour."

Kate closed the front door and bolted it behind her. She then moved to the staircase and sat on the bottom step, hooking one arm around a post as if clinging to a carousel pole. Round and round her mind went, the world spinning into a blur. She wanted to jump off, but it was going too fast. And there was no one waiting to catch her.

How did she end up here?

Regardless of how it happened, it was time for her to take control of her life. She was tired of being a victim.

She didn't know what she was going to say to Drew when he got home, but she knew it was going to change everything. For better or for worse.

Twenty Five

Kate leaned against the granite counter, arms crossed, eyeing her husband from across the room.

"We've got enough here to feed a small village," Drew said, smiling. "I was so hungry, anything that read 'Pao', 'Chow' or 'Special' ended up in the bag."

The smell of MSG and stir-fry intensified with each Chinese food carton he unloaded onto the glass kitchen table. Kate's gut felt as wrung as a washcloth.

Usually she loved Chinese take-out. Today though, it too closely resembled a new spin on a charitable pan of lasagna, the comfort food that brought no comfort. In the weeks following the death of Kate's mother, nearly every woman in the PTA had delivered some variation of the dish.

"Do you want me to make you up a plate?" Drew asked.

"No, I'm fine."

"Come on, babe—you've got to eat something."

"Because it won't do me any good if I get sick. Yeah, I've heard."

A wounded look flickered in his eyes before he turned back to the table and resumed his task, slowly, robotically. For a moment, she regretted her curtness. But then she reminded herself why the glow of this morning's reconciliation hadn't lasted the day. Besides, it was his turn to take some responsibility for their problems. His turn to be forthright and reveal some secrets of his own.

Drew flipped on the chandelier above the table, the light briefly stinging Kate's eyes. She hadn't realized the sun had disappeared. She hadn't realized a lot of things.

"The insurance agency's probably closed for the day," he said, reaching into a cupboard. "But I'll call them first thing tomorrow."

"I already took care of it."

"Oh...well, if there's anyone you need me to phone about the funeral—"

"I've made all the calls."

He stopped, plate in hand, his eyes locked on the tiled backsplash. "Ooo-kay," he said, heavily exhaling.

In silence, Kate watched him return to the table and crack apart a pair of wooden chopsticks. He shoveled sweet and sour dumplings out of a white box and onto his plate, followed by a mound of fried rice.

"I'm sorry it took a while," he said, as if he'd determined the source of her frustration. "Your car wasn't quite ready when I showed up. Then on the way back, there was a protest march blocking half of Union Street. Monday afternoon in downtown Seattle and they're saving the sequoias." He smiled. "I didn't realize there was a shortage."

Union Street?

Her simmering emotions were heating to a boil. "You went in to work?"

He looked up, his eyes half closing as if anticipating an exhaustive argument. "Kate..." His placating tone screamed, *Come, come, now—let's not get in a tizzy over something trivial.* "I had just picked up your car when I got a call about some case files they needed."

"And Beth couldn't find them for you?"

"Yeah, but—they wanted me to explain some of the documents. Look, I ran in and out. I wasn't there for more than twenty minutes."

"That's not the point, and I think you know that."

"Kate, I didn't have a choice."

"No," she flung back. "You *did* have a choice. You have all kinds of choices. I'm just never the one you pick." At least not for the right reasons.

"That is not true."

"Oh yeah? Then why was it so impossible for you to stay away from the firm for a single day? I mean, tell me, should I schedule the funeral for the morning or afternoon to best work around your appointments?"

His jaw muscles twitched as if wired shut. Finally, he tore his gaze from hers and back down to the table. After staring at his plate for several seconds, he unhooked the flaps of a sealed box. "Look. I know you're upset about your father—"

"Don't do that!"

Drew appeared as startled as she herself was by the outburst. Still, she couldn't stop from steamrolling ahead. "That is not what this is about."

He tossed his chopsticks onto the table and raised his hands in surrender. "Fine. I give up. What *is* this about, then?" His voice thickened with vexation. "Is it my job? The one I love so much? Kissing up and doing grunt work for no recognition?"

"I'm not talking about your job, I'm talking about your priorities. But, since we're on the subject, if working at the firm makes you so miserable, why don't you quit?"

His lips struggled to form a response. Of course, he didn't have to answer. Kate already knew the reason, even if he didn't.

"Actually," he said, "I'd quit today if I thought you wouldn't mind selling off the house, and our cars—"

"Right. You're hanging onto the job you hate for me. Because I care *so* much about where we live and what we drive."

Lower lip protruding, he folded his arms over fisted hands and issued a few brisk nods. "Well, good. I'm glad we cleared up that misunderstanding." His brows raised as he gasped in mockery. "Hey, I know. Why don't we both retire and move into a tiny storage room in one of your galleries?"

She loathed when he retorted with sarcasm. That was *her* weapon of choice.

"Why not?" she asked. "At least it'd be one way to get you to step foot into a gallery."

He barked a cutting laugh. "Ah, I see. We're still on that discussion. About how I don't support you enough."

She constricted her face. "You think you do?"

"Why else would I work so many flippin' hours? I do it for you, so you can paint whenever you feel like it."

"When I feel like it?" Her temperature climbed. "How gracious of you to allow me the means for my little hobby."

He groaned and yanked the scooped collar of his sweater from his neck. "I just meant I take pride in earning enough so you don't *have* to work. So you can run around and do whatever it is you enjoy doing."

Did she miss the moment Scottie beamed them into the year 1950?

When she rolled her eyes, he tossed her an incredulous look. "What in the world did I say this time?"

At least half of him had already left her. What harm would the truth do now? Maybe that's what their relationship had been lacking for far too long.

"Drew, you may not see my career as a valid one—"

"I didn't say that."

"—but at least I paint because it's something I'm passionate about. You, on the other hand, seem to hate your job. But you're willing to sacrifice everything for it, even us, just so you can become one of those snobby partners you complain about constantly."

"So what do you want me to do, Kate? Throw away all the work I've done because it's not *fun*?"

"I just don't know how you could ever feel good benefiting from other people's misery."

"That's not what I'm doing," he protested, though doubt wavered his voice.

"Drew, aren't you tired of pretending? It's not a competition. You're not your father."

Drew's complexion instantly reddened as if he'd been slapped by an invisible hand, her response leaving him stunned and verbally paralyzed.

Although the words needed to be said, Kate regretted the harshness of her delivery. She softened her tone and tried to explain. "This enormous house, your fully-loaded Beamer...how much will it take before you realize it's not going to make either of us happy?"

He took a deep breath and peered at her from beneath heavy lids. "If the house is too big," he ground out in a harsh whisper, "then we can certainly downsize. I *thought* we were going to need the space. For more than the two of us."

And there it was. The cardboard facade had fallen and exposed the puppeteers. There was no reversing the unveiling of naked, magic-less truth.

"We've talked about this," she reminded him, not sure how the spotlight had shifted onto her. "We said we—"

"Yes, what was it that *we* said?" His tone was confident, matter-of-fact, as if leading a witness to confess what the cross-examiner already knew. "That's right, you wanted to wait until your career settled down. Then again, since we're not *pretending* anymore, any chance you'd like to recant your claim?"

Apparently, Drew was resolved to expose the convenience of her excuse before the court. What he didn't know, however, was that she had irrefutable evidence that would swing the trial back in her favor.

Kate lifted an eyebrow. "I fail to see how us starting a family makes any sense, given that you're not planning to stick around." When she gestured her chin at Exhibit A in the living room, Drew's gaze followed. "Brian stopped by while you were out. He thought you might want your suitcase back."

Drew fell into a stupefied silence. "Kate..." he gravely whispered.

"Strange, I thought you'd at least leave a note. Or were you going to e-mail me from work?"

He turned slowly to face her. "To be honest...I didn't think you'd even notice I was gone."

She was about to sneer back at him in defense until she recognized the sincerity in his voice and eyes.

"Even when you're here," he said, shaking his head, "You're not really here."

She considered counterattacking with the argument that he was the only one taking business trips, preparing for hearings, entertaining clients at chi-chi restaurants. But then, that wasn't really what he was referring to. And she knew it.

Drew gripped the back of a kitchen chair with both hands. "I just needed some time to think."

"Yeah, well...maybe *I* didn't need to hear the news from Brian."

"I apologize for how it came out," he said, exasperated but firm. "But how am I supposed to know what you need? You don't tell me anything. All I know is you sure don't need me."

"Why would you say something like that?"

"You live your own life."

"And you don't?"

"Not by choice. Not like you."

"What does that mean?"

"The car insurance, the funeral arrangements. I'm just a bystander. Until last night, I didn't even know your dad was sick again."

His stinging words drove the air from her lungs. "That's not fair. I tried to explain it to you." Her voice cracked.

"I understand you were in denial, okay? I get that. But it doesn't change the fact that you don't want to rely on anybody. You don't want to trust anyone, especially me."

Unknowingly, he had tripped a wire camouflaged deep inside her. Not even Kate was aware how eager the bomb was to detonate. "Why should I trust you, Drew? You gave up on me. You gave up on us! You're no different than my father!"

Tears fell like ashes down her trembling cheeks. "When Mom died, my dad didn't just close himself off, he pushed me away. I didn't exist for him anymore. He refused his treatments without even bothering to ask how I felt about it. As if his decision wouldn't affect anyone but him."

Drew's gaze descended to the floor. After a long quiet beat, he raised his eyes and extended a look that reminded her of the sole reason he had chosen not to leave her.

Pity.

Setting her mouth in a bitter line, she wiped her cheeks with the sleeve of her button-down shirt. "I'm tired. I'm going upstairs to lie down."

He nodded solemnly. Before he had a chance to say anything that could make her feel worse, she headed for the stairs. She maintained a quick pace, though as she neared the top step, her quads softened like butter on a hot griddle. Sprints for her life were wearing on her limbs.

At last she reached the landing, but felt no accomplishment at crossing the finish line. She turned to her studio—her safe haven, her entrance to Narnia. She stepped through the doorway and closed the world out behind her with a click of the knob. In an instant, the scent of acrylics appeased her senses. She didn't bother to turn on the light; the moon's white glow reaching through the slanted wooden blinds lent her ample assistance. Not that she needed it. She knew this room inside and out, better than any other part of the house in fact.

She was Michelangelo in the Sistine Chapel.

Deftly, she serpentined around two propped easels, making her way toward the leveled futon, flush with the wall. Over an aluminum pan of brushes, then between stacks of crooked, artless frames, she maneuvered through this obstacle course of tangible imagination. At the mattress, she reached for the pillow topping two wadded blankets.

Smack!

She gasped and spun toward the sound. Her eyes strained to identify its origin.

"Hello," she said, hoping no one would answer. Then a muffled laugh filled the room and froze every muscle but her pounding heart.

Twenty Six

Kate braved two steps forward when...
Smack!
The wooden blinds bounced off the top half of the window. She'd forgotten she had slid the pane up to air out the paint fumes in her studio after Doris had called two days ago. Two days, two years. There was little difference anymore.

Be sure to lock the window or a burglar will crawl in and steal all your masterpieces.

Why had she always taken Drew's warnings so lightly? A lattice-covered wall leading up to the second-story balcony and open window practically begged for an intruder. Especially an obsessive fan.

Laughter echoed again, but this time she knew it came from outside. She approached with caution and squinted to see through the angled slats. To her relief, she spotted two teenage boys in baggy jeans strolling on the sidewalk with backpacks and skateboards in tow. Her hands quivered while she closed and locked the window.

Just as she turned back, a cup of paintbrushes toppled off a stool in the corner and crashed to the hardwood floor. She sucked in a breath as the slender tools went rolling. She was about to dash for the door when a small grey ball landed in a strip of light on the floor.

A low silhouette swayed toward her. It was Sofo,

singing a long meow, rallying acknowledgement for her rodent sacrifice. She slinked forward and curled her tail around Kate's leg.

"Not now, Sofo."

The feline tightened her coil, refused to relent until praised.

"Sofo, let go." Kate picked her up by the midsection, opened the door, and gently tossed her into the hallway. The cat twisted her head toward Kate, offering a pair of sad pewter eyes. Her meows resembled a baby's cry, a longing wail for affection.

"I just need to be alone right now," Kate said and slowly shut the door. She turned and leaned back against the Venetian plastered wall.

Alone. Was that what she really wanted?

Sure, it was safe and comfortable. But how long could she survive on loneliness? Longer than her father?

She closed her eyes. Her mind flashed scenes like a racing slide show: Drew rescuing her in the rain, the dream about her wedding day, leaving her dad's bedside the night he died.

Too many secrets, too many things unsaid.

Who was she to criticize Drew for becoming his father? She was no better. And her fate would be no different than Collin Flaherty's if she continued to allow pride to control her life, if she shut out the world and kept loved ones at a distance.

With a sharp sigh, she opened the door. She trudged down the stairs toward the glow of the kitchen light. When she reentered the room, the discovery curled her bare feet on the slate.

Her husband was gone.

"Drew?" she called. "Drew, are you here?"

He couldn't leave. Not yet.

She shuffled through the house—living room, formal room, rec room, study—calling his name, but there was no response. Her apprehension grew.

She was just passing the dining room when a familiar creak sounded from the backyard. She hurried around the formal table and chairs to the French doors, then peeked through a glass pane. There was Drew, seated on the patio swing, staring absently at a luminescent moon hanging low in the black sky. Concealing her relief, she opened the door. As she crossed the brick terrace, the man in the moon stared back, following her, just as her father had taught her it always would.

Drew glanced in her direction, then at the maple tree in front of him. Leaves ruffled in the dewy breeze as Kate sat next to him. She wanted desperately to apologize, but as usual her mouth refused to channel the words. *I'm sorry* was a phrase the Flahertys never voiced easily.

"Do you remember the day we found this house?" Drew asked unexpectedly, his eyes straight ahead. "The real estate agent must've run through a list of a hundred features—A/C, extra storage, landscaped garden with a privacy fence—but all you cared about was that it had a covered porch swing for two."

Kate glanced at the shadowed garden before them, the one she rarely noticed anymore. The scent of hyacinth bloomed from beside a two-tiered cherub fountain, the sound of trickling water reminding her of their presence.

She turned back to Drew. He sighed and shook his head, still gazing into the night. "I told myself I was doing it all for *you*—the house, the cars, the job—doing what was expected of a good husband."

"Drew..."

"You're right." He met her eyes. "I've been lousy at showing how much I value what's important to you. And I lost sight of what was really for us. My father's dead, but I'm still trying to earn his approval." He shrugged one shoulder. "Doesn't make much sense, does it?"

Oh, if Drew only knew.

"It makes perfect sense," she whispered. Empathy smoothed the rough edges between them. "I just think, at some point, we forgot how to make ourselves happy too. You and me, together."

As he nodded pensively, Kate realized they had arrived at a pivotal fork in the road of their marriage. One question would determine whether they would part ways or travel on as a couple. One question would determine what their future held in store.

"Drew, I love you. I couldn't love anybody more."

"I love you too, Kate—"

"No, please. Hear me out."

He sank back into the chair and waited.

"I know we've had some hard times, and I'd love to think we could get past them. But before we can, I need you to tell me why you're staying. I have to know it's because you really want to be with me, and not because of the car accident or my dad."

He took a deep breath. Then he rubbed his chin as if compiling his thoughts, every rub escalating her worries. "I'm not going to lie to you, Kate. Frankly, your car accident had everything to do with my coming back."

She forced a swallow, a gulp of pain, her eyes warding off a swell of tears.

"I don't mean that the way you might think, though." He laid his warm hand over hers, penetrating the chill left in the wake of his admission. "When I got your message, I was so scared. The whole drive, I was imagining what my life would be like without you. Nothing would have any meaning." He raised his palm and rested it on her cheek. "So, yes, the accident is what brought me back, but that's not what's keeping me here. What's keeping me is the hope that you'll remember why you married me. And that you'll have enough faith in our relationship to make it work."

He paused, the difficulty of expressing his next thought

evident. He looked into her eyes.

"I have to know that you need me as much as I need you."

Kate absorbed the earnestness of his words. Though she was scared to death to admit it, her heart gave her no choice. "I do need you." She layered a hand over his on her face. Through his words and touch, she recognized the man she had fallen in love with. "I need you more than anything in my life." A single teardrop fell and rolled over their laced fingers.

Drew wet his lips. He slid his hand to the nape of her neck and stared at her, into her, through her. With one smooth motion, he pulled her in for a kiss. One with such intensity, all of her swirling emotions instantly transformed into longing. Resurrected longing.

Her hands moved on their own accord, molding the curves of his broad shoulders. As she angled her face, his fingers traced the edge of her jaw as if outlining her features in his mind's canvas. Cradling her upturned face, he dusted warm, moist kisses across her cheek. His mouth lingered and grew more demanding as he traveled down the curve of her neck, beckoning her veiled passion. She leaned her head back further, relishing his touch, and blindly wove her fingers through his soft, fine hair. The musky scent of his cologne assaulted her senses, intensifying the desire she had suppressed for far too long.

"Hold on to me." His whisper sent a tremor through her body. With her arms wound snuggly around his neck, his hands moved beneath her thighs, guiding her legs to encircle him as he stood. It suddenly dawned on her that they were outside, that a world existed around them.

She kissed his neck as he carried her into the house, his skin smooth and salty on her tongue. When she glanced up, she noticed they were heading in the opposite direction of the stairs.

"The bedroom is the other way," she pointed out coyly,

"in case you've forgotten."

"Too far away." His lips hinted at a smile.

After a few more steps, he tenderly lowered her onto the chenille throw draping the couch, his knee taking their weight as they descended. The soreness of her body miraculously diminished, overtaken by a surge of anticipated pleasure. He brushed away a lock of her hair that had fallen over her eyes and kissed her again, deeply, more sensually than should be legal for any veteran married couple.

When she pulled at his sweater, he rose to his knees. He whisked the garment over his head and tossed it onto the floor. She kept him fixed in that position, running her fingertips through a streak of moonlight gracing his chest. Her fingers continued downward over his stomach, forcing a sharp breath from his mouth. He grabbed her forearm and held it at bay.

"Not yet," he said, his voice husky with emotion.

She looked up and was transfixed by his dazzling green eyes. Pity was nowhere to be seen, only love and yearning.

Ever so slowly, he lifted her hands above her head. He gave her crisscrossed wrists a light squeeze, directing them to remain there. He glided his hands down the length of her arms. Stretching out the moment, he unfastened the buttons on her shirt, one by one, his eyes never leaving hers. Despite the sudden heat that filled the air, an involuntary shiver rippled over her skin.

He peeled the divided halves of her shirt apart, and as his hands inched up her sides, he leaned down and gingerly kissed a tender spot on her shoulder. He moved his mouth along the contours of her body causing a breathless moan to escape her lips. Arching her back, she dug her nails into her palms and mentally begged him to never stop.

"Drew," she rasped.

He raised his head, angling his solemn face to meet hers. "I know," he said. And she believed he did know. He did understand how much she had missed him, how much she craved the closeness they had lost.

Her hands reached for his face, guiding his parted lips back to hers. The caress of their tongues quickened their pulses, feeding the hunger she thought extinct. There was no guarantee this ecstasy would last more than a single night. But for now, in this moment, the one certainty Kate felt in every pore of her being was that she truly loved the man in her arms and didn't ever want to let him go.

Twenty Seven

Drew couldn't remember when he'd last watched his wife sleeping. Or the last time she'd looked so peaceful, so beautiful.

On the chaise in the corner of their bedroom, he sat in his boxers, a glass of OJ resting on his bent knee. He studied the rise and fall of her back. The sound of her exhalations, accompanied by the soft pattering of rain outside, hypnotized him. Her auburn hair lay sprawled across the pillow. His gaze flowed over her bare shoulders, down her spine, and settled on her lower back, where her tattoo of a small black Chinese character peeked out from the sheet.

No wonder Kate loved to paint. A photograph could capture the perfection of the model before him, the elegant curves, lines, and shadows, but not the emotions the image evoked.

He glanced at the clock on her nightstand before realizing he didn't want to know the hour.

Too late. He'd seen the numbers: 9:37 AM.

After the night they'd had, he should be sleeping as soundly as she. The third time they'd made love, they'd finally reached their bedroom. Wrapped in the sheets, they'd laughed about nothing, snacked on moo shu pork, and held each other in peaceful silence. They had even talked about her father. Well, *she'd* talked about her father, and even recited his misdirected apology. Drew hadn't known quite what to say after learning about the indiscretion that ended in the ultimate tragedy. An affair that cost Collin Flaherty everything.

Her dad's civil but cool demeanor over the years certainly made more sense to him now. Their conversations had never gone beyond Seahawk and weather predictions. Drew was grateful to hear Collin's distance wasn't due simply to distaste for his son-in-law. And even more grateful he'd put on the brakes with Lindsey, preventing himself from making the same mistake.

Curse him for his night with Lindsey.

Granted, it could have gone much further than it did. And although no judge in the district would rule their brief make-out session an adulterous act, Kate might. The fact that it had gone as far as it did still nibbled away at his conscience. He was confident Lindsey had kissed him first—at least he would like to think so—but either way, he had hardly fought her off.

Should he tell Kate how close he'd come to betraying her? That he'd mistaken her icy behavior as utter disinterest in him? He could guess what Oprah would say: *Honesty will set you free.* But how free did he want to be? He certainly didn't want to be freed from their marriage, which is how he could end up after all was said and done.

Just then, Kate stirred. Yawning, she stretched her arms under the pillow. She blinked heavily and turned toward him. When their eyes met, a soft smile spread across her lips. And that's when he knew: Clearing his conscience wasn't worth the risk.

"Hey, there," she said.

"Hey."

"Whatcha doin'?"

He offered a slacked grin. "Watching you drool."

She dabbed the dry corners of her mouth with her fingers, then glared at him playfully. "Very cute."

"Yes, I am."

She pitched her pillow at him. He quickly raised his half-filled glass over his head to avoid splattering, but a few drops flew out and landed on the cream pillowcase. He set his glass on a neighboring table and tossed the pillow from his lap.

"Look what you've done." He stood and approached the bed. "Now I'll have to strip all the sheets and throw them into the washer."

"Don't you dare." She flipped onto her back and pulled the bedding up around her, fists clenched.

"I'm sorry, ma'am, but housekeeping insists we launder the entire set at one time." He tugged at the fabric, but her death grip rose to the challenge. He knelt on the bed and crawled toward her like a panther.

"Drew, quit it." She giggled and backed herself up to the headboard, exposing her legs from the knee down.

"Please, ma'am. Don't make this harder than it has to be. I don't want to have to call security."

She pushed against his chest with her feet, but her laughter weakened her efforts, giving him the upper hand. He grabbed hold of her ankle and pulled it toward him. A few kisses to her shin and her legs lost the fight. He continued a trail up to her knee before he raised his head, intending to confirm the magic of his touch through her expression.

She peered at him with a rigid gaze, eyebrow arched. "You're still not getting my sheet."

"What are you going to do? Lay in bed all day to keep it from me?"

"Sure. Why not?" The second she expelled the words, her face tightened—as if she had just remembered the reason she couldn't spend the day in bed. They had things to do to prepare for her father's funeral.

After a quiet moment, he asked, "You hungry?"

She nodded with a thin smile.

"Why don't you jump in the shower, and I'll throw

some breakfast into the toaster?"

"Sounds good."

He leaned on his arm and tenderly kissed her lips. "No dawdling now. Hotel checkout is at noon."

Her expression warmed.

He eased off the bed and headed for the hall, throwing a parting glance over his shoulder. "And please, ma'am, no stealing towels this time."

"I'm afraid you've mixed me up with another guest."

"What?" He halted in the doorway, feigning astonishment. He turned around and pretended to read numbers on the door. "This is the wrong room! I knew my wife couldn't have been that flexible."

A second pillow whomped him in the head. He flung it aside and chuckled while proceeding down the stairs. As he entered the kitchen, he heard the shower start on the floor above. He smiled at the thought of water cascading down Kate's body, tempting him to sneak back up to join her.

As if knowing his intent, hunger pangs regained his attention.

"Yeah, yeah, yeah," he answered.

He yanked open a bag of English muffins and dropped two in the toaster oven. The coils reddened like a branding iron. He needed a distraction to speed up the process. From the fridge he nabbed a jar of jam and a tub of cream cheese. He peeked through the toaster's window. The muffins were fending off their tan.

"Come on. Hurry up."

He thrummed his knuckles on the counter. Waiting, waiting. Usually, he would be reading the newspaper as his breakfast browned. But today's rolled-up headlines were staying out on the driveway. He didn't need any reports of senseless shootings and terrorist threats to encroach on the happiness he and Kate had resuscitated together.

The cordless phone chirped its ring. He was tempted to

let it go, but then realized the call could be about funeral arrangements. He snagged the handset from the kitchen table. Out of habit, he read the caller ID screen:

MILTON, SIDIS.

Why would the office be calling their house? It had to be an emergency.

"Hello."

"I'm sorry to bother you at home," Beth said without preamble, her usual honey-sweet voice sounding distressed.

"What's going on?"

"Milton's called a meeting to go over the Hanover case and wants you there."

"That's not my case. I was just helping Jim out with the research."

"I know, I know," she said. "I tried to explain that, but he still insists you be here. Said he might have some questions for you."

Drew grunted. "This is ridiculous. I promised my wife I'd help her with funeral arrangements today."

Beth paused. "What do you want me to tell him?"

He shook his head, frustration sealing his lips. Begrudgingly, he said, "When is the meeting?"

"Ten-thirty."

"Ten-thirty? That gives me less than an hour."

"Sorry. I left several messages on your cell." The cell he'd amazingly forgotten about.

"It's okay. My fault. How long did they say it'll last?"

"They didn't. But you know how long-winded Milton can be."

Drew sighed. He scanned the room, as if their stainless steel appliances might offer up a compromise. Instead, all he found was a house that his salary from the old geezer's firm had provided. "I'll be there soon."

So much for a leisurely shower.

He hung up and sped toward the stairs. He was three-quarters of the way up when the toaster chimed, freezing him mid-jog.

He'd promised Kate breakfast. He'd promised to help her with funeral plans. He'd promised her so much more than that. Yet here he was again, breaking his word to the one person who mattered in his life.

"Enough."

He lifted the phone still in his hand and speed-dialed Beth's direct number. Two rings.

"Drew Coleman's office. May I—"

"Beth, it's me again. I won't be able to make it after all."

"Really? I mean, are you sure?"

He nodded. "Yeah, I'm sure. Believe it or not, Kate needs me more than Milton does."

"Um…okay." Her tone didn't downplay her astonishment. "You're the boss."

"Jim should have everything gathered already. But if he needs copies from my file, they're all under 'Hanover.'"

"Sure thing," she replied. "Oh, and when should I tell them you'll be back in the office?"

"What day is it today?" A man whose life revolved around the calendar, he couldn't believe he didn't know.

"It's Wednesday."

"Tell them…tell them I'll see them Monday morning. And would you mind—"

"Rescheduling your appointments? Not at all." There was an approving smile in her voice.

"Now, if the phone's are quiet on Friday, you be sure and get out of there early."

"Are you…feeling all right?"

He grinned. "Never better."

Her laugh skittered over the line.

"Hey, by the way," he said, "Do you have any plans next weekend? For something non-work related?"

"Drew Coleman has leisure time? I was under the impression you slept in the basement here."

With the hours he put in, weighed against his commute through heavy traffic, there were times he'd seriously considered it.

"How about Saturday night at our place for dinner?" he asked. "Say, six o'clock?"

"Gee, I don't know. My people will have to call your people."

Her sarcasm came as a pleasant surprise.

"When did you become such a smart aleck?" he asked.

"When did you become such a slacker?"

He chuckled. "Whatever. Just mark your calendar, all right?"

"You got it. I'd love to be there. Unless…"

"Unless what?"

"Are you sure Kate will be in the mood for company, with the funeral and all?"

He glanced down the stairs, deliberating her valid point, and happened to catch sight of his honeymoon picture on the entry table. Even from a distance, he could see Kate's beaming smile in the photo. There was nothing he wanted more than to put that same smile back on his wife's face, as often as possible.

"Actually," he said, "I think a nice, relaxing dinner is exactly what she'll need."

"Then count me in," she said cheerfully. "Should I bring anything?"

"Hmm…how about one of your amazing chocolate cakes?"

"I suppose I can manage that."

"Good. Because Brian loves chocolate."

She gasped. "Drew—"

"Bye, Beth." He hung up, smiling as he imagined his assistant's cheeks blushing. She'd likely be too distracted to get much work done the rest of the day, maybe even the rest of the week, but it was worth it.

Several seconds passed before he realized his face still bore a grin, carved out like a comedy mask. Exhilaration filled him inside. Not just over his matchmaking scheme or because he'd finally found his wife again, but because he'd finally found himself. The him he didn't even know was missing, as if he'd stumbled across twenty dollars in the pocket of a suit coat he'd forgotten about. No, make that a hundred. Heck, make it a million.

"Meow."

Drew dropped his gaze and discovered Sofo beside his foot on the step, her furry white tail wound around his leg. She vibrated as she purred, looking up at him with affectionate eyes. Though cautiously, he leaned down and stroked her head. Her purring grew like the sound of a propeller on a plane about to take off.

"Well, what do you know?" Drew Coleman seemed to have won over the hearts of all the women in the house.

Now, if he could just keep it that way.

Twenty Eight

  Kate sat alone in the booth, bouncing her leg under the table. She scanned the wall of dated photos across from her. It had been Drew's idea to come back here.
  The place was different than the one in her mind's eye. Smaller. A little dingier. However, the aroma of garlic and baking dough was even better than she recalled.
  "Here you go," Drew announced over the clamor of the chattering lunch crowd and a looped mandolin track. He set down two cups of fizzing root beers and a deep-dish pepperoni pizza.
  "Finally." She licked her lips. The real Chicago deal, prepared in Capone's personal favorite style—or at least that's what Giovanni, the spindly Italian owner with a permanent grin, claimed. The hole-in-the-wall joint was so far off the beaten path tourists couldn't find it even if they were lucky enough to catch wind of the place from a local. One glance around the bustling, red-and-white checkered room and she could tell there were only Seattle natives here. As if it was a speakeasy that required a special knock—or Birkenstocks and a "Save the Planet" T-shirt—to get past Brutus the bouncer.
  Drew slid into the booth and scooped up two generous slices with a plastic server. Piled atop the crust, in upside-down order, was a layer of pepperoni, more than an inch of melted mozzarella, and a velvety blanket of red sauce.

Kate immediately brought the fork to her mouth, the thick cheese oozing off the prongs. She inhaled the smell of Italy before planting the mound on her tongue. Still hot, but some roof-burning of the mouth was a small price to pay. She sipped from her root beer to lessen the damage, then devoured another bite as Drew started in on his.

"Oh my word," she mumbled. "This may be the best food I've ever had."

"Even better than my gourmet English muffins?"

"Yes. Without question."

"Fine." Drew shrugged. "But let's not forget about the guy here who was responsible for working up your appetite to begin with."

She dropped her fork onto her plate and whipped her head back and forth in a panic. "What do you mean? Is my husband here?"

"Ha, ha. Touché."

Their laughs intertwined in threadlike warmth. Then in happy silence, they finished off their slices.

As Drew distributed a second round, Kate asked him, "Why in the world did we ever stop coming to this place?"

"I don't know." His eyes twinkled as he wiped something from her cheek with his thumb—red sauce—and transferred the small glob onto the edge of his plate. "Just have to remember how good it is so we don't forget about it again."

She nodded, knowing he was referring more to their relationship than to a restaurant. She ate a couple bites, and smiled at a memory. "You do recall this is where I managed to arrange our first date, don't you?"

He faked a cough while gulping down a mouthful. "Excuse me?"

"What?"

"I think you meant where I convinced *you* to go out."

"Hey, just because you did the asking doesn't mean you get full credit."

He picked at his pizza slice with his fork. "Well, I suppose it *was* your dropping that tank of an art book on my foot that sparked our conversation."

"Aha, you remember."

"Of course I do. I didn't realize you expected praise for it, though."

She peered into his eyes, her expression set as stone. "Who said it was an accident?"

His brow dipped. "But...I thought..."

"You thought what?" She gave him a smug grin as she sipped on her straw.

He sighed at the revelation, reclining into his red vinyl seat. "You mind telling me why you never mentioned this scheme before?"

"Didn't occur to me."

"And you're confessing it now because...?"

She looked him in the eye and replied with weighted honesty, "Because we're not keeping secrets anymore."

His gaze fell to the half-pizza pie between them. "Right." After a pause, he raised his eyes and gestured toward the front counter. "I'm going to hit the bathroom. You need anything?"

She felt the stickiness of her forefinger against her thumb. "Napkins would be great."

"Sure. I'll be right back." He smiled wanly as he scooted out, implying that his mission was born from a need to take a break from their conversation. Apparently, she'd divulged more information than he was prepared to process today.

She ate the rest of her slice, then sat back and pulled the top of her khakis away from her waist. The band was feeling snug, but Capone's favorite was worth the discomfort.

She glanced at her wrist, forgetting her watch—still broken—was in her jewelry box at home. Its absence also reminded her that her father was gone, this time for good.

Each entry on her to-do list today was there because her father wasn't. Just like when her mother died, Kate knew the void in her life would take a while to really sink in. Until then, she suspected the undercurrent of sadness streaming below the surface would remain a constant.

Might she feel different if she'd actually said good-bye to either of them? She would never know. So there was no reason to dwell on it. Instead she should focus on completing her tasks. With Drew at her side.

Absently stirring her drink with the straw, she peered out the window beside her. *A Slice of Heaven* was posted backward on the glass in adhesive letters. How fitting the name was, considering her situation. Not to mention its uncanny similarity to the engraved sign at her father's cabin.

She looked beyond the lettering and spotted a woman sauntering by with a small dog in her arms. Both of them boasted matching fluorescent pink hooded slickers. Good material for a painting.

Across the street a lanky guy in a blue jumpsuit was washing office windows. His softball-size bald spot was as shiny as the glass panes. When a middle-aged woman in a sweater set and slacks walked up to him, he paused. The lady mouthed words like an actress in a silent film, and the man turned and pointed down the street.

Kate hadn't noticed the toddler standing behind the woman until the round-faced, pig-tailed girl poked her head out. Staring directly at Kate, the munchkin waved hello with a wand adorned with shimmery streamers. Kate reciprocated with a small wave of her own. The girl giggled and covered her mouth. Then she disappeared behind the woman, presumably her mother, and jumped back out in a game of peek-a-boo.

The child wore a pink tutu outfit beneath her open raincoat, her feet in high-top tennis shoes. Either she was on her way to a dance recital, or insisted on wearing Halloween costumes year-round like Kate had done as a kid. Their gazes met again and held, warming Kate inside and stretching her mouth into a smile.

The mother tugged the girl's hand and led her down the sidewalk and around the corner. The window cleaner resumed his work, leaving Kate with a vast emptiness in her chest. As she had lost her own so early, she'd always feared she wouldn't be a good mother. Even under the assumption she could outlive her mom's thirty-six years, the fear had steadily increased over time. Now the unspoken exchange with the mini-ballerina reminded her of the joyful elements of parenthood she would have to sacrifice should she fail to conquer her trepidation.

A rumble interrupted her thoughts and she looked at the sky. The grey clouds didn't look dark enough for a storm. A little rain, for sure, but not thunder.

Another rumble.

She looked across the street, trying to find the source. It was the sick-sounding muffler of a truck.

A pickup.

Black and dusty.

With the driver's side in view, the vehicle inched over the asphalt, barely moving. A car behind honked, then swerved around it and sped off. Yet the truck continued to edge along.

The logical core of her being insisted she redirect her focus. There was no reason to stare. No reason to allow irrational fear to infest her mind like a recurring virus. Yet she couldn't tear herself away. In fact, she found herself narrowing her eyes and leaning forward, struggling to see into the vehicle. She couldn't make out the driver as the tinted window eerily shielded the person inside.

Her fatigued muscles locked in place. The hair on the back of her neck bristled.

The truck came to an abrupt stop. Another car veered around it. Still, the truck sat there, taunting her through the glass.

She sucked in a breath.

It was him. He had followed her here. She could feel it—in her chest, her limbs, her soul. Despite all her attempts to explain the intersecting "coincidences" of the past two days, nothing protected her from the terrifying reality that now gripped her.

A minivan, parked on the shoulder of the road, came to life and pulled away. The truck moved forward, muffler sputtering, and shimmied into the vacant space. The red taillights glared at her. Her pulse sped to a gallop.

"Should I get a box for what's left?"

She snapped around. Drew was standing beside the table. She flipped back to the window, unable to answer. The driver's face. She had to see his face. To know for sure.

The red lights shut off.

"Sweetie...?"

She held up her hand, cutting off Drew's question.

The driver's door opened.

A man's shoe.

A pant leg.

Her heart thumped like a rabbit's foot.

There he was...getting out...

A teenager?

The boy adjusted his low-hanging jeans, boxer shorts peeking out in adolescent rebellion. He closed the truck door and walked toward the hood where he linked up with his passenger, a petite gal in a denim jacket and miniskirt. They strolled off holding hands.

Kate slumped back in her seat. It was official: she was going crazy.

"Kate?"

She swung around to Drew. He looked at her with concern. "Are you okay?"

"Yeah, I'm good," she said before reconsidering. "I mean—" She swallowed, steadying her breathing. "No...I'm not okay."

He resumed his seat across from her, yet said nothing, as if waiting for her to volunteer what she was ready to share.

She glanced back at the truck, then over at Drew. Until this moment it hadn't occurred to her that by keeping silent about her suspicions, she could have put not just her own safety at risk, but her husband's as well.

And so, without worrying how it might sound to a sane person's ears, she recapped the events at the diner: Mick, her mother's photo, the telephone cord, her sprint that ended on the muddy bank of the river. She even threw in the strange phone calls, the gallery customer, and Wanda's dramatic report. A summary of Kate's reality TV-like life.

Drew stewed in silence, ingesting her words. Finally he said, "I'll talk to Brian myself."

"Honey, there's nothing to tell."

"But if he knew everything…"

"About the assumptions I'd made? About a nonexistent banana-split psycho? Yeah, he'd think I was one of those nutcases they make fun of at the station." She rolled her eyes. "Anyhow, I didn't tell you so you'd worry. Believe me, I've done enough worrying for both of us."

He nodded reluctantly, his expression still stern. "If something else happens, though, even if you feel silly speaking up—"

"I'll let you know. No matter what. I promise." She mustered a partial smile.

He reached across the table, lifted her hand, and kissed it tenderly. "Okay," he said, raising his eyes to meet hers. And in that moment, she felt a growing sense of safety and security wrapping her like a blanket.

"So," Drew sighed, stroking her fingers with his thumb, "What else can I do to help?"

She contemplated his question, reminding herself which duties remained. Then she scrunched her nose and asked, "Know anything about coffins?"

Twenty Nine

A cross between Tammy Faye-Baker and a drag queen. Kate knew that's what her husband was thinking as he gaped at the middle-aged receptionist. Hunched over the vertical metal cabinet, the woman sorted through files with her long acrylic nails—the airbrushed kind with glued-on rhinestones, bright purple to match her eye shadow.

Drew grinned at Kate sardonically.

"Don't," she ordered in a whisper.

"Don't what?"

"Behave yourself," she said, but then couldn't stop from breaking into her own smile.

"Mr. and Mrs. Coleman." A man's familiar reedy voice came from behind.

Kate swiveled toward the funeral director, who was just her height. Round as a barrel in his charcoal grey suit, he had a knobby nose and small beady eyes. He didn't appear at all like the man she'd expected to see, based on what he sounded like over the phone.

"I'm Paul Fawcett. Welcome to Owen and Sons."

She accepted his extended hand.

"First of all," he said, "let me express how sorry I am for your loss."

"Thank you," she replied.

He moved on to shake Drew's hand. "We have much to

do. So if you'll come with me, I'll direct you to our showroom."

She was grateful for his down-to-business attitude, as she wanted to get this over with as quickly as possible. As she followed him, she fixed her gaze on the back of his head where gelled black strands failed to hide a thinning area.

"Here we are." Mr. Fawcett turned beside an open doorway.

Kate halted. She stretched her neck forward, apprehension rising, and confirmed they were about to enter a chamber of caskets.

"Please. After you." He motioned with his open palm like a seasoned tour guide.

She didn't realize her legs hadn't budged until Drew said, "It's okay, sweetheart. I'm here." His hand gently touched her lower back.

She drew a heavy breath and stepped into the room. A gallery of death. A scene from *Interview with a Vampire.*

Once again, too many late night movies.

"Feel free to look around," Mr. Fawcett said. "I'd be happy to answer any questions you might have."

Synthesized music played softly on an overhead speaker—*Canon in D Major* mixed with crashing ocean waves and cawing seagulls. Kate surveyed the open caskets displayed chest-high about them, varying in size and color, each with a printed card listing relevant information. There were at least two dozen coffins to choose from, and all of them reminded her of her mother's funeral; the endless day she'd stood beneath an umbrella holding her aunt's hand as rain and tears pooled in the open grave.

"This one's nice, don't you think?" Drew asked, clearly sensing her unease.

"A fine choice indeed," the mortician chimed in, and toddled over to the black-lacquered casket with a silver bar. "This model, a popular one I might add, is the new deluxe version of the Going Home Classic. It's fully equipped with hand-tucked satin interior, has fourteen-karat gold stitching, and includes an adjustable bed. If you'll note, 'The Lord's Prayer' is inscribed on the interior of the lid."

Astounded, Kate couldn't help asking, "There's a prayer to read *inside* the coffin?"

"For the viewing guests paying their respects," he clarified.

"Oh…I thought…never mind."

Mr. Fawcett smiled. "Not to worry. You aren't the first to ask."

She gave a slight nod.

"Let's see, where was I?" he continued. "Oh, yes. You have several options for interior and exterior colors." Kate tried to ignore the similarity of terminology used for something she would drive off the lot. "The mattress is extremely well made, and I must honestly tell you, it is even more comfortable than my own bed at home."

She angled to catch her husband's reaction. Incredibly, he maintained a look of genuine intrigue with no hint of alarm or humor.

"Hmm. Good to know," Drew commented. "And this one here?"

"Ah, yes," Mr. Fawcett sighed in admiration at the sleek midnight blue casket beside them. "Our Final Farewell model." As he rattled off its long list of features, Kate was hit by the image of her father lying inside. Cold. Lifeless. Unmoving.

Drew placed his hand on her shoulder. "I think this one is perfect. Right, Kate?"

She gathered comfort from her husband's eyes, then faced the director and nodded.

"Splendid," he said. "Now, if you will both follow me to my office, we can take care of the final details."

Kate gripped Drew's hand as they shuffled down the

hall behind Mr. Fawcett. Once at the door, she relaxed her grasp. She had almost expected a tiny room as dark and musty as a bat's cave. To her relief, the medium-size office, equipped with only administrative essentials, had a large window that welcomed plenty of natural light.

"Please, have a seat." Mr. Fawcett rounded his desk.

Kate and Drew perched themselves on club chairs facing the man. A puff of air whooshed from Mr. Fawcett's cushioned high-back chair as he plopped down. He opened the lone manila file folder resting on the desktop and retrieved one of three identical pens from the mug beside him, a ceramic mug reading *Funerals can be quite an undertaking.*

So the quirky man had a sense of humor.

While Mr. Fawcett scribbled away, Kate looked over at the bookshelf on an adjacent wall. The King James Bible, Book of Mormon, Qur'an, Tao Te Ching, Hidden Words of Bahá'u'lláh—a smorgasbord of religious texts for people all over the world needing proof of the unprovable.

The funeral director cleared his throat, regaining Kate's attention. "Now that you've selected the casket, Mrs. Coleman—oh, I apologize, I see in my notes that it's Ms. Flaherty, isn't it?"

"Coleman's fine. Thank you." Out of the corner of her eye, she saw Drew's lips curve up.

"Well, then, Mrs. Coleman, based on our earlier conversation, I think we have just about everything covered. Per your request, I've scheduled one of our regular clergymen to officiate at your father's brief, intimate graveside service. Do I have your permission to pass along any information he may need?"

"Yes," she replied quietly. "Of course."

"Lovely." He inscribed a few notes in his file, then began to speak again. Kate struggled to focus on his words, but her jumbled emotions clouded her thoughts.

Eventually, she heard him say, "Mrs. Coleman?"

"What?"

Mr. Fawcett swiveled his roller chair, snagged a brochure from a neighboring credenza, and handed it to her. "If you're undecided about a viewing, this might be helpful."

She dared to look at the paper. Luckily, there were no photos of corpses, just text and a picture of the funeral home.

"We use only the finest cosmetics that include all natural ingredients. The results are truly miraculous. Erica does a wonderful job, I assure you."

"Erica?" Drew asked. "As in your receptionist?"

"We're a small business, so we do wear multiple hats. If you'd like to see any of the products she works with…"

The thought of Collin Flaherty going to his final resting place dusted in beige face powder with rouge smeared was unnerving. "We'd rather have a closed casket," she said. "I'm sure my father would want people to remember him at his best."

"I understand." Mr. Fawcett smiled courteously. "As for your father's attire, feel free to leave it with Erica if I'm not here."

Drew nodded and rubbed Kate's back. "Is there anything else?"

Mr. Fawcett flipped a page over and glimpsed at it before shutting his file. "I believe we're all set."

Kate sprang to her feet. The men rose and shook hands again, then Kate and Drew turned to exit. Halfway down the hall, Drew leaned toward her and said in a hushed tone, "Are you sure you don't want to at least take a look at Erica's work? She obviously knows the cosmetics from using them on herself."

Kate jabbed her elbow into his rib and hissed, "Not funny."

He released a soft chuckle then promptly dropped his expression and cleared his throat. "Sorry."

Maybe it was because of the sweet way her husband

looked right then, his eyes downcast like a kid chided for making an inappropriate joke. Maybe it was because she did need a mood lightener. Either way, she felt her burden lift a few inches off her shoulders.

She pinched his arm, a smile sliding across her face. "I can't take you anywhere, can I?"

He returned the smile along with a warm wink.

A few feet from the waiting room, a restroom sign hung beside a door. They had a good hour-and-a-half-long drive ahead of them to their next stop—her father's house. "I'm going to hit the bathroom before we go." Kate grabbed the metal door handle.

"Do you want me to wait for you?" The question wasn't asked casually. There was genuine care in his voice.

"No, I'll be fine. You go warm up the car. I'll be right out."

"Okay," he said. "Five minutes, though, and I'm blowin' this pop stand, with or without you."

"Oh, so you *want* to sleep on the couch."

He kissed her cheek. "See you outside."

As he strolled off she ducked into the restroom—a small, private space, spotless and white, lit by a fluorescent bulb.

She locked the door.

She'd shed too many tears in the last two days to have any liquid in her bladder left to relieve. What she did need was a quiet moment to collect her thoughts, her emotions. Her father's lifeless cabin and abandoned personal effects awaited her. But she was ready. Ready as she would ever be. She was facing her fears head on, immune to their control.

Too bad her nerves didn't seem as confident.

Thirty

Kate pushed through the exit door of the funeral home. As she crossed the street, she was surprised to see Drew standing next to his car rather than revving the engine. He was talking to someone in the outdoor city parking lot. The back of the woman looked familiar. Perhaps a paralegal Kate had seen in passing at a judiciary schmooze-fest. Judging by her jeans and windbreaker, she was someone who'd also taken the day off. The gal must have been playing hooky from the stuffy-shirt firm.

Kate liked her already.

Drew caught his wife's gaze as she approached. His expression had stiffened since they'd parted ways just minutes ago. Apparently, the coworker wasn't one of his favorites, or their discussion was an unpleasant one.

"I thought you were in a hurry to leave," Kate teased.

The woman turned around. She wasn't a paralegal. Or a coworker.

But Kate knew her.

"Lindsey," was all she managed.

"Kate, hi! How are you?" Lindsey's tone was too enthusiastic to be honest. "Long time no see."

"Yeah, it's been a while." Kate layered on a smile. She reminded herself there was no reason to feel threatened, despite the gal's cute face and cute hair, not to mention her even cuter body outlined by a snug black halter top and jeans. After all, Kate had been wrong to doubt her husband when he'd repeatedly pleaded his innocence in the infamous "Lindsey incident." And the past forty-eight hours they'd spent together assured her that he was still the faithful, loving man with whom she had exchanged vows for life.

"So—" Kate tried for idle chatter, as no one else was moderating. "Do you live around here?"

"Not really." Lindsey fiddled with one of her silver hoop earrings. "I'm just meeting a friend at a coffee shop round the corner."

"Oh, I see."

Silence enveloped their triangle, a lengthy silence that prompted shifting feet and averted eyes. It was clear Drew had told his old girlfriend about what now even Kate considered to be her immense overreaction to their friendly dinner.

"We'd better hit the road," Drew said at last.

Kate almost wanted to prolong the conversation, just to prove she no longer held any suspicions when it came to the former couple. But she appreciated the opportunity to slip away all the same. "It was nice seeing you, Lindsey."

"Yeah, you too," she said. "Oh, and I'm sorry to hear about your dad."

Kate replied vacantly, "Thanks."

"On the upside, I'm glad you and Drew here are working things out." When Lindsey tossed a glance his way, he dropped his set of keys on the asphalt. She quickly said to Kate, "I'd better go. See you around."

"Yeah...see ya."

"Take care," Drew mumbled, swooping up the keys. He unlocked the doors with a double beep, climbed in, and started the engine.

The tension permeating the moist air evaporated as Lindsey strolled away, her hips swaying rhythmically as she crossed the parking lot.

Kate made her way to the passenger side. She told herself there was no reason to discuss the encounter, perplexing though it was. If her husband wanted to talk about it, she would leave it to him to bring it up. And that was that.

She slid into the Beamer, feeling proud of her fresh outlook. By the time she buckled her seatbelt, however, Lindsey's words had fully registered, causing Kate to reconsider.

"Drew, you haven't—" She checked her tone, not wanting to sound accusatory. "I mean, have you and Lindsey been spending time together?" She longed for his answer to be "No, no way, not at all."

But he didn't reply. His gaze remained forward, his right hand gripping the gearshift between their seats. Several seconds dragged. He sat as motionless as the car. His silence was bundling her nerves.

"Drew?"

"Lindsey was…" He stopped and raked his bottom lip, as if his teeth were preventing his words from passing through. "She was at Brian's the other night when I went there to crash." He faced her, defending himself. "It was a total coincidence. I didn't know she was going to be there."

"It's okay, really," Kate offered with as much zeal as she could. "I was just wondering how she'd heard…you know, about us."

His eyes brimmed with sincerity. "She happened to see my suitcase. I didn't give her any details."

Ah, yes. The same suitcase Brian had returned. What was Kate thinking? Even if Drew hadn't told Lindsey, her brother surely would have.

"Kate, I'm sorry."

"Honey, it's fine," she assured him. "So you told her we were taking a break. No big deal." Truthfully, Kate would prefer that her husband not have heart-to-heart chats with a woman with whom he used to have an intimate relationship.

Still, she touched his shoulder and said, "I'm just glad you told me. I'd rather you be honest than keep it from me."

When his features didn't brighten, she decided to toss playful sarcasm his way. "Now, if it were up to me, I'd have told her you and Brian were just having a little slumber party, but hey…" She smiled.

He jerked his gaze back to the windshield, muttering something she couldn't decipher. Then he exhaled slowly and returned his eyes to hers, his expression so forlorn her heart missed a beat.

Why was he looking at her like that?

Her smile fought to hang on, though it only half-succeeded. She didn't want to ask, but she had to. "What's wrong?"

His lips parted, then closed, then parted again, as though he was debating whether to respond. At last, he said, "It never should've happened."

A tidal wave of panic came crashing down on her. Inside, she flailed to stay afloat. "*What* shouldn't have happened?" she demanded in a horrified whisper.

"Kate, it was nothing really…just a stupid mistake. I didn't think you loved me anymore."

She stopped looking at him. Her ears blocked his words. Facing the window, she squeezed her lids closed, wishing this was a dream. But no. This was reality—a reality from which she couldn't awake. She opened her eyes to the absence of light. The world had darkened around her. Only muted shades of misery covered the landscape, rendering every object unrecognizable.

Was this what her mother had seen out the windshield as she raced away into the night?

"Did you sleep with her?" The voice came out of Kate's mouth, but it seemed as if someone else had spoken the question.

"No," he insisted. "*No.* We just kissed. That's all. It

didn't mean anything."

"And that's all that happened?"

"Yes. Well...basically." He touched her hand resting on her lap. A chill crept up her arm.

Basically. Her mind seized the word, stretching and pulling its implications into unbearable scenes.

"Hon, you have to believe me—if I could take it back I would."

She refused to look at him. She didn't want to see the apology in his eyes. She didn't want to hear any more.

Kate yanked her hand away and ran her palms over her face and down the back of her hair, swiping a protective shield around herself to keep her emotions in and Drew's out.

He sighed. "I don't know what I was thinking. I shouldn't have told you this now, not with everything. I just didn't want to lie to you." He groaned at himself. "You have to know how much I love you."

She was too numb to respond.

"Baby?" He waited. "Please. Say something."

"We should go," she said coolly, still gazing out her window.

After a quiet pause, Drew shifted gears. And on they went, forward yet backward, together yet apart. With every passing mile, Kate felt her soul retreating into itself. Further and further than ever before.

Perhaps beyond return.

Thirty One

"Wow," Drew said under his breath as they turned onto the dirt driveway, the first word uttered between them since they'd left the city. Out of the corner of her eye, Kate noted the surprise on his face, reminding her that his last visit was more than eight months ago.

The Lincoln Log-like home, as well as its once lush property, had deteriorated as quickly as her father had. Chipped paint, missing shingles, torn screen door, rusted gutters. Evidently the old saying was true: A house does thrive on the energy of the people within it.

There was dark irony in it, really. The closer her father had come to death, the more his "Lil' Bit O' Heaven" had gone to hell.

The instant Drew shifted into *Park*, Kate unfolded from the car and headed straight for the front door. For the past few days she'd been dreading this trip. Yet now, the house represented an escape. The car ride there had been torturously long with silence and betrayal as the main passengers. Even if their drive had ended at the Bates Motel, Kate would have checked in just to free herself of the automotive trap.

Atop the doorframe, her fingertips searched blindly for a spare key. Nothing but a layer of dirt. Could be unlocked, a hopeful notion.

She opened the creaky screen door, kept it ajar with her

elbow, and tried the knob. She turned and jiggled the tarnished orb to no avail. One of the hospice gals must have inadvertently taken the key.

"I'll go try the back," Drew volunteered.

Kate nodded without turning. When she released the spring-tight screen door, the metal frame banged closed, then bounced open, leaving an inch-wide gap. She grabbed the handle and tested it for proper closure. It failed. She didn't try again.

As Drew rounded the side of the house, she approached a screenless window off the family room and gave it an upward pull. It wouldn't give. She then leaned forward and peeked through the dusty, raindrop-marked pane. She shaded her eyes from the dull light of the overcast sky with her hand. The room seemed different from this view. Less familiar. It was strange being on the outside looking in.

Maybe this was how her father had always seen it.

Her impatience was growing, though she didn't know why. She was in no hurry for the drive home. Another ninety minutes of staring vacantly at the passing scenery—make that over a hundred with the inconvenient detour—all the while doing everything in her power to control her thoughts. She had no intention of pondering anything but the assignments on her list today. No tears. No emotions. She wanted to feel nothing, only to rely on herself, the one person she could trust.

As she waited, she looked around absently until she connected with the shed off to the side, nestled among the towering trees. Didn't her father keep an extra key in his toolbox? It was worth a try.

She made her way over the bumpy, weed-infested ground and around an ancient scarred stump where her dad used to chop firewood. The final image she had of her father was of a man who didn't have the strength to lift a spoon, much less an ax.

Just then, a memory nudged into her thoughts: her dad

whistling as he split a stack of logs, pausing only long enough to flash her an occasional wink. Her mom hollering out the kitchen window for Collin to keep her at a safe distance. A warning he later heeded in every aspect.

It took a few hefty shoves for Kate to slide open the shed door as rust and the caked dirt on its track hindered the process. She fumbled for the light switch. *Blink, blink, blinkety-blink.* The florescent bulb overhead came to life. She wiped the maddening, invisible cobweb threads from her face as she moved inside.

Through the dust motes, she located her dad's large forest green toolbox in the center of his worktable, a thick slab of plywood propped up by a pair of sawhorses. She opened the metal lid, which raised its tiered shelves. In light of the condition of his home, she expected all the items in the box to be in disarray. Instead, everything was neatly stored in compartments. Screws, nails, nuts and bolts, all separated by size in clean baby food jars. Like a time capsule from his earlier life.

For a moment, she almost forgot what she was looking for.

She was about to rifle through the case when she spotted a ridged item duct-taped to the inside of the lid. She pulled at the stretchy, silver adhesive until she gained access to the copper-colored key.

"Kate, where are you?" Drew yelled.

"I'm in the shed." Though she wasn't sure if he'd heard her, she didn't repeat herself.

She closed the lid and wiped her hand on her pants to rid her fingers of the tape's sap-like goo.

"There you are." Drew neared the shed doorway. "I climbed through a bathroom window that was cracked open, so we're in."

She nodded, not bothering to tell him about her find, and slipped the key into her pocket. As she moved toward the door, the bottom of her pant leg caught on something, sending her into a two-step stumble. Drew reached for her just as she steadied herself.

She pulled back.

He dropped his hands.

Glancing down, she identified her latest offender: a swooped leg of the worn walnut rocking chair stored near the wall. Carved roses adorned the headrest area of its broad camel back; the ends of the armrests curled into spirals. The chair swayed back and forth, reminding her of the last time she'd seen her father seated in his handmade creation. Gently, it slowed to a stop.

As Drew muscled the shed door closed, Kate plodded toward the open front door of the house. Upon entering, she prepared her nose for the hospital odors that had plagued the home just days ago. To her surprise, only trace smells remained. In fact, there was an added strawberry scent. Like that of an air freshener.

Of course—Doris. She'd take on the responsibility of improving the air quality in the home after her patient had been taken away. No question, she was a woman with a good heart, a woman Kate's mother wouldn't have minded traipsing around in her domestic territory.

A creak followed by a metallic slam let Kate know Drew had joined her, but she kept herself from twisting her head toward him. She had no desire to see his further dismay over the condition of her parents' once-charming dwelling.

"Do you want me to gather his documents?" Drew's tone seemed unfazed.

"Sure." She started down the hall. "The safe is in the basement. Key should be in the kitchen drawer by the oven."

The basement stairs were off the back of the kitchen, which sent Drew in the opposite direction of her own destination. She was grateful for that as she needed space. Unfortunately, the narrow hallway provided little. The faded trail of missing frames and stolen memories seemed to draw the walls closer together as she approached her father's now-empty bedroom.

At the doorway, she stopped, her feet still planted safely outside the bedroom. The amber lamp no longer beckoned with a haunting glow. The air had lightened in every way. The black weight of cancer that had draped each object, every breath, in the dying man's room was gone, whisked away like the cloak of the banshee who had awaited her father's surrender.

Again, Doris had left her mark. The hunter green curtains were swagged to the sides, inviting light under the sleepy eyelid of the matching valance. The floral bedding was made up perfectly, with quarter-bouncing tautness, sham ruffles uniform, and tossed pillows pleasantly staged. Even the Celtic throw was laid meticulously over the foot of the bed. Such symmetry usually irritated Kate, like an unreachable itch, but instead she merely acknowledged the benevolence of the caregiver's gesture.

She released a thin sigh and moved toward the closet. A glint from atop the nightstand caught her eye. Her father's eyeglasses. There they rested, neatly folded, unaware their rightful owner had left them behind. How she wished she could have been a speck of dust on one of those lenses, to see what he saw, to understand something, anything, about the man who'd given her life.

She gripped the closet door handle and opened it as slowly as a yawn. The scent of cedar and mothballs tickled her nose and tugged her lips into a thin smile. She recalled the countless times she'd crouched behind a curtain of her mother's Sunday dresses, trying to hold in the giggle that would betray her fail-safe hiding spot. No matter how often she used it, her father still struggled to find her. To and fro he would stomp, calling out in the gruff voice of a child-eating giant, "Fee-fi-fo-flass—I smell the blood of an Irish lass."

Her mother's dresses were now packed away. Although Kate missed the powdery fragrance of perfume in those pastel fabrics, she had since found a better hiding place, elusive and reliable, deep within herself.

Just get his clothes and get out. Her anxiety was building.

The choice was simple. There was but one suit hanging in the closet. Solid navy, save for a sprinkling of lint on the shoulders. She tried to remember when she'd last seen him wear it. Must have been the first and only art show opening of hers he'd attended. Well, made a brief appearance at anyway.

She wiped the thought from her mind.

To accommodate his final rail-thin form, she liberated a black belt from a wall hook. A split second later, she realized how pointless the accessory was. As if his pants might actually fall down. She kept the belt regardless.

Picking up her pace, she collected undergarments, a white tab-collared shirt, and a faded blue striped tie. Now all she needed was shoes and she could be on her way.

She surveyed the floor beneath the bottom shelf. Shabby hiking boots, tennis shoes, house slippers. No dress shoes.

Come on, he owned a suit. He had to have a pair of wingtips in here somewhere. Mr. Fawcett had categorized shoes as optional, but for some odd reason, her father's ensemble would seem incomplete without them.

She rotated in a slow circle, visually sifting through his shelves: flannels, T-shirts, jeans. She stopped when she landed on a small cardboard moving box tucked in an alcove above the closet door. Poking out from the top were the lids of two shoeboxes.

On her tiptoes, she reached up and clutched the outfaced bottom corners, wrinkled at each point. She wiggled the box forward, then lowered it to the wooden floor. Brushing the dust from her hair, she guessed at which shoebox to try first. As bright as a Halloween banner, the orange lid jumped out at her. She flipped it open.

Papers and envelopes. Just a bunch of junk.

She tried the light grey box next, and found the shoes she had been looking for: navy Florsheims, slightly scuffed, laces tucked under the tongues.

She replaced the lid, her fingerprints remaining in its dusty layer, and placed the box of shoes aside. When she reached for the orange box, however, the dried pasta she noticed inside halted her.

Confusion grew as she retrieved the raw macaroni noodles linked by a thread. Tied into a loop, they formed a necklace fit for an Italian peasant. Before her thoughts explored the accessory, she noticed a seashell half-buried in the clutter of the box. A small conch shell, scrubbed clean of sand, its inside shiny and smooth. Her fingers traced the pink, white and brown ripples on the rough exterior.

A memory swam to the surface. She was five or six. Strolling on the beach with her mom, searching for a shell to give her daddy. Kate didn't want him to feel left out. She'd brought him home a magic shell that carried within it the sounds of the ocean.

She knelt on the floor, confounded.

Out of the box, she pulled a piece of sunshine yellow construction paper folded into a card, trimmed with tiny rips. In crayon letters, slanting this way and that, it read *To: Daddy*. Attached to the middle of the page was what appeared to be a quarter of a brown cookie—gingersnap, based on a quick sniff. The zigzags of dried glue indicated the cookie had originally been whole, but had crumbled over the years. Surrounding the morsel's remnants were crayon-drawn hearts. A child's experiment in multimedia art.

She opened the soft, heavily wrinkled card.

Your nice and sweet

like my favarit treet
even thow you snore
I love you more
than all the cookies in the grosery store.

Happy fathers day!
love,
Katie
XXXOO

PS – *My 7 birthday is March 3. I want a purple Barbee car.*

The air in the closet thickened with her realization that these weren't just random items tossed into a junk box. They were keepsakes of her father's, all gifts from *her*.

She snagged another paper. It was a sheet out of a coloring book; a printed outline of a kitten in a basket. On the left bottom corner, written in her dad's graceful penmanship, was *Katie, age 10*. But the picture was uncolored. Even back then, she'd clearly failed to see the point of completing someone else's artwork or keeping within predetermined lines.

So why had he kept this—a page without so much as a child's scribble?

She flipped the paper over and found her answer. On the blank side was a freehand drawing. A man with a moustache, waving from inside the cab of a semi. A little girl crying in the window of a house. A winged angel sitting on a cloud. The meaning behind the picture tore at her soul. Her buried pain began to rise, but she swallowed the emotion down.

Her self-preservation instincts warned her to seal the box. But her fingers had already reached in and closed over a small manila envelope. One of its long edges was bent to fit inside. She shook the contents onto her lap, unable to stop her investigation.

A pile of newspaper clippings covered her legs, each article perfectly trimmed, some yellowed from age. Moisture rimmed her eyes as she leafed through the headlines. The local announcement of her wedding day. The prestigious award she'd received from the Oil Painters of America. Calendar listings of her gallery show openings. *The Seattle Times. The Journal. Mason County News.* Among them, packets of letters, cards, scribbled notes—all tied together in chronological order. He'd saved them all.

Then came pictures. Pictures! He had pictures!

Kate as a toddler, holding a snow cone at a Fourth of July parade. Kate again, a bit older, making a goofy face while standing in front of a monkey cage at the zoo.

Biting her bottom lip, she tried without success to stave off the tears welling in her eyes—tears of joy, so heady and overpowering she barely recognized the feeling. Here, in her hands, she held actual evidence that in his heart he'd cared. A silent fan on the sidelines.

She flipped faster and faster, defying the skeptical whispers inside that were sure to belittle her find as insignificant.

Her last day wearing braces. Sledding on a snowy hill in her preteen years with friends. The high school graduation snapshot Aunt Sophie had taken as Kate crossed the stage in a royal blue cap and gown.

Kate shook her head, a lifetime of comprehension whirling in her mind. All these years, he'd kept his love for her buried in a box. If only she'd known, perhaps their relationship could have been different. Knowledge of his unexpressed feelings could very well have empowered her with just enough strength to reach out to him more. To try harder to break through the seemingly impenetrable barrier that he...no, *they* had allowed to separate them.

Had she missed the signs? Had the pride he held for her always been subtly woven into his words, his gestures, his eyes? Had she been too wrapped up in her own selfish torrent of anger and self-pity to notice?

A teardrop surrendered and slid down her cheek. Then another. And another.

She felt overcome with frustration, as her discovery had occurred far too late for it to have any practical meaning. She hastily wiped her sweater sleeve across her nose and cheeks, then gathered the disturbing mementos and pushed them back into the shoebox. Had she simply chosen the grey container first, she would have been none the wiser.

She exchanged the shoeboxes and attempted to release her emotions through a sharp exhale. The car ride back had gained its appeal. However, when she started to get up, she spotted an item that pulled her down again. In the bottom of the moving box was a single crackled, gold-embossed word on a tan leather cover: *Memories.*

Her fingernails clawed at the side seam of her pants, debating, debating. Did she really want to know what filled those pages? Chances were these memories were best left unshared.

Unless, of course, they served as the hidden links she'd always sensed were missing from her life. A history. The family past to which every child was entitled.

She had no choice. She had to know.

She tugged the album out from under the orange shoebox and sat cross-legged. Bracing herself, she lifted the cover.

Property of: Collin Flaherty

Next page: a farmhouse, a tractor, a barn. Then a sunset, a lake, a tree house. More pages of still lifes—vehicles, boats, shorelines. No people, no interaction. The majority of her father's life as she knew it.

Questions—she should have asked more questions. About who he was, what his life was like. Before the accident. Before tragedy stripped him of his warmth, his dreams.

She was about to skip ahead when she noticed a folded newspaper page peeking out from the back of the album. She pulled it free. It wasn't one she recognized.

A scandal involving a local politician and an underage prostitute gobbled up the top half. Below the fold were stories about a school fundraiser fiasco and a house fire in Shelton. No article was clipped or circled. No phone numbers were in the margins, and there were no familiar names in the captions.

She didn't see a reason for him to keep the page, yet he had. *Why?*

She turned the paper over and skimmed the headlines. Still nothing. Her father's life was an infinite black hole of the unexplained.

Kate tossed the page aside just as her eyes did a double take. She reclaimed the paper from the floor. Two inked words jumped off the newsprint: *Flaherty* and *Jail.*

Thirty Two

FORMER CONVICT RECEIVES HUMANITARIAN AWARD

The Daniel J. Loughery Humanitarian Award was presented to Paul Crane on February 28 at a well-attended banquet in Seattle, raising funds and awareness to fight drunk driving. Crane is no stranger to consequences resulting from this burgeoning crime. In 1981, while driving home intoxicated from his sister's wedding reception, he collided head-on with driver Iris Flaherty, 36, who was killed upon impact. Crane underwent seven surgeries as a result of injuries incurred to his right arm and knee.

Crane, who at 22 had just graduated from Lewis & Clark College and had never been in trouble with the law, served three years and six months for vehicular homicide at King County Jail. Since his release, he has dedicated his life to promoting the prevention of driving under the influence (DUI). He and his wife, Megan, both volunteers for various charitable causes, have together raised upwards of $160,000 for Mothers Against Drunk Driving (MADD).

Beside the article was a photograph: Paul Crane shaking hands with a foundation executive while accepting an engraved plaque.

Kate studied the murderer's face, the murderer who

didn't look like a murderer. Not the cold-blooded killer she'd painted in her mind all these years. He wore a suit and tie, his dark hairline as square as his jaw. The image was a bit grainy, but she could see kindness in his teardrop-shaped eyes, his brilliant smile, his lone-dimpled cheek. He could easily have been one of her old teachers, or a school friend of Drew's—even one of her collectors.

"Did you find what you needed?" Drew stood in the closet doorway, papers in hand.

She shoved the newspaper page along with her uncertain feelings into the album and set both in the moving box.

"Here, I'll give you a hand with that." He reached for the container.

She was about to stop him, wanting to leave behind all but the essentials she came for, then realized there was no one but her to claim her father's possessions. Eventually, she would have to take everything anyway.

"Is that it?" Drew asked, box held to his chest. "'Cause if you'd like more time…"

"I'm ready to go."

He nodded twice, then turned for the hall.

She bundled up the suit and accessories and headed out. Once she reached the woven doormat, she pulled the key from her pocket and was pleased it fit in the lock. House secured, she returned to the car. With burial attire and boxes in the backseat, they rumbled toward the old mountain road.

They covered the winding highway, followed the detour, and flew past the waves of the Puget Sound. The mottled sky dimmed mile after mile. Silence in the car remained a constant. Even if she wanted to talk, she couldn't, as she was too busy trying not to think. About the driver's acts of retribution, and why her father kept the article; about the trinkets, cards, and photos he'd stored away. She only wished he had saved at least one photograph of her mother—some evidence she'd existed—regardless of his guilt.

She clenched her locket, grateful for the one picture she did have. If not for the terrifying end to her diner visit, Kate would have offered Mick just about anything for the framed snapshot of her mom on the wall...

"It can't be," she said.

"What's wrong?" Drew asked.

Kate's throat cinched, shallowing her breaths. Images whizzed through her mind. She unbuckled her seat belt, twisted around, and scrambled through the box.

"Kate?"

She grasped the photo album and sat back in her seat. Her hands trembled as she reopened the book and flipped past the first few pages. When she reached the one she had left off at, the earth slowed on its axis.

A picture of the ocean at daybreak with seagulls soaring. She knew this photo. And the ones around it. The entrance of a drive-in. A lineup of '60s hot-rods.

A rush of déjà vu swept over her. It couldn't be possible!

Heart drumming, she dared, guardedly, to turn the page.

And there it was.

The sight compressed the air in her lungs. Her hands cupped her nose and mouth.

It wasn't just any photo; it was *the* photo. The one of teenage girls clustered beside a parked Chevy, the all-too-familiar diner in the background. And in the sea of Coke bottles and hair flips was Kate's beloved mother, Iris.

"Sweetheart, what is it?" Drew's concerned voice projected faintly over the sound of her own strained breathing into her domed palms.

She dropped her hands and frantically scanned their surroundings.

They hadn't missed it. Up ahead was the old highway bridge. Then the railroad tracks.

"Turn left, up there!"

"But—"

"Drew, please." She faced him, pleading in desperation. "Just do it."

His features clouded before he replied, "Okay."

She stared straight ahead, gripping the open album as if it were a life raft. She felt Drew shifting his view between her and the highway. Despite his obvious bewilderment, he followed her order and turned onto the dirt road.

Slowly, they bumped over the tracks and down the uneven path. She craned her neck, searching for the diner's large illuminated sign. After her core-shaking encounter with Mick, she never imagined returning. But now, she had no choice: she had to understand why the walls of the restaurant displayed the same photos as the ones in her father's album. There had to be an explanation.

Was her dad a photographer? Was he friends with the owner? How else could—

"This is it!" She pointed to the sign on the right. The letters were filthy and no longer lit, though still legible.

Gordy's Diner.

"Kate, you sure this is a good idea?"

As the mouth of the gravel lot opened to their car, she met his eyes. "There's something I need to know. Please—come inside with me."

He turned back to the windshield and jerked the car to an abrupt stop. His jaw slackened and the lines on his forehead creased. She followed his gaze toward the diner, a nostalgic checkerboard pit stop, just as she'd remembered. But the site had been altered. Drastically. Horrifically.

"I don't understand," she said in a choked whisper.

The very window she'd sat behind two days ago was now covered with weathered sheets of plywood. Each board was vandalized with red and black spray-painted gang markings. Shattered beer bottles littered the ground. A dingy

No Trespassing sign hung crookedly on the door.
 There was no denying it. The diner had been closed for decades.

Thirty Three

Kate sat alone in the armchair, slumped in the shadows of her living room, as motionless as a still life. Relying only on light from the Tiffany lamp in the entry, she stared at the final page of the photo album on her lap.

A wedding portrait: her mother in a white gown, lace up to her neck and bouquet in hand, seated beside a man in full dress Navy uniform. Kate knew his boyish face and twinkling eyes. They belonged to the man from the diner.

In reality, though, his name wasn't Mick—it was Collin. Her father. The handwritten caption provided validation.

Collin & Iris Flaherty
Married October 24, 1969

It all made sense now. The quiet ride home had given Kate ample time to formulate a logical explanation behind her hash-house encounter. Correction: *imagined* diner encounter. Chances were she'd never even left her immobile car that night, not until soon before Drew showed up to rescue her from…well, from herself.

Her fleeting belief that a deranged lunatic had been stalking her almost made her laugh. She had to give Drew credit; he'd been quick to offer assurances, in spite of how nuts she must have appeared—gawking at a dilapidated diner while swearing she'd been served coffee there the night before last.

Rather than vowing to have her committed to a padded room, he'd insisted her delusions were understandable after her head injury from the accident as well as her compartmentalized "emotional distress" following her visit to her father's house. Lawyer talk in a husband's caring tone to say she wasn't crazy.

And she'd agreed with him. What else could she do?

Everything at the diner seemed so real, it was nearly impossible to believe it had been a figment of her imagination. Yet clearly, she couldn't have been there. Not since she was a kid. Back when her dad must have looked like the sailor in the portrait. And the kind diner employee, who lacked glasses and stubble on his cheeks and chin. No thick neck and round belly. No moustache or prematurely aged hair.

Kate had never had a family photo album of her own, so it was no wonder she'd failed to recognize him in his youthful prime. A little calculating and everything could be reasoned away: reminiscent songs and amusement park trips, scenic snapshots she must have peeked at as a kid, an aspiring truck driver with a young daughter, a "new guy" at work permitted to handle the till all alone.

How obvious it all seemed now.

Somewhere in her memory, like the sentimental pictures on the make-believe wall, she must have filed away his image from his livelier, more jovial days. Days when he smiled and cracked jokes. Days when he listened to her talk and earnestly gave her advice. Days she longed for even now.

It's funny how the mind works. Certainly that's what a tweed-jacketed, pipe-smoking psychologist would tell her while analyzing her dream, or hallucination, or whatever it was—which, by the way, she had no intention of ever recounting again. Legs crossed and notepad in hand, he would sit in his wingback chair, linking each component of her eventful evening to any number of emotional cravings buried in her subconscious.

It would hardly be a difficult task.

Of course she wanted to ask her father why he had cheated on her mom. And it was too late for Kate to accuse him out loud of ending her mother's life, even though the brutal accusation had brought her right back to blaming the drunk driver who was actually responsible.

Through it all, she never had stopped hoping for her daddy's approval. She needed to hear that imperfections in people, and relationships, were not only acceptable but expected; that, in spite of her flaws, she was a good person and could be a good parent; that it was solely the devastating loss of his wife that had turned him into an absentee father rather than any of Kate's shortcomings as a daughter.

And perhaps, most of all, she simply desired to spend one more day with her father, to share a warmhearted, lucid conversation before losing him forever.

"I'm heading up to bed." Drew's even tone spurred Kate to look up from the album. He stood across the room beside the china closet, hands in his jean pockets, expression as worn as she herself felt. "Is there anything you need? Something I can get you before I go up?"

She automatically shook her head. "No, thanks."

He paused and nodded slowly. "For what it's worth, Kate—" He peered sorrowfully into her eyes, "—I do love you. And I'm sorry I hurt you. I really am." His gaze lingered as if he were memorizing the features of someone he was saying good-bye to. Then he turned for the stairs.

"Drew. Wait."

He angled toward her.

She didn't know what to say. Her emotions, her memories, her discoveries—all twisted and swirled. But she knew she didn't want to lose him. She loved him. Not the same as she did on their wedding day, when her father had put her devotion to the test, but ten times more than that. She and Drew were no longer a blissful young couple who were never supposed to argue, or whose love would never be challenged.

They had matured while building a history together. Their paths had separated and at last rejoined. And now it was up to her to permanently bind those paths together, having faith that rocky times didn't mean their marriage was doomed.

That is, if she loved him enough to fight for him. To fight for *them*.

"I'm the one who's sorry," she offered.

He squared his shoulders to her, looking confused. He didn't move or answer, either waiting for her to continue or stunned by her apology.

She glanced down at the wedding portrait on her lap. Her gaze flitted from her father's dark brown eyes to her mother's light blues, then back to her father's, and what she found in both sets was love. Not a fairy-tale love, but real love. The kind that caused the person left behind to struggle, sometimes without success, to find meaning in life without the other. The kind of love only attained through vulnerability and understanding.

"I didn't want to trust you, not completely." Her eyes remained on the picture as she spoke to Drew. "I guess part of me was waiting for you to leave. Thinking you'd choose someone or something else you loved more—your job, or Lindsey. I didn't want to let you in, because I didn't want to get hurt. But all I was doing was hurting both of us."

When she raised her head, she noticed Drew had moved toward her.

"For most of my life," she went on, "I thought my dad didn't believe in me. But I was wrong. He just didn't know how to tell me." She made no attempt to fight the tears misting her vision. "Drew, I don't want to make the same mistake with you. I don't ever want you to think I don't believe in you."

"Are you...saying you forgive me?" he asked through tight lips, his tone hopeful.

"That's what real marriage is all about, isn't it? Learning from our mistakes, then moving on—together?"

He drew a deep breath before his mouth eased into a smile. The lines of doubt on his forehead disappeared as he crossed the room and knelt in front of her chair. He moved the album to the floor and gently cupped her face with his hands. For several seconds their gazes mingled, communicating in a secret language. A language with a vocabulary that promised to grow with each passing year.

"I don't know what I'd ever do without you," he said softly.

"Me, too," she whispered.

Drew tenderly pressed his lips to hers, then laid his head on her lap, his arms encircling her waist. She smoothed his golden hair with her hand. Her thumb caressed his temple, over and over, until his eyes closed. And at that moment, the two of them encased in a world of their own, Kate finally understood the real love her parents had shared.

Thirty Four

Kate drummed her fingernails on the beveled glass kitchen table five more times before crumpling the paper into a ball and flinging it at the pool of discarded wads on the floor. She planted her elbows on the table and buried her face in her palms. The space between her hands was just wide enough for her to see another blank page glaring at her.

She glanced at the clock on the microwave. It was already past noon. Aunt Sophie would be flying in tomorrow morning and checking into the Fairfield Inn, her effort not to burden them as a houseguest. In less than twenty-six hours, a limousine would be pulling up to their house and after one quick stop to pick up her aunt, they would be on their way to the funeral.

Yep. Twenty-six hours and counting, and not a word of the eulogy drafted.

Why was this such a struggle? There would be, what, all of seven or eight people attending the service? And her father wasn't going to hear any of it. So why couldn't she scribble more than half a dozen sentences before deciding each attempt was garbage and should never be read aloud? Either too formal or too cheesy, too phony or just plain forced.

It wasn't helping that her mind refused to let go of all her recent revelations—revelations that had crushed her world as quickly as they'd replaced it with a foreign one. She'd stepped off the spinning merry-go-round of her life only to land on a Ferris wheel with merely a different view of the same carnival.

Kate straightened and exhaled a determined breath. She placed the pen on the page and started: *Collin Flaherty. What can I say about Collin Flaherty?*

If she knew, she would be done with this by now.

A spurt of male laughter echoed through the house, stole her focus. She peeked around the corner into the entry where the French doors of Drew's study were cracked open. Sofo must have left the room she'd suddenly formed such an attachment to. Kate's search for her feline friend that morning had ended when she spotted a white feathery tail extending out from under Drew's massive mahogany desk. Lack of movement indicated Sofo had discovered a new cove for napping, one surrounded by legal books and the smell of leather and courtroom injustice.

Kate returned her attention to her paper. She attempted to add to her pathetic opening line, but laughter invaded again followed by shushing. She grumbled as she jumped to her feet and marched toward the study. Brian was supposed to be helping Drew write her dad's obituary, and no one should be able to laugh until she'd finished her own challenge.

Her gaze honed in on the seated figures shadowed by the frosted glass panes of the study doors. She'd intended to reproach the terrible twosome, yet as she approached, curiosity over the source of their humor halted her.

"Okay, how about this one," she heard Brian say. "Retired and highly decorated Police Chief Brian DiSanto, an officer who shot through the ranks after single-handedly rescuing a dozen grateful bikini-clad Playboy bunnies from a hostage situation, died at the age of ninety-eight. Even in his final days, DiSanto bore the charisma and astounding good looks that twice earned him his famed title as *People* magazine's most eligible bachelor, as well as Viagra's leading spokesman."

When Kate burst into giggles, the study fell silent. She didn't have to see the guys' faces to know they'd be expressing a mixture of surprise and guilt. She took a few more steps through the entry towards them before the doorbell chimed.

"Saved by the bell, fellas," she hollered. She smiled as she made a sharp left and reached for the front door. Having spotted a *For Sale* sign in the neighboring yard that morning, she'd concluded the parked truck she had previously fretted over simply belonged to a real estate agent or prospective buyer with an inside scoop.

Now, her sense of safety fully restored, she didn't bother to use the peephole. She swung open the door, basking in relief that quickly vanished. "Wanda." Kate forced herself to sound pleasant. "How are you?"

"How am *I*?" She sang out the *I* in a long drawl as if a doctor were checking her tonsils. "Well, aren't you sweet as pecan pie to ask, when the real question is, 'How—are—*you*?'" She paused between each of the last three words for emphasis, her brow knitted in daytime-drama concern.

Obviously, news of a death in the Flaherty family had already reached Wanda's ears. However, this time Kate was actually impressed more than irritated. How on earth did this woman accumulate her reports? And so quickly? Put Wanda Finch within a hundred feet of the grassy knoll during Kennedy's final parade and in a matter of minutes she would have solved the case of the "magic bullet."

"I'm fine." Kate managed a flimsy smile, keeping her body wedged in the open doorway to serve as a barricade. "Thanks for asking."

"Here ya go, sugar. I brought this for y'all." Wanda handed over a large rectangular glass casserole dish wrapped in overlapping sheets of aluminum foil. "Nothin' soothes the soul like a big ole plate of comfort food, my mama always says. You just pop that there in the oven for an hour, covered, at three-hundred-fifty degrees, and you'll have yourselves a meal that'll last you a week."

"I appreciate it, Wanda. You really didn't have to go to so much trouble." With the pan no longer in Wanda's hands, Kate could observe the woman's full fashion ensemble: Kelly green pedal pushers, a pale yellow turtleneck, and a floral vest that reminded Kate of the Von Trapp family's curtain-made garments.

"No trouble at all—it was my pleasure," Wanda replied. "Oh, and lookee here." She reached down and retrieved a FedEx envelope propped between the corner of the thick welcome mat and the door frame. "A package," she announced. "I'll put it here for ya." She placed the bulging, document-size casing on top of the dish's tinfoil covering.

"Thanks. I didn't hear them deliver it."

Wanda sighed heavily. "You know, my own daddy—God rest his soul—he passed away five years ago come November."

"I'm sorry to hear that."

"It was a blessing, really. See, he went into a coma on account of him hittin' his head during his third heart attack. Had it in the middle of one of our potluck family reunions. He and Uncle Dick were having a friendly debate as usual. Weed whackers, I believe it was about."

Just when Kate thought she'd heard it all.

"For two months, doctors said it was just a matter of days. Then my sister's son Jimmy finally came home from the service—of all the grandkids, we always knew he was Daddy's favorite, even though he'd never admit such. And wouldn't you know it, Daddy passed away that very next mornin'. It was like he was waiting for Jimmy to come pay his respects."

Wanda's cheeks suddenly drooped, as if she'd just recalled the mournful nature of her visit. "Dear me, would you listen to all my rattlin'. I'm sure my family's tribulations are the last thing you needed to hear about today."

"That's quite all right." Kate raised the heavy pan in her hands. "Thanks again for the…"

Wanda perked up. "Lasagna."

Lasagna. Kate felt the giggles inside her returning. One day she would make it her life's mission to seek out, confiscate, and destroy every copy of the merciless cookbook she was convinced existed: *Pasta for the Grieving Daughter's Soul.*

"Oh, and I should warn ya," Wanda added. "The red sauce has a little zip to it. I was hoping y'all wouldn't mind a smidgen of cayenne pepper. It tends to give Carl heartburn, so I don't make it as often as I'd like."

To try to keep her laughter in, Kate locked her gaze on the pair of red cherry-shaped pendants hanging around Wanda's neck. The bold accessory screamed Home Shopping Network louder than a set of Ginzu knives. Kate's urge to giggle gained momentum until she couldn't fight it anymore.

The outburst stopped Wanda mid-sentence. The neighbor stood there, eyes squinted and face crumpled in confusion. The woman was speechless.

Wanda Finch was speechless!

"Don't mind me." Kate tamed her laughter. "It's just the stress of it all."

Wanda nodded, eyeing her skeptically. "Well, awright," she said, edging away. "I best get back to my ironing anyhow."

Kate cleared her throat, her smile retaining its hold. "You have a good day."

"Uh-huh. You too." Wanda reciprocated with an uneasy smile as Kate closed the door.

Kate shook her head, imagining how swiftly her neighbor would spread word that grief-stricken, non-cooking Kate Flaherty was losing her cotton pickin' mind.

"That woman and her stories," Kate muttered to herself.

As she journeyed toward the kitchen, she mentally replayed a few of Wanda's highlights. Pausing on the tale of

Jimmy's hospital visit, she wondered if her own father had similarly held on, waiting until his daughter came to see him a final time. Perhaps nothing more than a hopeful notion, but a nice one all the same.

"Kate?"

She spun around, her heart stalling.

"Brian," she sighed. "You scared me." She was relieved she hadn't released her grip on the dish handles. Scrubbing pasta and zippy red sauce off the slate floor would have been no easy feat. Especially a week's worth.

"Sorry," he said.

"Not your fault—I just didn't hear you." She looped around the kitchen island and set the pan down.

"No, I mean I'm sorry...about that." He motioned toward the study, his eyes lowered and face drawn, like a remorseful kid in the principal's office.

She'd nearly forgotten about his amusing rendition of his own obituary. "It's okay," she assured him. "I needed something to lighten up the day."

He nodded, his expression loosening.

"Would you like to stay for dinner? I've got lasagna here that should be great, provided you don't mind a little heartburn."

He shoved his hands into the back pockets of his jeans and shrugged. "Wish I could, but duty calls. Working the nightshift."

"Oh, that's too bad," she said. "I hear you're joining us for dinner on Saturday, though, right?"

"Actually, I just told Drew—the sheriff's office is having sort of a banquet thing I have to go to."

She raised an eyebrow. "You're not making up excuses, are you? That's three invitations in a row you've turned down this week."

"Hardly." He grinned. "Believe me, I'd take a home-cooked meal any day. Me and the Pizza Hut delivery guy are on a first name basis."

"We'll reschedule soon, then?"

"Sure thing."

"Especially since there's a certain legal assistant who will be pretty disappointed."

His olive skin instantly flushed a muted red. "Yeah, well, Beth...she's, uh...well, she's going to the banquet too. With me."

Kate's jaw dropped.

"I know, I know," he mumbled, rolling his eyes.

"After a year of our prodding, you're finally giving that girl a shot?"

"I've always liked her," he asserted.

"Uh-huh," Kate murmured in disbelief.

"I *did*. I just..." He shrugged again. "Wasn't quite ready to go down that road. You know?"

Kate, of all people, could relate to the challenge of tackling emotional stages, one cautious, gradual step at a time. "I understand." She smiled.

"Hey, if all goes well, maybe we can all meet up for dinner at my parents' place in the next week or two. My mom's been wanting to make you two another big pot of her legendary spaghetti."

Fabulous. More pasta.

"Tell her I'd love to. And please, thank her for the flowers." A curvy chartreuse vase displaying the colorful spring bouquet Brian had delivered rested on the kitchen counter beside the sink—right next to her mangled wallet. A gas station attendant had apparently found her ransacked pocketbook beneath drug paraphernalia in a bathroom trashcan. The cash and cancelled credit cards were missing, but the most valuable item had been left behind: Kate's driver's license.

"Thanks again for helping me get my wallet back," she said to Brian. "It's been...a little nerve-racking without it."

"Eh, don't mention it. Just fulfilling my civic duty,

ma'am." He puffed his broad chest and tipped an invisible hat atop his head. "I'm glad you can finally put your concerns to rest." He glimpsed his wristwatch. "Jeez, I'd better run."

"Yeah, you wouldn't want to keep those *Playboy* bunnies waiting." She tried for a straight face, but the corners of her lips shot up.

"Well, I did take an oath."

She waved him off. "Get outta here."

He raised his hand and chuckled as he turned to leave, a devilish glint in his eyes.

Poor Beth. Combine Brian's charm and suave Sicilian looks with a crisp blue uniform, and that girl's heart didn't stand a chance.

Thirty Five

Kate waited to hear Brian's car drive away before shifting her gaze to the still blank, still waiting pages on the kitchen table. She grabbed the FedEx package from the island and returned to her chair.

In a blatant act of procrastination, she ripped open the envelope and fished out the contents: a hardcover book, a key, and a small, folded yellow paper. She flipped the book over to view the front cover.

Heaven's Light.

A gift from Doris. The caregiver must have an unlimited supply.

Kate smiled fondly as she unfolded the enclosed note:

Dear Kate,
I had accidentally taken these items with my belongings when I left your father's house. I realized the book was his when I happened across the inscription. Assuming you might need the key before the funeral, I am overnighting this package. Please know, I would have preferred to hand deliver these, but I'll be busy tending to a patient for the next couple of days. Please feel free to call me should you have any questions or concerns.

My heart and prayers go out to you and your family during this challenging yet rejoiceful time.

With warmest regards,
Doris Shaffer

Kate's eyes returned to the word *inscription*.

She picked up the book and opened the front cover. Sure enough, there was a handwritten dedication:

Collin,
May the messages within these pages
bring you comfort as you journey
back into God's tender embrace.
Your dear friend,
Ron

Kate immediately closed the book to verify the author's name on the front cover. *Ron McGary.* With thoughts chasing through her mind, she turned to the back inside flap of the dust jacket. The slender man in the black-and-white portrait had a saintly look about him. His jaw line looked strong, yet softened by a joyous smile. His grizzly hair appeared as billowy as cotton, the skin surrounding his eyes wrinkled from a life spent serving others.

She skimmed his bio in search of a connection to her dad.

Dedicated pastor...Shepherd's Gate Christian Church...inspirational speaking tours...lives in Portland, Oregon, with his wife and two sons.

Kate read the author's inscription again, stunned. Sure, her father had been a Christian, but he'd always been more of the casual non-practicing type—a man who'd found more redemptive value in an underdog collegiate football team's Hail Mary pass than visiting a sanctuary on Sundays.

So where did this pastor, one who considered himself a dear friend of her father's, come from?

A thought occurred to her: perhaps her struggle over

composing the eulogy was due, in part, to the lack of a personal connection the rest of the funeral was seeming to have to her dad's life. If it weren't too late, enlisting the help of this pastor—someone who apparently knew and cared for her father—could be the element she needed to add.

She nabbed the nearby cordless phone and dialed directory assistance. Within seconds, her fingers had punched the number for Shepherd's Gate. A receptionist assured her she would relay the urgent message about Collin's service the moment Pastor Ron returned from lunch.

After hanging up, Kate headed back toward her husband, toting the book. A glimmer of newfound hope lightened her stride. The pieces of her father's life were popping up one by one, like stepping-stones leading to a destination she'd resigned herself to believing would be forever unreachable.

In the study Drew was planted in his throne-like chair, hunched over his desk, engrossed in a paper held in his hands. His usual case-study pose.

"Hey," she said. "I've got good news. I just…"

When he jerked his head up, his dark expression reined in her words. The arc of her lips leveled. "Is everything okay?" she asked.

His eyes, hooded and foreboding, twisted her stomach into a tightly wound ball.

"What's the matter?"

He didn't respond.

She glanced at the paperwork fanned out on his desk, noting her father's name. "Are those the documents you found in his safe?"

As if suddenly gathering his bearings, Drew folded the paper in his grip and hastily stuffed it into an envelope. "It's nothing," he said half-heartedly, not looking at her. "Life insurance, a copy of the will, etcetera."

She stepped closer to the desk. "Drew," she persisted,

trying not to sound panicked. "What is it? What did you find?"

Kate stood firm in her decision that secrets had no place in their marriage. But that didn't stop fear from prickling her skin. Fear of what was to come as a result of their uncompromising honesty.

He raised his eyes, heavy with angst. "Really, all of this can wait."

Her open palm instinctively lunged out. "Please."

His gaze swept over the ominous envelope. He pulled out the collapsed page and placed it gently in her hand. She was about to unfold the paper when Drew touched her forearm.

"Baby, you'd better sit down first."

With those words, she already knew reading what she held in her hands was something she would regret. But it was too late to turn back.

Thirty Six

In elegant cursive, at the top of the page, appeared the date: *December 15, 2007.* Below it: *Dear Collin.*

Obviously it was a letter. Penned five months ago. The longhand was graceful and perfectly aligned. A woman's handwriting, familiar to Kate.

Kate's daughterly instinct warned her against perusing her father's personal correspondence. But then she reminded herself he was gone.

She took Drew's advice and sat down in one of the armchairs facing his desk. She was about to continue reading when she noticed her husband had swiveled his chair slightly to face the window capped with a sienna-brown cornice. Atop the papers on his desk, his elbow propped a fist that covered his mouth. His eyes were averted to the clouds in the sky. By all accounts, he appeared lost in thought, though Kate sensed he was merely giving her space while still remaining in the room for support.

Why she would need his support after reading this letter to her dad, she had no idea. She took a deep breath, knowing she would soon find out.

Dear Collin,
I know it has been a long while since you have heard from me. I had contemplated writing you countless times since

I moved away. I even went as far as beginning a few drafts over the years, but the words always appeared too small for the letter that needed to be written, and as usual, silence seemed a better solution than another irreversible error in judgment.

I am so sorry about the health challenges you have faced. I had kept abreast of your treatments and their successful outcome. It was, then, with as much sadness as surprise that I learned of your cancer's recurrence. Upon hearing of your decision to forego further treatments, my first inclination was to phone you and ask you to reconsider. But then, who am I to make demands on your life? And who am I to prevent you from reuniting, at last, with your beloved wife, an angel who is no doubt awaiting your arrival?

Not a day goes by when I don't think about what happened between us, about the mistake that shattered our lives because of a single night. Even now, I find myself imagining how different our lives would be if only I had called someone else for help. Strange, isn't it? One phone call and our worlds were thrown into a tornado spin that eventually slowed, yet never stopped. Had I simply misdialed or summoned a girlfriend of mine instead, you and Iris would surely have been married for almost forty years now. Perhaps I, too, would have found someone to share my life with and raise children of my own. Unfortunately, I have discovered, there isn't room enough in any relationship for growth when guilt insists on taking up so much space.

The reason I am writing you today is to tell you it is time you released the self-blame that I know still binds your heart. You are a good man, Collin. In your final days on this earth, I ask that you allow the burden of guilt to rest on my shoulders alone, and let peace and forgiveness be yours.

As always, I will respect your privacy. Yet please know, if you need anything at all, I am here for you.

Yours,
Sophie

Kate's eyes zeroed in on the name *Sophie*. She knew the handwriting because it belonged to her aunt.

Aunt Sophie.

Her mother's sister.

Her father's *mistress*?

Kate suddenly felt lightheaded. Slowly raising her head, she gripped the arm of the chair with her free hand. If she weren't sitting, she would have crumbled to the floor.

"My aunt?" she barely whispered. "The woman he had an affair with was my *aunt*?"

Drew's consoling gaze reached for her across the desk. His fist remained against his mouth as if providing a reason for his inability to speak.

When a realization dawned on her, her body became a cauldron of bubbling and bursting emotions. "So that's why my dad stayed on the road. That's why he and my aunt hardly ever spoke." The volume of her voice climbed, despite her words being directed more at herself than Drew. "And this is how I find out?" She clenched the page in her hand. "Through a frickin' letter? It wasn't enough that I lost both my parents? Now I have to lose my aunt too?" Her eyes raged with tears, blurring her world.

Drew, a fuzzy silhouette, lowered his hand onto the desk and leaned toward her. "I'm sure there's a lot more to it, sweetheart."

She shook her head. Disgusted. Shocked. Furious.

Her entire childhood was a mirage, a house of cards built upon secrets and lies. And the crumpled letter in her hand was the gust of wind that had just blown it all down.

"Maybe you should talk to Sophie about it," Drew suggested, "after the funeral tomorrow."

Oh, Kate was going to talk to her all right. But whether she could hold off speaking her mind until *after* the service was a whole other question.

Thirty Seven

Kate stared at the empty square decanter in the limousine bar, wishing she could funnel her emotions into the confines of its etched glass walls. She would seal them with the cork, then drive along the Puget Sound. Standing through the open moonroof, she'd hurl her compacted feelings into the waves where they would sink like a rock to the bottom of the sea. Lost. Discarded. Forgotten. The way she'd felt for too many years of her life. And a glimpse of her aunt being escorted by the chauffeur out of the hotel's revolving glass door reminded Kate why that was.

She tensed in her smooth black seat that faced the rear windshield. As the suited driver reached for the exterior door handle, Kate wondered if she'd made a poor choice in facing her aunt's bench seat rather than sharing it. Hiding an onset of scowls would be an easier task if Kate were situated beside Sophie and able to simply turn toward the side window.

She started to stand on the cushy carpeting to switch seats, but the door flew open and her body pulled down, as if linked to a cord on a pulley.

A black pump—low-heeled, with a small bow embellishment—entered the six-passenger limousine. It tapped the floorboard first to gain footing, testing the waters for safety. Suntan-colored stockings covered the leg, shown below a black linen A-line skirt cut modestly past the knee. Kate detected subtle traces of spider veins and sunspots on her aunt's calf, yet couldn't deny that the shape of her legs—kept slender and toned from Stairmaster workouts and ladies' hit-n-giggle golf outings—retained a youthfulness at sixty that rivaled Tina Turner's.

Guided by the chauffeur's hand, Sophie ducked into the vehicle and slid gracefully into her seat. Her black dress jacket, a set with the skirt, featured overly large buttons, each fastened up to a pointed collar. Her forearms, peeking between her three-quarter length sleeves and black gloves, evidenced more sun exposure than Kate remembered from when she visited her aunt in Scottsdale just over two years ago.

Sophie leaned forward, arms outstretched, clutch purse in hand. "Goodness, Kate, I've missed you."

Kate's neck stiffened as Sophie embraced her, yet she managed to pat her aunt's back once to give the illusion of a reciprocated greeting.

The door closed.

"How are you holding up, honey?" Sophie drew back a bit and touched her gloved hand to Kate's cheek.

She fought the reflex to push her aunt's hand away.

"Any other stops, ma'am?" The driver's voice, deep with a smoker's rasp, rescued Kate. Welcoming the opportunity to break connection with Sophie, she twisted her head toward the open privacy window.

"No." Kate held eye contact in the rearview mirror. "Just straight to the cemetery."

"Yes, ma'am." He nodded and started the engine.

"Drew isn't joining us?" her aunt asked.

The limo bumped out of the parking lot and veered to the right. The women swayed left, then returned upright. Kate pressed herself to answer, both to kill time and to elude suspicion.

"He went on ahead, to make sure everything was in order with the funeral director, and with Dad's pastor."

Sophie's penciled eyebrows scrunched together. "Your father had a pastor?"

"Apparently."

"I had no idea."

"Neither did I until yesterday." Kate shrugged. "But then, there are all kinds of things I didn't know about him." Berating herself for slipping, she whipped her face toward the window. She gazed at the cars flying past as the limo merged with the freeway traffic. Internally she willed the driver to floor the gas pedal.

Kate shifted in her seat. She had an urge to keep her distance until disembarking at their destination. But she knew her neck would soon insist on uncoiling, and nothing would prompt an "Is everything all right?" inquiry faster than obvious avoidance. Sophie did have the advantage of ten years of learning Kate's behavioral tendencies. A decade spent playing her mother's role.

Kate felt repulsed at the thought, but ushered the feeling away. She directed it to a waiting room, requested its patience until she called its number. It wouldn't be long; a thirty-minute drive, a thirty-minute service. If Collin and Sophie could swing twenty-five years of deceptive fronts, Kate could handle an hour.

As the limo rolled on, she angled back around. She straightened and lowered her shoulders, a proper habit from years of Sophie's prodding. Then, in quiet rebellion, Kate slumped her lower back into the seat, perhaps daring her aunt to admonish her.

But Sophie didn't. Instead, she sat quiet and ladylike, ankles crossed, hands folded on her lap. Her silver-blonde hair swept into a French roll was just as prim. Her thin lips were meticulously lined and painted antique pink. Save an edging of white lacy trim from her slip at the hem of her skirt, she was as poised as Jackie O. A picture-perfect mourner.

In lieu of conversation, Kate was tempted to scan static-free channels on the small television beside her knee. She held off though, aware chances were high her hands would shake from the anger that yearned to show itself.

She turned to her aunt, took a stab at idle pleasantness. "How was your flight?"

"Oh, fine, I suppose. They don't give you much legroom anymore, though. And, I had a screaming toddler behind me who kept running up the aisles and kicking the back of my chair."

"Well, kids can certainly be inconvenient." Kate swiftly pinned the corners of her lips up to cover any edge that may have seeped into her tone.

Sophie playfully wagged a finger. "Not if they're your own." Her copper eyes gleamed and her mouth slanted into a smile, accentuating the hint she was dropping.

Unbelievable. Her aunt actually had the gall to pressure her about becoming a mother. Who was she to talk? Oh, that's right: there wasn't enough room in Sophie's life for such relationships when guilt took up so much space.

Too agitated to speak, Kate stayed silent. Finally Sophie cut through the awkwardness by continuing, "So…are you and Drew thinking yet of having children?"

"No," Kate replied flatly.

"Mmm." Sophie smiled wanly over her disappointed hum.

"In fact, I'm not sure we ever will." Kate couldn't keep from slinging the additional comment.

"Oh," Sophie said. "I guess I misunderstood your plans. I thought you were just waiting for your careers—"

"Well, you thought wrong." She wanted to smash her aunt's hopes like a brittle leaf beneath her shoe.

A pause. "I see." Sophie tilted her head slightly. "Would you mind if I ask…?"

Her question was posed respectfully, but Kate found no reason to let her finish. "Because I wouldn't make a good mother."

"What?" Sophie touched her pearl necklace and released a soft "don't be silly" chuckle. "Why in heaven's name would you think such a thing?"

A point-of-no-return alert blinked in Kate's head like the flashing lights on a police car. Still, the impetus to hurt her aunt was too great to hold in. She steeled her gaze at Sophie. "I didn't have a mother when I was growing up. So I wouldn't know how to be one."

Sophie's eyes dulled. She tucked her chin and studied her niece as she'd done countless times when seeking honesty behind the usual teenage defenses. "Honey—are you all right?"

"I'm fine." Kate pursed her lips and retreated to her window. Why couldn't her parents have chosen plots in a closer cemetery?

"Kate." Her voice was firm. A no-nonsense, don't-even-try-to-fool-me-young-lady tone. A mother's approach that suddenly infuriated Kate.

"My father died," she blurted, glaring at her aunt. "How do you expect me to feel?"

Sophie remained stone-faced, her angular features unreadable. A moment of silence lingered before she looked past Kate's shoulder and leaned forward. "Excuse me, sir."

"Yes, ma'am?"

Kate had forgotten they weren't alone.

"Would you mind raising the divider, please?" Sophie's request was a polite yet uncompromising command.

"Not at all, ma'am." He answered so quickly it was obvious he'd been listening. Not that he'd had a choice in the matter.

The mechanized wall whirred as it rose, dimming the back of the limo. And with that, Kate and Sophie were face to face without an escape.

Kate swallowed. What was she thinking? Drew had encouraged her to wait until after the funeral. Why didn't she listen?

Kate smoothed her hair behind her ears. She lowered her tired eyes, hoping her makeup and Visine drops still concealed her sleeplessness from the night before. As she picked an imaginary piece of lint off her pantsuit, she felt Sophie's unrelenting gaze.

"Well...?"

"Well, what?" Kate muttered, not knowing why her own eyes were downcast. Her aunt was the criminal here, yet somehow Kate couldn't shake the feeling she was about to be grounded for skipping school.

Sophie exhaled deeply and waited.

The heady scent of her aunt's Estée Lauder perfume, likely from the bottle Kate had given her for Christmas, contended with the smell of the vehicle's new leather upholstery. Still, nothing in the air was as strong as the tension between them.

Sophie folded her arms. "Kathryn, we're not leaving this limousine until you speak your mind."

Kate knew from experience her aunt meant what she said. A forty-five-minute silent standoff in a parked car with her aunt during Kate's sophomore year of high school had proven such. But what was Kate going to say?

The hypothetical confrontations she'd imagined at three in the morning failed to factor in the intensity of seeing her aunt in person. Articulate accusations were currently not at her disposal. Besides, now wasn't the time. Too much information and Kate might not be able to maintain her facade at the funeral. Too many details and she might never be able to say good-bye to her father.

"Really," Kate explained, "I'm just upset about my dad, that's all."

"Try again."

Kate shot her an astonished look.

"All I mean is," Sophie said, as if backing up, "I'm sure

that's part of it. But your curtness on the phone last night, and now here...I know you well enough to realize there's something else going on."

Kate squeezed the edge of her seat, containing her mounting fury.

"Come on now, let's hear the truth about what's bothering you."

A sharp huff blasted out of Kate's mouth. *"Truth?"* Her aunt's word choice yanked the pin from the grenade Kate had been carrying inside for nearly a month. She exploded, "What would you know about truth?"

Sophie peered at her watchfully for a moment before offering, "Honey, if you and Drew are having problems..." But Kate could hear a trace of fear in Sophie's voice, as if she were suddenly uncertain where the conversation was headed.

Kate charged on, her raging emotions grabbing hold of her like an undertow. Surrendering to the current, she unzipped the purse resting beside her hip and extracted the tri-folded letter. Without a word, she handed it to her aunt.

Sophie looked puzzled, but she accepted the pages and warily opened them. She looked at the first lines, then her head snapped up, her face instantly pallid.

As the limo rumbled, traversing the freeway, their unblinking gazes held. For minutes that clung like hours, they said nothing.

At last, Sophie melted into her seat, shoulders hunched. Her left hand, barely holding the letter, fell limp in her lap. Her right hand clutched the armrest on the door as she shifted her gaze to the side window.

"What happened that night?" Kate demanded.

Sophie's eyes glossed over.

"What happened," Kate repeated, "the night you called my father?"

"Kate..." she rasped. "I... don't think now is the time—"

"Aunt Sophie, you have to tell me. I have a right to know."

A long, stifling moment passed. Finally, her aunt inhaled deeply and began to speak.

"We liked movies," she said. "Black and whites, the classics."

Kate shook her head, impatient, confused. "What are you talking about?"

"Collin was the new kid in town. He'd just moved here from Iowa, so he didn't have many friends. I used to spend every Saturday seeing a matinee, even before he started working at the movie house." Her voice was distant, as if relating a hazy-edged dream.

"It was a tiny theater," Sophie continued. "Not more than a dozen folks on weekend afternoons. So he'd often join me, sneaking in after the lights went down. We'd recite lines back and forth, laugh at all the same parts. He'd tease me and make jokes, and I'd throw popcorn at him." Her mouth suggested a smile. "I knew he saw me as more of a kid sister than anything else. He was seventeen; I was fourteen. Even if he *had* looked at me differently, I wasn't allowed to date yet. Not that it stopped me from doodling his name in my diary, or marking off the days until I could see him again."

Kate reclined in her seat, attempting to bridle her thrashing emotions. Had the affair taken place when they were teenagers? An adolescent love triangle whose ripple effect wasn't felt for years to come?

"When he dropped out of school and enlisted in the Navy, I secretly cried my eyes out. No one really understood what was going on in Vietnam—it was on the other side of the world—but we all knew war was dangerous.

"The last day I saw him before he shipped out, he made me promise I'd write. So I did. Fairly often. Though never with a message indicating I expected more than friendship, mind you." Again, the corners of her lips rose a fraction. "He loved care packages the most. Cookies, candy bars, and magazines." She sighed before going on.

"I was so thankful when I heard he was finally coming home. He'd spent all of his leaves in the Midwest. His parents would meet him there to visit family and friends. Which I didn't mind entirely, because the longer he was away, the more time I had to grow up. He was supposed to come back and see me, and just like in the old movies, he'd realize I wasn't a kid anymore. That the girl he thought of as a little sister had matured into the woman he wanted to marry."

Kate shifted uncomfortably, overcome by the feeling she'd made a mistake in unlocking the cage of her family's dark history. Once the beast was set free, there was no way to draw it back in before permanent damage was done. A voice of warning screamed inside her, commanding her to halt Sophie's claw-ridden purge. But she ignored the order. Kate's need for truth far outweighed any consequence of her aunt's words.

"Once he was settled," Sophie went on, "we decided to meet up for a movie. I was so excited, I couldn't sleep a wink the night before. I must have gone through a dozen outfits. I told my parents we were just friends. But since I wasn't quite seventeen, I had to have a chaperone. So they made Iris go along."

Sophie paused, the letter quivering in her hand. "She hated old picture shows. Told me she'd wait until after the movie started to slip out, in case any of our parents' friends were there. But that all changed when I introduced her to Collin. I saw it in their faces the second they met. The way they both acted so shy at first, then stealing glances during the film." Sadness flowed into Sophie's eyes. "She stayed for the entire show. And when he invited us out to a diner afterward, looking at Iris the whole time, I knew it was over. They'd gone to different high schools, but they were the same age and had a good deal in common.

"The next morning, she asked me if I had feelings for

Collin, but what was I going to say? He'd clearly made his choice. Besides, part of me was still holding out hope that things wouldn't work out between them. And as months went by, I had even more reason to believe it. They were always fighting and making up. I kept thinking that sooner or later they'd called it quits. But then..." She took a breath. "Then he proposed."

Sophie nervously kneaded her gloved palm with her thumb. "Eventually, I started dating other guys. It was impossible not to compare them to Collin, so the relationships never lasted long. Of course, I never let Iris know that was the reason. If anything, she thought I'd become too critical of Collin." She turned and connected with Kate's gaze. "I tried my best to stay away, I did. But I didn't want to miss your childhood, all because of my selfish feelings. I'll admit the pain never went away, but seeing the love your parents had for you made it worth being there."

Sophie's inimitable sincerity tugged unexpectedly at Kate's heart.

"Your father showed your pictures and art projects to anyone who had a set of working eyes," Sophie added. "For years, their marriage was as smooth as one could be. It wasn't until you were about seven that things got rocky. Three years of trying to get pregnant again wore on them both. With all the tension, tiffs became more frequent..." Sophie's voice cracked. She returned to the window, her jaw visibly tightening.

"The guy I'd been dating was a real charmer, but he was also a nasty drunk. He'd thrown back a few too many that night and put his fist through a wall in my apartment. When I tried to take his drink away, he slapped me across the face."

The idea of Sophie as a victim was so disarming Kate had to fight the impulse to reach for her aunt's hand.

"Once he realized what he'd done, he apologized, then left for good. I called to talk to your mom, but she was out of town, visiting a friend. Collin heard me in tears and rushed right over." A tremble invaded Sophie's words. "He was determined to hunt the guy down, but I was so shaken up, I begged him to stay. So he did. He held me, made me feel safe. After drifting off, I woke up and saw his face next to mine. I thought I was dreaming at first."

Sophie paused, the pale skin of her cheeks flushing. "One thing led to another, and before we knew what happened, it had gone too far. I didn't realize until that night how much I still loved him. But I also loved my sister." A pool of tears gathered in her eyes. "We both agreed it was a huge mistake. We swore we wouldn't tell a soul. It was never going to happen again, so there wasn't any reason to make Iris suffer."

Kate's mind tried desperately to keep up. Dumbfounded, she stared at a single drop rolling down Sophie's face as her aunt continued.

"For months, life went on. Collin and I avoided one another as much as possible. When Iris demanded he tell her why we were being so cold to each other, he came to me. He wanted to come clean, said the guilt was tearing him apart inside. He planned to beg for her forgiveness, praying she'd still love him. I'd intended to see her the next morning, after you went to school, to do the same…" She trailed off, tears streaming.

When Aunt Sophie first stepped into the limousine, Kate was fully prepared to transform all the love she'd held for the woman who'd raised her into ice-cold hate. Like the revealing letter to her father, the situation was laid out in black and white. Simple as that. Adultery and betrayal.

Yet now, after hearing details of the account, the entire world seemed filled with shades of grey. A tragedy of Shakespearean proportion for all involved.

Sophie pulled a handkerchief from her purse and wiped her cheek. She turned to Kate with solemn eyes. "I cannot begin to tell you how sorry I am," she said softly. "I would do anything, truly anything, if I could undo it all."

Kate wanted to console her but was too consumed with grasping her own feelings, her own frenzied thoughts, like sand slipping through her fingers.

Finally she said, "Aunt Sophie...I...can't..."

A click sliced through her words and drew their attention to the door. The chauffeur was unsealing their vault. Sunlight breaking through the cloud-strewn sky poured into the back of the limousine.

Kate wondered how long ago they'd arrived.

The driver held out his hand. The ladies remained in their seats.

Kate wiped the nervous sheen on her palms onto her slacks. "We have to go," she managed.

Sophie nodded, keeping her gaze low. She briskly dabbed under her eyes and pulled a compact from her purse.

"Kate!" Drew rushed up to the limo door, his tone urgent.

She was afraid to ask, but couldn't stop herself. "What is it?"

He hesitated, eyes widened. "You're not going to believe this."

Thirty Eight

Kate tightened her grip on Drew's hand, her anxiety about to erupt. He led her between a pair of cars in the parking lot without saying a word.

"What is it?" she asked again. "Did something go wrong?"

"Just come see." His expression gave away nothing.

As he pulled her around a small, brick cemetery building, worst-case scenarios queued up in her mind. The wrong flowers. The wrong coffin. Oh no, the wrong body!

She was about to demand an answer when, in the distance, a flag-covered casket propped just above ground came into view. She hadn't visited her mother's grave in years, but she knew that was the general area. Then she recognized the floral arrangements as the ones she'd chosen, both displayed on metal easels by the coffin. Nearby, at least thirty people shrouded in black attire quietly conversed in groups, trading hugs and handshakes.

She tugged Drew to a stop, horrified. "They booked a service right next to my dad's? At the exact same time?"

Drew shook his head, his lips drifting into a smile. "They're here for your father," he said. "All of them."

"What?" She jerked her eyes back to the group and searched for familiar faces. Amidst the unknowns, she found the hospice duo, Doris and Sarah. Then Christina and Kevin from the gallery. Mr. Fawcett with a younger version of himself, presumably his son. And a few elderly couples she had seen in the mom-and pop stores near her dad's house. But what about the others?

"I don't understand," she said. "Who are they? How did they know about the funeral?"

"Apparently, through your aunt and Pastor Ron, word reached quite a few people who wanted to pay their respects."

Kate took in a full breath of air scented with freshly cut grass. As she scanned the attendees again in disbelief, a man emerged from the crowd. He walked purposefully toward her—a tall, somewhat hefty guy in a simple black suit, his thin hair pure silver, matching his neatly trimmed beard.

"Pastor Ron," Drew said to the approaching man. "I'd like to introduce you to Kate."

The pastor reached for her hand. His powder blue eyes glimmered. "Oh, Katie, it's such a delight to meet you after all these years."

Wait. Tall gentleman. Silver beard. The visitor Doris had mentioned.

"You visited my dad," she said, confirming the realization, "a week or two ago."

He smiled, reflecting. "I did. I had some business to attend to up in Port Angeles." He sighed. "Had I known how poorly your dad was doing, I definitely would've stopped by sooner."

Her lips failed a couple attempts at forming words before she said, "I'm sorry. I just didn't put it together, from the way Doris described you. I guess I'd pictured you exactly like the photo on your book cover."

"Ahh, the one from my Calvin Klein modeling days." He chuckled and shot her a wink. "Lucky for me, my wife's a big fan of the Kenny Rogers look."

That's when Kate noted the same sweet crinkling at the corners of his eyes and the radiation of goodness she had sensed in his photograph. Already she knew she'd made the right decision in phoning him.

"Pastor," Drew said, "do I have time to swing through the restroom before we get started?"

"I'd say that's up to your wife here." Ron arched an eyebrow at Kate.

"Of course," she answered Drew. "Aunt Sophie's in there right now, freshening up. We'll start when you two get back."

Once Drew zipped around the corner of the building, Ron presented his elbow to Kate. His other hand held a small black Bible. She smiled politely as she hooked her arm around his. In step, they headed toward the people who were now congregating near the gravesite. Though still dazed, Kate had reclaimed enough rational thought to tender her appreciation.

"Thank you so much for doing this," she said as they waded through the moist grass, flanked by rows of headstones. "I know it was extremely last minute."

"Please—I was honored you asked."

The question *So who are you?* collected on the tip of her tongue. Yet to save herself from a tactless moment, she swallowed the words.

While they walked, she gazed over at the laurel hedge that framed the cemetery, interspersed with well-groomed oak and maple trees. Halfway to their destination, Kate opted for a more delicate approach.

"My father...he was in a congregation of yours at some point?"

Ron laughed good-naturedly. "If I could have gotten Collin into church on Sunday...now that would've been one for the books."

Okay, so they both knew that much about her dad. But that still didn't enlighten her as to how the two men became "dear friends." She wanted to come right out and ask. However, as she hadn't bothered to find out before she'd invited him to officiate, the inquiry now felt awkward. Particularly as it risked telling this kind man that her dad had never spoken of him, or at least not to her.

She feigned contemplation. "I forget, how long did you and my father know each other?"

"Goodness," he sighed. "Must be well over forty years now. Amazing where the time goes."

She stumbled over a dense clump of grass. The pastor tightened his elbow around her arm, saving her from a fall that carried the increased potential of embarrassment before a mass of spectators.

"Thanks," she said, straightening.

"My pleasure, Katie." His tone was so soothing, she didn't mind that he called her Katie although her parents were the only ones who'd ever done so. She had been adamant about going by *Kate* for as long as she could remember, as *Katie* was a little girl's name, while *Kathryn* connoted being in the doghouse. Now, though, hearing how easily the nickname rolled off the pastor's tongue, she felt a comfortable connection to her past, and to him.

Before they could resume their stroll, she peered up at him and said, "Pastor Ron, I hope you don't mind me asking, but...how did you and my dad meet?"

"Oh, I'm sorry, I thought you knew," he replied. "He and I served in the war together."

"You were in the Navy?"

The broad smile he flashed made it clear she hadn't veiled her surprise.

"Hard to imagine now, I suppose." He lifted his Bible to punctuate his words. "Not many folks in my church would picture me running around on an aircraft carrier."

"I didn't mean to imply...I just didn't know he kept in touch with anyone from the service."

"I probably didn't give him much of a choice. He'd saved my hide more than once during our tour. So as I saw it, he was stuck with me for life."

"Did you see him often? Through the years?"

"Not as often as I would've liked. Mostly, we kept up through a letter or phone call. We'd meet for coffee when his deliveries brought him out my way. He was a good man with a good heart, no doubt about it."

Hearing someone speak of her father with such admiration brought warmth to her cheeks.

The pastor shook his head. "I just wish it hadn't taken all these years for you and me to meet in person. After your mom passed away, I didn't hear from him as much. But whenever we did touch base, he'd brag up a storm about you. How proud he was of you. How fast you were growing up."

With those words, snippets of the last several days flickered through her mind: the dream of her dad in the chapel dressing room, the "proud Papa" conversation she'd imagined having at the diner. Mere incarnations of her deep-seated desire for her dad's approval. But now, at last, she had received confirmation from a dear friend of his—proof that the keepsakes in the shoebox she'd found did reflect paternal pride.

"Yes, indeed," Ron added, "he sure was a huge fan of yours. If I had a nickel for every time Old Mick brought your name up…"

Old Mick? The name echoed in her ears, ignited a shiver that raced up and down her back.

"Shall we?" The pastor raised his elbow.

She must have misheard him. "What did you say?"

He tilted his head, puzzled, and retracted his arm.

"Just a second ago," she urged. "What was it you called him?"

His brow knotted and held for a moment before he relaxed his face. "Oh heavens, I hope you don't think I meant any offense," he said apologetically. "With our ancestries, mine being English and your dad's Irish, 'Limey' and 'Mick' were all in fun between us. Not quite PC these days, I realize."

So "Mick" must have been a moniker Kate had stored in her memory. From another acquaintance of his. Sure. That made sense. She hadn't pulled the name out of thin air.

That is...assuming...

She anxiously wet her lips. "So other friends knew him as 'Mick' too, then?"

"Actually," he said, chuckling, "he probably would've decked any other guy who called him that. But I couldn't tell you for certain."

See—Ron didn't know. Someone else could have called her dad that when she was a kid. It was definitely possible...so why then, was she getting the nagging feeling that her skeptical theories were disintegrating?

She spared a glance to her right where the mourners were tightening their circular formation. To her left, she glimpsed Drew escorting Sophie around the corner of the building. Time was running out.

"Pastor Ron, do you...?" Kate hesitated, fearing she would sound as ridiculous as a grown woman asking if the Easter Bunny really laid eggs, but forced out the sentence anyway. "Do you believe people who are dying ever come to say good-bye?"

"You mean their spirits?"

She nodded sheepishly.

"Now, that's a good question."

Thankfully, he didn't look at her like a nutcase. Or like a naive youngster.

"Theories vary, of course," he said with a stroke of his beard. "Come to think of it, a girl in our congregation—back when she was about eight or so—shared something to that effect. She had a dream she and her grandpa were walking by a cliff. He slipped off, and she barely caught his hand. Told me she'd held on, trying to pull him up. Her grandpa kept insisting it was all right to let go. After a while, as small as she was, she couldn't hold on anymore. Next morning, come to find out he'd suffered a massive stroke and passed away during the night."

Kate struggled with his message. She knew firsthand how easily kids placed blame on themselves, wondering what they could have done to prevent the loss of a loved one. She fought to control her incredulity. "You're saying he could have lived, if she'd held on?"

"No, no. Not at all," Ron said with a caring smile, his response a relief to Kate. "Just that it was his time to go, and he wanted to tell her it was okay. That he was ready to cross over."

Even if the little girl's nightmare wasn't pure coincidence, his story didn't address the question of whether Kate's encounter at the dilapidated diner actually happened. The realness, the clarity, the details. Defying rationale, the memory of that night seemed less and less like an illusion. As if a camera lens were bringing the images into crisper, cleaner focus rather than blurring and fading with each passing day.

"So you believe spirits can visit while you're sleeping." Her tone bordered between a question and a statement.

"I think it's a period when our souls and minds are open to receiving more, without being scared of what we don't understand."

"But what if you're awake?" Kate's voice projected a tad louder than she'd intended.

He stroked his beard again, as if the answers to the universe would be released once his whiskers were sufficiently warmed. "Folks can get tangled in all kinds of heated debates over that one. Now, if you're asking for my opinion…"

She nodded.

"Well, I for one think there's a whole lot out there we can't explain, no matter how hard we try. You've got medical miracles not even the world's top doctors can find reasons behind. On the other hand, there's just as many silly ghost-hunting shows on TV that make me wonder sometimes."

"And...?" she persisted, hungry for the verdict.

"Do I believe a person's spirit can visit us while we're awake?" He drew a pondering breath. "Yes. Yes, I sure do."

She shrugged dubiously. "Even though there's no way to prove it?"

He folded his arms, hugging his Bible to his chest. "You see, Katie, that's what makes faith so tough to grasp. But also makes it so wonderful. It's all about believing in something—whether it's God, or other people, or even yourself—when you've got nothing else to go on. Nothing but a little voice inside telling you it's more than a hunch."

Just then, Drew and Sophie glided around them and continued toward the casket. Kate's gaze trailed Drew's sandy-blond hair. Only days ago, she had nearly lost her husband, a man whom she loved with all her heart, over a lack of faith on her part. Not just in him and their marriage, but as she now realized, an absence of faith in herself. And all the while, her father, perceived as the major source of her insecurities, had been harboring more faith in her than she'd ever suspected.

Perhaps her dad—if he had in fact intervened in her life—was trying to prevent her from continuing down the same lonely path he himself had taken.

She looked up at the pastor and simply said, "Thank you." The two words seemed inadequate to communicate her gratitude, but from the single nod he gave her, he appeared to understand.

She again slipped her arm around his, and together they went onward. Meek smiles and limited eye contact from the attendees greeted her as they wove through the crowd. Drew guided Aunt Sophie to one of the white garden chairs in the trio lineup, then seated himself on the opposite side, leaving the center chair open for Kate. Whispers and murmurings evaporated as if houselights in an opera house had dimmed.

Ron eased Kate into her seat and made his way to the head of the coffin in preparation for the show. The only sounds disturbing the quiet stillness were the faint chirping of birds and the humming of car motors in the distance.

The pastor cleared his throat. "Ladies and gentlemen, dearly beloved. We are gathered here today to honor and celebrate, not the death, but the life of Collin Flaherty. Collin was a kindhearted Irishman whom I was blessed to have called my friend. With this in mind, I thought I would begin today's service with an old Celtic blessing."

As Ron began his recitation, the red stripes of the American flag on the coffin seized Kate's attention. Since arriving at the cemetery, it was the first time she'd remembered that the casket beneath the patriotic drape was no longer an empty product on Mr. Fawcett's showroom floor; her father was now inside. His body anyhow. The body he'd ended up with, not the stalwart man she knew. Not the charming diner employee who quite literally sent Kate running back into her husband's embrace. Not the youthful sailor who never recovered from the most harrowing storm of his life.

Oh, how she yearned for a sense of closure. Something to sweeten the bitter aftertaste left in her soul after she stumbled across her aunt's incriminating composition.

A notion pierced Kate like a spear: What if her discovery had been no accident? Kate was his only child, his next of kin. Her dad had to have known she would be the one to sort the documents in his safe. Then why? Why intentionally tarnish her memory of him?

Could it be, deep down, he'd always wanted her to know? That it was the only way she'd find out it was guilt that had kept him away, not lack of caring?

She'd been so furious with him in his final weeks. The timing of his morphine-induced confession had barely allowed her an opportunity to digest the implications, much less forgive him. Then again, maybe, just maybe, in the end, her forgiveness wasn't what he sought.

Maybe it was his own.

Out of the corner of her eye, Kate studied her aunt. Sophie sat primly, hands on her lap, large sunglasses resting on her narrow nose. Then came a sparkle. The sun, streaming through the clouds, glistened on the tear that fled the cover of her aunt's dark lenses. Sophie brushed away the drop with the back of her glove so briskly that had Kate not been looking, she wouldn't have known her aunt was crying.

Kate grasped the locket hanging from her neck and closed her eyes, seeking her mother's guidance.

"Sweetheart," Drew whispered and gently tapped her hand, pulling her from her trance.

"Yes?" she whispered back.

"Do you still want to say something?" His intonation indicated he was reiterating a question the pastor had already asked.

She swung a glance across the arc of attendees and found all eyes resting on her, the grieving daughter. Not a sound in the air. Even the cars and birds seemed to have silenced themselves in anticipation of her response.

"If you've changed your mind—"

"No. No, I'd like to," she said, and rose.

As she headed toward Ron, she reached into the front pocket of her slacks and retrieved a folded paper: the eulogy she'd somehow managed to draft the evening before.

Pastor Ron gave her a tender smile, then stepped off to the side.

Kate took her position and unfolded the page. She was about to read aloud when she noted she was standing only a few feet from her parents' now-shared gravestone. Their names sandblasted on the granite surface reminded her how close their remains would soon be.

She attempted to focus on the paper in her hand, but instead her gaze sifted through the sea of faces surrounding her—people who cared for her father, or her, or both—and her premeditated speech teetered. Perpetrating the front her family members were experts at maintaining now seemed inappropriate. The eulogy she was about to give belonged to the old Kate, not the Kate she'd become, or the Kate she wanted to be.

She slid the paper back into her pocket. At last, when it came to her father, the time had come to be guileless.

Thirty Nine

Kate briefly glanced at the white stars on the flag covering the coffin before her, then back up to the attentive listeners. "I've decided not to read the eulogy I wrote for my dad. So if I stumble over my words a bit, I apologize." She raked her bottom lip, feeling small in a circle that now appeared to number a hundred. "I had no idea my father had so many friends."

Mumbled laughter trickled through the group. So far, her honesty was well received. Her courage was growing.

"I'd planned to say a few nice things. Nothing profound, just the standard things I figured a daughter should say about her father—a man she loved, but didn't know very well. I have to admit, in some ways, with seeing you all here, I feel like I knew him even less than I thought I did. Up until yesterday, I didn't realize one of his oldest and dearest friends was a minister." She glimpsed Pastor Ron's face and was relieved by his warmhearted expression. "Truth is, the only prayer I ever remember him reciting at all went something like 'God come down with a wiggly twist, and give me a biscuit as big as Your fist. A-a-a-men.'"

Another wave of soft laughter rolled through her audience as Kate's own lips curved up.

"At least we all agree he could make people smile." The grins she caught sight of proved her point and further lightened the somber mood. She moved onto what she did know about her father.

"Strong and independent are the first traits that come to mind when I think of my dad. He was a hard worker. He could be a man of few words, but those words were never wasted on complaints about anything he had to do. He would just buck up and do it. Not even during his battle with cancer did he gripe, or ask 'why me.' At least not out loud." Recalling his brutal physical reactions to chemo treatments brought tears to Kate's eyes.

"My father was a pro at hiding his wounds. I remember this one morning, he was up on a ladder, cleaning out the gutters, when he fell—come to think of it, I'm pretty sure he fell every time he got on a ladder." Her comment unintentionally prompted another spackling of giggles and delayed her for a moment.

"He did his best to hide his limp for a week, never saying it hurt. He'd just go about working on the house as usual." Images of her dad's home came to mind: the cabin he'd built from scratch, the handful of detailed furnishings inside he'd carved out of walnut. Not until then had she recognized the origin of her artistic inclinations.

"My father taught me a lot," she admitted. "He taught me the box step. How to catch fish and dig for clams. How to drive a boat, and secure it to the dock with a bowman's knot. And, of course, there's the Irish stubbornness my husband will gladly attest to." She looked at Drew, who responded with a smile. His eyes projected loving acceptance, encouraging her to continue. "Given that my dad never had a son, he even tried to teach me about car engines. And fence posting. And plumbing."

A warm glow filled her body as an obscure memory swooped in from her childhood. "I must've been about six..." She shook her head, unsure why she was divulging such an embarrassing tale. "For two whole days, my dad was baffled as to why every toilet in the house kept overflowing. He couldn't figure it out. He took pride in fixing everything himself, but was so stumped he had to call Roto Rooter. Well, it wasn't long before the guy was able to identify the cause of the pipe blockage: it was the pair of Strawberry Shortcake underwear I had tried to get rid of after having an accident."

She felt herself blush. "I thought for sure he'd be livid. But, surprisingly, he just grinned and said something like, 'So that's where my rag went.'"

She savored the expressions of delight and endearment encircling her. Yet when the true lesson of her recount emerged, her smile dissolved. Her eyes lowered to her father's casket, then shifted to her mother's grave beside her. She saw now that his message then was no different from the one he'd offered by leaving Sophie's letter in his safe.

"I guess my father was trying to teach me something for quite some time," she said. "He was showing me we're all human. That we make mistakes. But that doesn't mean we don't deserve another chance. Or to be forgiven." She gazed at her aunt's face. "Sometimes forgiving ourselves is exactly what we need to do, no matter how hard it is." Tears tumbled from Kate's eyes. She returned her attention to the guests standing behind Sophie, Doris Shaffer among them, their eyes just as moistened.

"Like I said, there's a whole lot I didn't know about my dad. Clearly, as I discovered today, I'll never know how many lives he touched. But I do know he loved me. And he loved my mother. And I know, wherever his spirit is right now, he's with her, smiling at all of you today, and thanking you for being here."

Kate paused before returning to her chair. The second she sat down, Drew clasped her hand. She glanced at her parents' gravestone. Relief and pride blossomed within her in equal doses. She was certain both Iris and Collin would have approved of her speech.

Pastor Ron invited up any others who wanted to say something. A large man with the weathered look of a lumberjack but a teddy bear demeanor stepped forward, hand raised. He introduced himself and launched into a humorous story from her dad's trucking days.

Meanwhile, Kate subtly turned her focus to Sophie. Following her heart, she slowly moved her free hand to rest on her aunt's. A familiar scene, minus the cold drizzle.

She felt Sophie shaking. A new tear appeared at the bottom rim of her aunt's glasses, then streaked her face. This time, though, Sophie made no effort to wipe it away. Without turning her head, Sophie piled her other hand over Kate's and squeezed tight. It was a gesture as comforting to Kate as the acknowledgement that her aunt's hand had, in fact, been there for her in more forms than she could ever count. An applauding hand. A guiding hand. A heavy hand to keep her on the right track. While no one could truly take her mom's place, Kate realized she had been wrong about not having a mother all these years. In many ways, she'd been fortunate enough to have two.

The service carried on for well over an hour. One by one, attendees volunteered to speak in honor of Collin Flaherty. Spurts of laughter alternated with tears. And with every speech and every anecdote, Kate felt a swell of joy knowing she was learning that much more about her father.

Finally, Mr. Fawcett presented Kate with the flag he and his son had ceremoniously folded into a perfectly tucked triangle. Everyone bowed their heads for Pastor Ron's concluding prayer before being dismissed. Many guests filed past Kate and greeted her with handshakes and hugs. Unlike at her mom's funeral, there was no trace of pity in their condolences.

Pastor Ron was right: this had been a celebration spotlighting her dad's life rather than his death. From then on, Kate promised herself, she would do the same in regard to the memory of her mother. Her family had spent too much energy focused on Iris's tragic end instead of emphasizing the wondrous person she was when she was alive.

"Now, if you ever need a thing, I'm just a phone call away," Doris said while hugging Kate.

"Thank you." Kate rocked back and peered into the woman's eyes, aware no words could justly express her appreciation, and simply repeated, "Thank you. For everything."

"It was my pleasure, dear."

As Doris shuffled toward the parking lot, Kate's thoughts suddenly zoomed in on the caregiver's final night with her dad. More importantly, his final minute. Why hadn't she thought of it before? Obviously, Doris would have been the one to record his time of death. Kate's watch was stored in her jewelry box, crystal still cracked, hands frozen from the accident. If the times matched, then Kate would know for sure that her dad had come to see her at the diner on his way to…his ultimate destination.

"Doris! Wait!"

She pivoted around. "Yes?"

Kate had started toward her when she caught a glimpse of Pastor Ron talking to a couple nearby. The mere sight of him brought back his words, halting Kate's feet. Here she was, still searching for proof to support her faith. And for what? She already knew what she believed. No recorded details could possibly change that.

"Is everything all right?" Doris appeared concerned.

A smile stretched across Kate's face. "It is," she said. "I just wanted to say thanks again—for tidying up when you left my dad's house."

Doris humbly waved her fingers. "Oh, it was nothing."

Kate nodded. "You take care."

"You too, dear." Doris swung back around and toddled off.

Kate felt a broad hand on her shoulder.

"Are you ready to go?" Drew asked.

She shifted her gaze to the casket, which now sat alone as guests strolled off to their cars. "Actually," she replied, returning her eyes to her husband's, "I need a minute. With my dad."

He kissed her cheek gently. "I'll go help Sophie back to the limo. Take your time."

"Thanks, Drew."

As Kate returned to her father's gravesite, she paused at one of the flower arrangements. From the center, she plucked a single stalk of green buds—Bells of Ireland—and approached his midnight blue casket.

She sighed. "I guess we've covered just about everything, haven't we, Daddy? For now, anyway." She kissed the floral stem and laid it across the middle of the coffin. She took a few steps back, the words from her dream crystallized in her mind: Love, Faith, Forgiveness. The stained-glass elements now shining in her life. Elements once forgotten, but always there under the surface, awaiting the chance to bring her parents back together again.

"Goodbye, Mick," she whispered. "I love you. Give Mom a hug for me, okay?"

Kate lingered in that spot for an extra minute, relishing the light breeze and warm rays gracing her face. She turned and headed toward the limousine, relieved at how easy it had been to say good-bye. No deluge of tears, no quivering of her voice. Just a nice, peaceful farewell.

Then she realized why: something told her their parting was purely temporary. Someday, somehow, she and her father would see each other again. Even if it were only in her dreams.

Forty

In the south corner of the Sunnyside Memorial parking lot, blanketed by the shade of an overgrown maple tree, Paul sat in his car. Watching. Waiting.

The girl in the distance was now a woman: Kathryn Grace, Iris Flaherty's only child. This was the first time he'd seen her in person. He could hear and feel a tremble in his breathing. Perspiration coated his palm. He reached for the door handle, but immediately yanked his hand back, as if the metal were ablaze.

For years he had thought of her, wondered about her life. He'd sent a letter of apology to her father long ago. The fact it hadn't boomeranged *Return to Sender* had brought him a trace of comfort, assuming Mr. Flaherty hadn't shredded it. When it came to the little girl he'd stripped of a mother, however, his hands always refused to pen any words.

Then, several weeks ago, Paul's wife, a hospice volunteer, had informed him she'd heard that a patient by the name of Collin Flaherty was on the extensive care list. Hence the idea of contacting the man's daughter resurfaced. Not just resurfaced like an occasional, fleeting notion. It consumed every idle moment of thought, whether he was stuck in traffic, in line at the grocery store, lying in bed awaiting sleep.

He'd tried to approach her, but cowardice cut short each attempt.

When he'd caught wind of today's funeral, he had no intention of showing his face. Yet his vehicle seemed to have steered itself to this spot. He wasn't sure why. No, he knew why. But still, even given the opportunity, he didn't know what he would say. His presence alone, specifically on this mournful day, could cause her more harm than good.

And so he merely watched, veiled by his windshield and dark sunglasses. The sun shone on the woman's loose auburn hair as she made her way to the sleek black limousine, where a suited, broad-shouldered man stood—her husband, he guessed—leaning on top of the open back door. In a matter of minutes, she'd be gone.

He had to make a decision.

What if he simply refrained from introducing himself? He could offer condolences as a guy who knew her father—an anonymous apology masking a deeper meaning. Chances were slim she would know who he was, especially if he kept their exchange brief.

He grasped the door handle again, this time with dogged determination. One foot out, then the other. He was about to charge forward when Kate met her husband's welcoming arms. As they embraced, strands of her hair covered her eyes, soaking up what must be a flood of tears from the loss of yet another parent. An outpouring of pain that never ended.

She raised her head and gazed up at her husband. Strangely there were no etched lines of grieving or sadness on her face. Instead, she was smiling. Her expression was calm and content. Her husband touched her cheek with his hand. Their mouths moved in conversation. She nodded and smiled again, then they both climbed into the limousine.

The sound of the door swinging closed boomed through the parking lot, startling Paul into action. He had to hurry. She was going to leave.

His brisk walk turned to a jog at the revving of the

limousine's engine. The wheels began to roll. He should run. But there wasn't time. He had waited too long.

The limo fled from reach, and out the driveway she went. Down the street. Out of sight.

Now he was alone.

There was nothing left to do but return to his car. However, he'd only traveled a few yards when something inside stopped him. Feet planted on the asphalt, he turned his head to view the destination he'd never had the courage to visit.

Could this be the real reason he'd come? He wished there were another means of finding out.

At last, he trudged toward the stone marker that displayed his crime, his legs weighted with remorse. The tendons beneath a surgical scar on his knee—a permanent reminder of that horrific night—ached more with every stride, like a guilt detector nearing its source. Over the pavement, through the grass, across cushioned soil that threatened to swallow him whole, to deliver him where he would have gladly gone had he been able to switch places with his victim.

More than once, he was tempted to retreat to the safe haven of his vehicle. But somehow he resisted, willing his feet to continue until he reached a respectable distance from Mr. Flaherty's casket. Far enough away from the space he had no right to invade, yet close enough to read the engraved headstone.

Iris Flaherty
1944 – 1981
Collin Flaherty
1944 – 2007

He closed his eyes and bowed his head, girded himself for a slide show of memories to tear through his mind—shattered glass and crushed metal, fire engine lights, a zipped black bag on a gurney, the cell wall he'd stared at month after month—all images that haunted his dreams, though less frequently with the passage of years.

To his amazement, though, he saw nothing. Just the orange glow of the afternoon sun on his eyelids. He opened his eyes and read the bottom inscription on the gravestone.

May they rest in peace.

The couple he'd divided was finally together. The thought kindled a warm sensation in his chest.

He'd made a mistake—a deadly, life-altering mistake—and he had paid dearly for it. Always he'd craved forgiveness from the Flahertys, the family he'd wronged. Though even if they granted it, would his soul be any less burdened? As he stood here, facing his past, he uncovered his answer: no.

For the sake of his wife, his son, his own sanity, he needed to retire the agony of self-blame and find peace within.

He looked at the couple's graves one final time. Then he turned and walked away, eyes forward, the ache in his knee lessening with every step. Or so it seemed as he retraced his path with a decidedly lighter gait.

Once behind the steering wheel, he released a long, heavy breath, one he had been holding for decades. And without looking back, he started the engine of his dusty black pickup truck and headed for home.

Epilogue

Four months later

Kate stared at the illuminated numbers above the door in the elevator. Her hands wrung faster and harder the closer she came to the sixth floor.

Ding.

The doors swooped apart, hitching the air in her lungs mid-breath. She exhaled. Lowering her shoulders, she stepped out and walked down the spacious hallway. Dull brown shades of paisley carpet led her past a water fountain and a series of black doors with silver handles. Freight forwarding, secretarial services, kids' dentistry. Maybe she'd gotten the suite number wrong. She was about to turn around and check the directory board when she found it.

The last door on the left: *D&K Advertising.*

Upon entering, her heightened senses took in the world surrounding her. Magenta, azure, violet. From the swirly coffee table to the couch shaped like gigantic lips, every piece of decor in the waiting room emanated the vibrancy of an elegant funhouse.

She crossed the shag throw rug to reach the reception desk. A funky green bamboo potted plant sat atop the frosted glass counter. Business cards, brochures. No receptionist.

She glanced at her wristwatch that, with its replaced

crystal, now appeared brand new. Half past noon. Lunch hour. She would have to find his office herself.

Taking a chance, she went left around the receptionist's station. Other than a few phone rings and the birdlike trill of a fax machine, the spacious room was rather quiet. Almost completely abandoned. These people actually stopped working to eat lunch!

The surprises didn't end there. Instead of the usual maze of individual, confining cubicles, serpentine partitions created community sections filled with desks and beanbags and doodle-covered wipe-off boards. Family photos and kids' crafts rivaled the number of framed ads hanging on the walls. Light years away from the starch-collared galaxy of Milton, Sidis & Stricklen.

Rounding the corner, she spotted a familiar profile through a gaping door. Her heart thumped half a beat faster.

She rapped twice with her knuckle. "Excuse me, sir. Is this the ladies' room?"

Drew lifted his gaze from the moving box on his desk he was unpacking and beamed. "Hey! What are you doing here?"

"Well...I heard D&K hired a new, hot corporate attorney. So thought I'd check him out for myself."

"And...?"

She eyed him up and down, admiring the strong curves of his neck and biceps left uncovered by his polo shirt. A backdrop of sunlight shining through the floor-to-ceiling, city-view window highlighted his artfully unkempt hair and smooth skin. His tan still lingered from their trip to Maui.

She pursed her lips. "Hmm...overrated."

Biting his bottom lip, he grabbed a fist-sized foam basketball out of his box and prepared to pitch it in her direction.

"Watch it," she yelled with a laugh, instinctively covering the small pooch of her belly. "Pregnant woman here, in case you've forgotten."

"Forget? How could I possibly? I'm reminded every time you beat me to the fridge and clear out half the shelves."

She dropped her jaw in a huff. "That is such an exaggeration."

"Oh? Let's recap, shall we?" He tapped the basketball on his chin, gaze toward the ceiling, contemplating. "This morning's breakfast: two bowls of oatmeal, cranberry juice, yogurt, a banana, a boiled egg, Pop Tarts..." He looked back at her with smirking eyes. "Have I forgotten anything?"

Wow. Listed aloud, it did sound like she was gorging before a winter-long hibernation.

She planted her fists on her hips. "Okay, food police. Then what's *your* excuse?"

"For?"

"For eating half a pint of cookie dough ice cream straight out of the carton last night?"

He wrist-flicked the orange ball into an arc that connected with a mini-hoop on the vertical file cabinet against the wall. "Sympathy weight," he replied, grinning.

"Leave it to a lawyer to have a clever answer for everything."

And leave it to *her* to tiptoe around the real issue at hand.

She cleared her tightening throat. "Listen, the reason I stopped by is that, um...well..."

Before she could finish, his cell phone rang. The phone—one of her least favorite inventions, holding firm in third place below a dentist's drill and gynecologist's stirrups.

However, Drew's attention remained steady on Kate.

She motioned toward the device hooked to his belt. "Go ahead," she said. She masked her impatience with a smile that implied there was no gravity to her upcoming words.

He glanced at the caller ID screen and raised the phone to his ear. "Hey, Bri, what's up?" He perched on the edge of his oblong desk.

Kate sought an activity to harness her nervous energy. She turned to a half-empty box resting on a diamond-shaped chair that resembled a metal spider web. She pulled out a few worn legal books and stacked them on the wall-mounted shelf next to the painting he'd already hung. *Her* painting—the one she'd given him last week for their anniversary. Peaceful waves of lavender, joyous splashes of spring green. A reflection of the emotions she now openly shared.

Next from the box, she retrieved a dual frame housing photos that made her smile: one of the two of them snuggled together in a sleek gondola in Venice, and the other of her stretching her arm out to the side, pretending to support the leaning Tower of Pisa.

"I don't know, let me ask her." Drew lowered the mouthpiece. "Hon, Brian wants to know if there's anything he and Beth should bring this weekend."

With her mind so occupied lately—crammed with concerns regarding nutrition and nursing, midwives and epidurals—Kate had almost forgotten about their monthly excursion to her father's cabin. Well, technically it was Kate's cabin now, but she couldn't imagine calling it anything but her father's.

She and Drew had been looking forward to this trip for weeks, not only because they were eager to witness Brian's inaugural crabbing experience, but because this would be their first stay there since the new carpeting was laid. Every repair and cosmetic touch had aided the house in earning back its "Lil' Bit O' Heaven" title, and had given Kate, Drew, and Sofo good excuses for convenient getaways together. With Wanda as the ever-reliable volunteer, they could relax knowing someone was keeping a close eye on their suburban home while they were away.

"I think we're pretty well set," Kate replied. "But we could use a few games."

"You catch that?" Drew asked into the phone, then paused, listening. "Yeah, just don't bring Twister again. I almost ended up in traction last time." He chuckled and said good-bye. After hanging up, he returned his focus to Kate. "You want to grab some lunch? I don't have a meeting until two thirty."

Kate propped the frame next to the books. "I'd love to, but—" She dragged out her words." First, I have a favor to ask."

"Uh-oh." His eyebrow peaked. "We're not repainting the nursery again, are we?"

"No," she said tentatively. "But...we do need a new crib."

"A new crib?" He dropped his head back and groaned. "Babe, you're killing me. It took me a hundred hours to assemble the one we have."

She crept toward him, chin tucked. "I'm not talking about replacing anything."

He looked befuddled. "Okay, you're losing me here."

"What I mean is—" She swallowed, standing before him toe-to-toe, "We're going to need a *second* crib."

Digesting the clarification, Drew became a pale statue. A long moment passed before he blinked and said, "Are you saying...?"

She nodded stiffly.

"But how...you were...when did...?" His words tumbled, his mind clearly spinning, just as hers had been upon receiving the news at the clinic.

"I guess we brought home one more souvenir from Europe than we thought."

Color returned to his face as he gazed down at the barely visible bump of her belly, then back up to her eyes. "Are you sure?"

"Right after you left the house, the doctor's office called. They had a last-minute cancellation this morning," she explained. "Since they wanted to confirm how far along I am, they snuck me into an ultrasound. And, that's when the technician found...the other one."

He paused before nodding, his eyes still dazed. "We're having twins," he said quietly, as if testing the phrase out on his lips. Then a broad grin stretched across his face. "Holy cow!" he exclaimed and swept her up into a whirl of circles. "I can't believe it! We're having *twins*!"

When he finally set her on her feet, his expression tightened. "Sorry, sorry," he gasped and loosened his hold. It must have just occurred to him that his tight grip and aerodynamic spin could be harmful to an expectant mother. "Are you okay?" He gingerly placed his hand on her belly.

She couldn't help giggling. "Yeah, I'm fine."

"With the news, though—are you okay? With all of this?"

"You mean, am I scared about juggling two babies at once?"

He nodded, his brow tense.

"Oh, no, I'm not scared," she told him. "I'm actually terrified."

He let out a deep sigh, confirming that his mixture of joy and apprehension equaled hers.

"But—" She framed his jaw with her hands. "That's how I know it's worth doing."

His eyes reflected the love expanding within her.

"Besides," she said with a smile, "we're in this together. Right?"

"Always," he answered and lifted her hand to softly kiss her fingers, followed by her lips. Then he nestled his face in her neck. And as they held each other in that moment of abounding hope—perfect not despite but due to its uncertainties and imperfections—Kate felt her dad smiling down at them from above, a guardian angel with the twinkling eyes of an Irishman.

A Personal Note From The Author

I sat before my computer writing FLAHERTY'S CROSSING as a source of personal therapy after losing my beloved father to colon cancer. You might say I was angry at him, at God, at the world in general. However, after writing this story, I had the opportunity to really look into my soul and consider the fact that so many other sons and daughters have had to deal with similar and even worse situations. Rather than a memoir, this novel evolved into a fictional journey which brought about the resolution I needed to find. I never expected this exercise in writing to go to press, touch lives, or win literary awards. But as a result of my good fortune, I have arranged for proceeds from the sale of this book to go directly to the cancer research at Portland's Providence Medical Center. I am now convinced and proudly share my belief that good things can grow out of the worst times in our lives if you just take the time to open your heart.

Kaylin

About Kaylin

Linda Yoshida, writing as Kaylin McFarren, minored in English in college and for the past twenty years has led PR/marketing efforts for several companies within her family's international conglomerate. She is a wife and mother of three, and resides in Oregon. In addition to serving on numerous foundations and boards, she actively works with multi-published critique partners and is a member of several writers' organizations, including Willamette Writers and Romance Writers of America. Although *FLAHERTY'S CROSSING* is Linda's début novel, it has already garnered numerous awards and received recognition as a 2008 Golden Heart® Finalist.

Visit our website for our growing catalogue of quality books.
www.champagnebooks.com

Made in the USA
San Bernardino, CA
27 October 2014